"You are the oddest creature."

Andreas reached forward and one finger touched her chin. Her breath caught, heart picking up speed quickly. His eyes were intense on hers, and so near.

"You are one of the most confident people I've ever encountered, with a core so vulnerable to hurt. Do you realize what you are doing, showing me such vulnerabilities?"

Phoebe swallowed. "Perhaps it is stupid of me. I cannot help but be interested in you. And I do little by halves."

"I as well." He said nothing further for long moments. "When I take something, I take *everything.*"

She had the feeling that he was giving her an opportunity to turn tail and run.

She tilted her head. "When I give something, I give everything."

So many expressions chased across his face that she was uncertain what to even attempt to read there. Need, victory, despair.

"I know," he whispered. Then his lips parted hers, and the tinder exploded into flame.

Romances by Anne Mallory

In Total
Surrender

ANNE
MALLORY

A V O N
An Imprint of HarperCollinsPublishers

This is a work of fiction. Names, characters, places, and incidents are products of the author's imagination or are used fictitiously and are not to be construed as real. Any resemblance to actual events, locales, organizations, or persons, living or dead, is entirely coincidental.

AVON BOOKS
An Imprint of HarperCollins*Publishers*
10 East 53rd Street
New York, New York 10022-5299

Copyright © 2011 by Anne Hearn
ISBN 978-0-06-201731-4
www.avonromance.com

First Avon Books mass market printing: October 2011

Avon Trademark Reg. U.S. Pat. Off. and in Other Countries, Marca Registrada, Hecho en U.S.A.
HarperCollins® is a registered trademark of HarperCollins Publishers.

Printed in the U.S.A.

10 9 8 7 6 5 4 3 2 1

To the usual suspects—
May Chen, Mom, Matt, Dad, and S.

Chapter 1

He had expected revenge. Had anticipated it keenly enough to move all of the papers that incriminated them. Still, the loss of Building Twelve at the docks was irritating.

And while they had been dealing with the fires, other events had been in play around the fog-shrouded East End of London.

The aftermath would be spectacular, especially without his brother around to deal with the chaos. All in all, it had been an absolute *beauty* of a night. One that could simply not grow worse.

"Mr. Merrick, we will get the man responsible. I won't fail you again."

Andreas looked coldly at the underling standing on the other side of the desk—he hadn't bothered to learn the man's name, that was Roman's concern, knowing the names of those around them. But names were meaningless and easily exchanged. Or thoroughly discarded like the anchor they were. He knew that better than anyone.

No, Andreas knew all he needed by the way men

held themselves before him. Whether they could be trusted or needed to be *dealt* with.

The human bulldog curled his fingers into a fist but held steady otherwise. Andreas pinned his gaze on the man for an excruciating half minute more. Two fidgets ensued.

Andreas drummed three heavy beats onto the desk with his forefinger, his blackened cuff brushing farther up on his wrist than it had earlier in the night when it had been pristine. The man stiffened in front of him, understanding the threat. He was better than many, if unimpressive still. "Do it." Andreas picked up the envelope in front of him, not bothering to look up again as the man retreated.

He didn't need to. He knew exactly where the man stepped and when and how he turned. Could feel and hear it in the sounds and curl of the displaced air, the bend of the boards. It was death not to pay attention to anyone within fifty paces. A hundred paces out in the open. Though difficult, the shot could be made.

The old wound twinged, but he didn't scratch it, even alone as he was now. His lip curled derisively. His bastard of a *sire* would be pleased.

He stabbed his opener into the half-exposed throat above the wax seal and ripped.

Dear Brother,
   Charlotte and I arrived in Italy to a bloody fantastic . . .

Blah, blah, some festival drivel, blah, blah, happiness, blah. Andreas skimmed the barely legible note—a full page of sentiment. Roman was going completely soft—that woman making him lively and blissful.

Emotion wound through him—something that vacillated between satisfaction and disquiet. He carefully placed the note on his desk to read more fully later.

He picked up another note, eyes narrowing on the name Pace, before slitting it open.

Another politely worded refusal for a face-to-face meeting. Another note laced with words far too empathic. Another quick-witted and clever response underlying it all.

Needless to say, the serial correspondence he had engaged in with James Pace for the last six months had made him . . . interested in the family.

White dresses and warm smiles.

He banished the unwanted images to the depths of his personal hell and refocused his thoughts.

Andreas avoided meeting with people, but he kept offering a face-to-face meeting with James Pace. He didn't know why. The dark laughter of the eternally damned slithered through him.

He might see Pace's daughter.

No. Something about the man's damn sunny outlook annoyed him, and he wanted to reconcile it with the shrewd businessman Pace had once been.

Sparkling eyes full of interest, head tipped perennially in curiosity.

He tapped the edge of the thick paper harder against his desk. Dammit.

Pace continued to decline tactfully. In a manner

that would tie anyone with a modicum of restraint into knots. And no one declined a meeting with Andreas.

No one.

He could have issued a pointed threat to Pace after the first refusal and unleashed hell after the second; but something had made him hesitate. The dark laughter echoed internally. *No.* The hesitation was easily explained—he needed Pace & Co. of London under his thumb in order to further his own plans.

White cloth under his thumb, writhing and moaning.

Goddammit. He felt as if he'd contracted some sort of weakening sickness. Infected by a single glance.

He should never have sent those men to make inquiries even though he always gathered complete information on everyone with whom he did business. It was standard procedure to find out who could be bought in a household. Who had access to information. What secrets were already willing to be sold.

Not one servant had been receptive. And the Pace craftsmen, who had been willing to gossip about each other, their business partners, and rivals in the carriage company, had turned frosty when discussion of the Pace family was broached.

It had been a singular moment when he had received those reports. And reason enough to see the family for himself. Anyone who inspired that type of loyalty—or fear—was worth a personal look.

The problem was that James Pace was a recluse.

Only occasionally attending the theater with his family before retreating to his inner sanctum.

Andreas had found himself hidden in the shadows of the Claremont Theatre in order to divine his answers. But James Pace hadn't been there. Andreas normally would have left the instant he realized that. He hated theater.

He had stayed the entire performance. He had stayed for the revels afterward. The audience had started to *empty,* and he'd still been there, stuck, frozen in his shadowed seat.

It had been immediate. How the hell that could be, he didn't know. But her eyes had connected with his, somehow, as she'd entered the box on the opposite side of the theater—connected with his even through the dark shadows he surrounded himself with. And her mouth had bestowed a warm smile on a random stranger in the crowd.

Barbed warmth sinking under his skin, biting and clawing.

Her body had been cloaked in the color of innocence, but her lips were passion-stained. The warmth of the lamps seemed to converge on her at all times, no matter where she moved, or with whom she spoke—a bright spot pushing back the shadows.

A bright look on her face mixed with something she had been trying to conceal. Bone tired, but pushing past that exhaustion and engaging the people around her during intermissions. He had nearly recoiled when she'd sent another soft smile his way, head tilted in question.

He had attended the Theatre Royal later that

week to see James Pace. There was no excuse for going to Covent Garden to see *Richard III* or to watch Grimaldi as a country bumpkin, nor going to the Haymarket Theatre or to the Olympic, without result. He wasn't a lackey. And he hated theater with all of its trumped-up dramatics. But there he had been, absorbing *her* delighted reaction to Madame Vestris performing in breeches as Cherubino in *The Marriage of Figaro*.

She was probably one of those women who swooned for the incompetent lover spewing useless words beneath her window. Or the man who emasculated himself in the end for *love*.

He sneered at the page in his hand, looking at the curve of the letters. The sincerity and empathy ever present in the words. Earnest. Like father, like daughter perhaps. He balled the paper in his fist.

Familiar footsteps strode down the hall, and a firm rap followed. "Merrick?" a low voice said on the other side.

Andreas stared hard at the door, but Milton Fox, their head casino manager, wouldn't interrupt him for a mere chat. If there was something wrong with one of the hells tonight too, someone else was going to die. Slowly.

"What?" he barked, paper still crushed between his fingers.

Red hair and a stocky frame emerged from behind the portal. "I know Fred was just here to report on the leader, but we picked up a trail on a few of the others. About three hours from now, I expect."

"Good." Andreas smiled. Irritation bleeding to anticipation.

Milton kept his face blank, nodding, but Andreas knew he was as unnerved as every other person was, bar Roman, when Andreas's lips moved in that direction. Milton was just better at hiding it.

Milton's eyes drifted to Andreas's wrist, and for a moment Andreas thought he might stupidly say something about it, or inquire if he wanted *help,* but the other man displayed his keen intelligence when he simply cleared his throat. "I'll give them a nudge before you get there, shall I?"

"Yes, do that. And put Fred, was it, on assignment somewhere else for a month." He narrowed his eyes at his manager. "Or get *rid* of him."

"Yes, sir, of course. And only the men on gaming duty will be here for the next hour, sir."

As requested, went unsaid between them. Milton had been with them long enough to know a dismissal without being given one, and he ducked back through the portal.

The knotted anticipation corded. It wouldn't be long now, especially with the end of their conversation purposely echoing into the hall. Good. He could have the building locked down at any time so that no one could get in, but not tonight. Tonight it would remain unlocked. Dealing with a good assassination attempt always relieved his tension. Hopefully, they wouldn't send amateurs this time.

Besides, it would keep eyes from other places in the city. From white dresses and warm smiles.

Andreas tightened his fingers around the balled parchment and ignored the dull ache of the burns as the skin pulled. He looked to the side—at his brother's letter. Roman would want to know what was happening, and there would never be anyone he'd rather have at his back; but if Roman knew the circumstances, he would return from his honeymoon. And the constant need within Andreas to assure his brother's happiness overruled all else. Andreas had lied and told Roman that his plans would be set in motion *after* he returned to London. To keep him safe.

Stupid emotional connections.

Easier to rule alone and with fear. Simple and true. Elemental. He had always claimed fear as a willing servant, but had long ago realized that, together, he and Roman could do anything. And they had done so both in London's underworld and above for the twenty years since they had incongruously met. A relationship stronger than any of true blood.

But now that Roman's life was tied around another's, his brother's happiness could be assured. Their own tie could be loosened.

He tossed the crumpled paper.

Change. It was all around him. Poking, retreating, laughing maliciously. Change was fate, Roman always said. Well, Andreas loathed Fate, that bitch.

A faint noise in the hall raised the hair on his neck. Footsteps that were faint enough to belong to one of the young boys that Roman always took in, but the steps were far too hesitant, slowing as they progressed down the hall. It was possible Milton or one of the others had sent up a new recruit to give him an additional message—it had been a busy night—but they usually knew better. The last sapling hadn't emerged from his room belowstairs for three days afterward.

Faint steps. Specially crafted shoes.

Andreas calmly reached into the drawer to his right, his burned wrist brushing the lip of the wood, and withdrew the expensive pistol there, checked it, then put it in the specially made holster on the back side of the desk. Easy to pull at a moment's notice. The desk itself, brilliantly crafted with its special . . . features . . . made other methods of self-preservation obsolete, and he had inspected the panels and mechanisms earlier as he did each night. Perfectly oiled and powder-filled.

But only a stupid—and dead—man relied on a single plan.

The footsteps stopped outside the door. The comforting steel of two knives strapped to his upper arms and one long blade pressed against his left forearm easily pulled him to center. The hidden pocket in his right sleeve which had housed the lower blade's twin had been damaged earlier in the evening along with the skin underneath. He should have changed his shirt. He waited, perfectly still, irritation simmering below his awareness, as the person worked up the nerve either to knock or crash through in an attempt to kill him.

Though crashing through *would* take him by surprise. He'd place his stake some sort of *lady* stood on the other side of the door. A woman with soft slippers, just like the ones he'd heard every morning outside his rooms for the first decade of his life. He kept his fingers loose and ready. Only a fool underestimated the female half of the population.

A second set of footsteps shuffled hesitantly down the hall, stopping outside the door as well. One more? That was all? Last week they had sent four and had barely given him a sweat.

"You must not—" A reedy voice said, then devolved into low, furious tones, followed by silence.

A stronger rap than he had anticipated sounded on the solid oak. When he didn't answer, the person knocked again.

"Good evening? Mr. Merrick?"

The hair on his neck stood straighter. The voice seeped through unknown fissures in the wood to dip and soar through the open air and wrap around him. The ropy silken strands of a noose.

Something hit the floor with a thud. He only barely registered the pain in his elbow and the missing statue of the scales of justice and vengeance—usually upright and immovable on the edge of his desk.

"Is . . . is someone there?"

It was a voice filled with light—showing a spirit that would not be contained. Andreas gripped the desk mechanism, instinctively reacting against the threat of it.

He let the silence hang. The creaking sound of the metal handle being pushed down was loud in the stillness. The woman's hesitancy and determination were equally obvious in every sound she made.

He should have run and locked the door the moment he heard that voice.

A cloaked head peered around the edge of the

wood, lit by the sconces near the door, the light placed exactly to give him an advantage in seeing whoever might enter, momentarily blinding the visitor.

Reflecting off brown eyes too big.

Red lips too full.

A serious, drawn look to her features, but he could picture the overlay of joy easily in his mind's eye—enjoying the newest farce or spectacle at the Claremont, where she held a damnable subscription.

"Mr. Merrick?" She entered the room fully. Without the oak between them, her voice was clearer though still the slightest bit smoky.

A reedy man to match the reedy voice took a jittery step behind her and into the room, closing the door reluctantly behind him. He looked ready to bolt at the first sign of trouble.

The cloaked woman walked toward Andreas, small hands pushing the hood back from light brown hair as she drew closer. As she peered into *his* shadows, relief—and something else—graced her features. "Yes. Yes, you *are* Andreas Merrick." It was said almost under her breath, like a whisper against satin sheets. White satin sheets.

His fingers jerked along the edges of one of the desk's mechanisms before he ripped his hand away. Half an inch more and he would have accidentally shot her. He looked at his hand for a second, then focused back on her, eyes narrowed in anger, pinning the entire incident where it belonged.

The man took a step back, pressing against the closed door, pure terror in his gaze.

"I . . ." The woman cocked her head, eyes widening at his expression, before she frowned. She looked down, seeming to ponder something. She seemed to find the answer in the toe of a suspiciously dirty but finely crafted slipper. She looked back up, brilliant smile once more in place, eyes meeting his. Just that edge of loss there in the back of her gaze. Loss that had not been present four weeks ago.

"My name is Phoebe Pace, Mr. Merrick." The smile and eyes stayed bright. It was exceedingly rare that people met his gaze, no less seemed *happy* about meeting it. "I apologize for bothering you this late in the evening."

Most people would qualify the hour as *morning* at this point, but he didn't bother to correct her. That would mean speaking.

"I wouldn't normally do such a thing, you understand." She looked at him in some sort of universal feminine appeal that had never previously worked on him. But suddenly he felt the need to scrub the lingering brushes of it from his skin. "No, well, that is untrue. I might, you see. Mr. Harris says I'm no end of trouble."

She gestured toward the other man, obviously Mr. Harris, who looked even more terrified as Andreas turned his gaze his way.

"Still," she continued, "it is rather a frightful neighborhood you reside in, and I found seeking you out to be quite the adventure indeed, one I might not have taken under normal conditions. But I'm quite at the end of the rabbit's tail, you see."

A small hand smoothed her skirt, just the barest tremble visible.

"I discovered . . ." Her mouth hovered open for a moment, unable to form whatever words had been planned to follow. Her fingers slipped into the folds of her cloak, revealing for a brief moment a bright, rose-colored skirt as her hand rippled along it.

He tensed at the action and the unfinished words, forefinger against the trigger, ready. She looked fresh from a ball, not as if she were carrying a weapon, but he couldn't trust anyone. And *she was here*. He had specific instructions for two men to watch and report this woman's actions. That she was *here,* in front of him, meant that at least one person would need to be severely punished later.

Her fingers reemerged, empty, clasping together in front of her cloak. He didn't relax his position even half a fraction.

He stared at her, waiting, and wasn't disappointed when she rushed on after a few beats of silence. She had too much forward momentum for conversation lulls. "But I jump ahead. May we sit?"

"No."

He watched the beat at her neck pulse at his tone, her lips part at the single word. "No?"

He didn't respond, continuing to look at her coldly. He *hoped* that was how he looked. It seemed far safer than any other action he might take. The outward ice a cover for the suddenly frozen inaction of his limbs.

He thought of cold betrayal and let the response rise to his features. Mr. Harris fell over his own feet, sprawling on the floor against the door.

Phoebe Pace turned and blinked at her companion, then hurried to help the man. "Dear me, are you well, Mr. Harris?"

"Yes, fine." His eyes didn't leave Andreas.

"Perhaps"—she bit her lip—"you would feel more comfortable in the hall?"

Andreas sure as hell didn't want to be alone with her. He narrowed his eyes, intending to say just that. The man tripped up before he could, fumbling for the handle, then nodded frantically and scurried out.

Phoebe Pace stared after him, nonplussed. "Well . . . excellent. There are matters on which I need to speak with you in private anyway, Mr. Merrick. Most of the matters, really."

She turned, bright eyes determined as she started forward again, undoing the clasp at her throat, then clutching the side of the cloak and pulling the fabric in a long, graceful arc to rest over one arm. The vibrant fabric of her dress spilled into the light—even here in his comfortingly dark den the light seemed to track her.

"May I sit?"

It would be easy for her to have hidden a weapon underneath her cloak and be pointing it at him as she moved. If it had been anyone else standing before him, they would no longer be able to stand. "No."

She stopped, staring at him like a startled owl for long moments. "I . . . I must say I do not have the first wit for how to speak with you, Mr. Merrick." She sounded truly bemused underneath the socially polite and cautious words. The requisite touch of dread he effortlessly gifted to people laced the edge of her voice, waiting to take hold.

Something dark curled inside him, but he simply pushed it into the pit of equally dark emotions that always swirled.

"Good. The door is behind you."

She absently smoothed her free hand down the side of her waist, pulling the rose material along hidden curves. "Yes, Mr. Harris just used it."

He could do nothing but stare at her. Her eyes searched his for a moment, then a warm smile curved her lips, and she relaxed a measure. "It is good to finally meet you, Mr. Merrick. I have business with you that is of vital importance."

Of course it was, to her at least, or she wouldn't be standing here, in a room alone with a stranger, in one of the seediest sections of town. He watched one small hand smooth her ball gown again, a light touch against the satin, shoulders pushing back with purpose.

His eyes traveled down to the hem of the gown, stained and dirtied along with her slippers, as if instead of using one of her family's fine carriages, she'd trudged the long distance from the west of town—Mayfair, the bane of London's existence— by foot. He pushed the feel of her smile away and sneered. "Doubtful."

She took another quick look at her slippers, then met his eyes once more dead-on. He had to credit her—she had grit. Roman and Nana would love her.

The ice in his veins grew harder at the thought. He touched the cord at the wall, then wrapped his fingers around it. He'd pull it and have Roman's runts bodily evict her, then have them carry the spineless fool in the hall out. Just a normal night. He'd deal with the aftermath, punish some minions, and dismiss her from his mind completely.

Guilt was a useless emotion only fools felt. He had never been accused of being a fool.

She stepped toward him, eyes tracking the motion of his fingers. She opened her berry-stained mouth—her lips were always so *bright,* as if raspberries had been crushed upon them, overly ripe juice dribbling into every crevice—then pressed her lips together, looking at the toes of those damned slippers once more.

He gripped the cord but didn't pull it. *Why?* He clearly wasn't going to like whatever she had to say. He should have *sprinted* to lock the door as soon as he'd heard her voice. Should have had someone shuttle her from London weeks ago, as soon as he realized he was going to that damn theater *again.*

She looked back up, determination set in every innocent feature. "I have a proposition for you."

Every tightly controlled instinct screamed at him not to respond, and yet she pulled the dark words from him like some damned Greek siren. "Oh? And what could you possibly have that I might want?"

"Me."

Chapter 2

He stared at soft lips, slightly parted. Uttering something that must have been a different language entirely. If he hadn't learned enough Latin, French, and Greek by the time he was out of his nappies, he might have confirmed such a thought.

"*You.*"

"Yes." She looked so . . . earnest. He almost recoiled from the sincerity he saw in her gaze.

It was like something out of a dream, a nightmare. Unreality bleeding into conscious thought.

With another person, his continued silence would have long since pulled a twining net over her, tight and uncomfortable. But even in this, she defied expectation.

"That emerged in a rather blurted fashion. I must confess you make me feel somewhat pubescent and awkward, Mr. Merrick. Quite a talent, that." She looked . . . cheerful. Andreas discreetly pressed the burned flesh of his wrist, and whiteness blurred the edges of his vision. Not dreaming. "I am getting off track though . . . I confess to nerves. May I sit?"

She took a step toward him, and his shoulder automatically dropped so that he was touching the mechanism again. Her head cocked at the action, assuredly not understanding how close she was to certain death.

"May I sit?"

Again he said nothing.

She peered at him through the low candlelight on the desk. "You know, you rather look like a picture I observed once of Mephistopheles. Never quite emerging into full focus, making one guess at the full face just out of view. Arresting and dangerous."

She stepped around the seat of the chair across from him and promptly lowered herself, arranging her skirts as she might at tea, cloak on the back of the chair. "And I confess that I find that quite intriguing when combined with your reputation and correspondence. My father is James Pace." She looked at him expectantly. He could do *nothing* but coldly return the gaze.

"My brother is Christian—"

"I know who you are"—his sudden interruption was tight and vicious—"and who your brother was."

A clenched wave of despair rolled over her face at his use of the past tense, dimming her internal light for a fraction of a moment.

"You requested a face-to-face meeting with my father," she said quietly. "I would like to negotiate with you in my father's place. He has given me permission to do so."

"No. Leave." With another person, he would expect the command to be followed immediately. That this woman would not do what she ought to was becoming apparent.

She stared at him, gripping the edge of her chair as if the force of it alone would keep her in her seat. "Please. I have much to offer you."

The words coiled around him, squeezing, and he fisted all but his first finger and threw his hand toward the door. "Get out."

She didn't move for long moments, her gaze locked with his. And that awful warmth she exuded slithered toward the darkness in his gut.

She cocked her head suddenly, her body *relaxing*, the echo of his black command hovering awkwardly in the extended pause. Forced tension stole over him at her peculiar reaction to his anger, and his whole body tightened, survival instincts rearing. He suddenly knew he was going to do something he would regret before she left. And he never regretted anything.

"There is something quite familiar about you, Mr. Merrick. Apart from seeing you at the theater, of course. I hadn't realized it previously, seated so far away from you. Have we been introduced before?"

Ice froze the blood in his veins, both at her admission that she recognized him from the theater and that he resembled someone she might know. "No."

The Paces might be a few generations removed from the peerage—and too steeped in trade—to be invited to the haughtiest functions, but they were still a part of London society. A social sphere he kept as far from as possible for many reasons.

"You remind me of someone now that I can see you up close." A single finger rubbed the bottom of her lower lip, and she leaned forward. "Who—"

Unwillingly, he pulled farther into shadow. It had been a long, long time since he had felt any need to retreat. The thought of it blackened his mood further. "What do you want?" His voice was rough. He felt like prey for the first time in fifteen-odd years.

She smiled—completely without fear. A warm, unnerving smile. *Relaxed.* "I have a proposition for you, as I said."

"I'm not interested," he said bitingly.

She cocked her head again, and he thought he might be beginning to hate the gesture. "I think you are interested. And that for some reason I frighten you."

He unexpectedly gave a dark laugh. Unnerving even him. "Your entire species is terrifying. Now get out."

"I do not desire to terrify you. Though you enjoy promoting fear, do you not? Your reputation precedes you."

His gut clenched, and some strange feeling collected there. "You should believe every inch of that reputation."

A normal person would not be behaving as the woman in front of him was. The daughter of a wealthy man—or at least a previously wealthy man—should be out worrying about the state of her clothes and her marital status. Definitely not looking as if she wanted to take tea with the devil—and warmly chat about the lovely weather while she did.

He again eyed the cloak behind her and the set of her hands. But she only seemed to be carrying the weapon of her lips.

She cocked her head. "Yes, of course I should believe it. The longer I watch you, though, the more secure I feel. You remind me of—"

"What do you *want*?"

The response wasn't terse enough because hope bloomed across her face. Hell, the devil himself could tell her he was taking her straight to hell, and she'd probably smile in idiotic anticipation of a balmy trip to the tropics. She thrust a hand into her bag, and he didn't even tense. Perhaps she would shoot him and end his misery. She extracted a sheaf of papers.

"My father was taken in by frauds and cheats, as you know."

"I know nothing of that nature." There it was. That tingle of guilt that had no business exploding in his brain. "Your brother publicly claimed such a thing. However, the evidence suggests that your father is in fact one of the instigators of the scam."

"Yes, the perpetrators were quite thorough in casting him in that role." She nodded. "Before his absence from society, my father began to invest the company's funds in the New World markets. Brazil and Chile, most notably. People took note and followed suit. My father was . . . encouraged . . . to start a fund. It will be no secret come next month's report that the fund is defunct. The money gone. And we are now embroiled irreparably."

The great James Pace had forgotten to separate his own finances and those of his company from those of the fund. It had been a singularly grave mistake on the man's part that still made Andreas wonder as to his sanity. The man's brilliance in his letters made the whole question that much more intriguing.

Phoebe Pace leafed through her papers, grabbed a sheet, then leafed through for another. "I tell you this freely as you are assuredly aware of it already, and I do not desire to show doubt in your intelligence or intelligence gathering. You have undoubtedly been keeping an eye on us, as I have been going through our accounts, and it seems we owe you quite a bit of money, Mr. Merrick."

His gaze sharpened on her as she sifted through the pages in front of her. Her face was concentrated on the task, as if she were getting ready to start at page one, then continue through infinity. He had the most absurd feeling that she would somehow manage to freeze him in his seat until the end of time.

"You owe more than 'quite a bit,' Miss Pace."

"Yes. And it was good of you to buy so many shares of our debt. Helps 'quite a bit' in making it easier to pay back."

He thought of the figure. They'd never be able to pay it back. He had engineered it in just that way. Their accounts were completely tied up at the moment in land, facilities, contracts, and the dirty speculation fund. "You think you can pay it back?"

"Yes. With time. I have a plan that will benefit us mutually."

"I am only concerned with what I gain."

"Yes, of course." She continued flipping and pulling out pages. "And I will guarantee that you will double your investment in five years."

He opened his mouth to coldly state that they'd never be able to pay back a tenth of the money they owed, much less doubling his money, but something else emerged entirely. "Why are *you* here?"

She stopped her motions and interlaced her fingers on top of the pages, eyes steady on his. "My father was unable to come."

Her body proclaimed her words true, but a truth that concealed something else.

"And your man of business?"

The derisive slur to the words gave her obvious pause. "Mr. Harris is our current man of business."

Andreas allowed his thoughts on the matter to show.

"Yes, I think he might have been put off by your manner." She leaned forward. "But I find you rather intriguing and quite a humanitarian."

He had experienced this feeling once before. When he'd encountered a strange, colorful insect on the sill. Bright blues and greens mixed with dark veins of rose. It had been the most absurd-looking creature he had ever encountered. That it had survived a day in the colorless world of east London was astounding. Squashing it promptly was the only way to put it out of its misery.

"The Collateral Exchange?" she asked, her voice warming *more*. "Is that what you call it? Making loans to wealthy merchants and nobles on the security of tangible, negotiable collateral—mortgages on real estate, cargoes on ships, pledges on merchandise, precious stones, or livestock. Helping people consolidate their debts in order to more easily repay them. It is quite lovely."

Dear God. He stared.

It was perhaps the most merciless endeavor they had ever undertaken. Slit throats in the night were merciful when grabbing a man by his pride and twisting one's fingers to the point of dark pain—social, political, personal safety—and removing all hope for a future not consisting of dirt, grime, and humiliation.

She patted the papers in her lap. "I would like to discuss the terms of paying back our debt. Lord Garrett is becoming quite insistent with us on our need to enter betrothal negotiations."

Both endeavors which would never occur. Outcomes—due to his direct involvement—of which he was sure. "Perhaps you and your *man of business* missed the turn to *Mayfair*."

"No." She smiled. "I am exactly where I need to be. I have no desire to enter negotiations with Lord Garrett and his heir."

He couldn't keep down his dark pleasure at that.

"However, I am—I mean my family is—ill equipped at the moment to handle these matters when we are at the end of our credit most places. Quite frankly, I—we—need you."

The dark offer was on the tip of his tongue. He kept his lips closed, though, swirling it around, thinking. There was something quite . . . unsettling . . . in the air. Making any type of offer, especially one so clearly springing from his own dark needs, would be unwise. The scent of choice and decision hung. He had lived far too long with Roman not to recognize the weaving of a fated web.

"You come highly recommended from multiple sources. Ruthless, but fair. Quite frankly, I have a number of things I would like to hire you for, should our negotiations continue favorably."

Continue favorably? He stared hard at her, trying to read beyond the obvious and overwhelming naïveté.

Brown hair arranged in some absurd looping style framed the set of her earnest eyes and over-generous lips, which were determinedly pressed together. Honey-coated steel. Others referred to this woman as "truly nice," whatever the hell that meant; but she'd never give up. Ejecting her from his office was not going to stop her from seeking him out again. He'd seen that damn insect flutter-ing stupidly outside of his window a week later, far, far outliving its life span.

"Have your father make an appointment."

A twofold request, as he wanted to meet and observe James Pace. The question of the man's complete commercial downfall, then absence from social and political life was one he desired an answer to, especially considering the sharpness of the man's correspondence.

And he wanted the woman across from him gone. He continued to swallow the other words— words the ever-present darkness filling him wanted to say to her. Dangerous.

"I would like to go over this matter with you myself, Mr. Merrick, if you don't object."

"I do."

Damn tilting head. "Is it because I am a woman?"

He leaned forward past the light of the candles and into the shadows between them. "That you are sitting alone in a room with me? Or that you are trying to negotiate with me?"

"Do you seek to protect my virtue?" Her lips curled, without a trace of guile. It was alarming. "I knew you would prove to be an honorable man."

Dark, dark words rose, and he swallowed them again. Forcing them back down. They would prove more dangerous to him than to her, if accepted. "I am a vile man." He gave her a feral smile, letting the darkness rise. "The absolute worst you will ever meet."

"That is absurd, Mr. Merrick." The darkness froze, then began undulating, snapping at an unseen threat. "How do you know what kind of men I might meet in the future?"

Tilting head, tilting head, tilting head ... it would feature prominently in his nightmares tonight.

"As to my virtue, I would like to keep my reputation intact, of course. But time proves itself the enemy. What good is an unsoiled reputation if my father is thrown into prison to rot and my mother and I are tossed to the streets? I daresay a good reputation will not survive such circumstances. Therefore, I would rather hammer out details, if you please. I am willing to offer much."

The Paces were in danger of losing everything. He didn't need to look at whatever it was she had brought with her. He knew the business of everyone of social, political, or financial importance in

London. It was part of the job of running it all behind the scenes.

"Even had I a care for your circumstances"—most men would be cowering under the silken words, yet she perked up as if he were being complimentary—that he *did* care—"your company has become an investment security risk."

"We've had an unfavorable year because the speculation fund has been tied to the company's finances, it is true." She nodded decisively. "But our company produces the finest carriages in England, and we are on the mend."

Truth. From her, and in the black-and-white figures. Things would turn around for the family if they could keep her father from prison and hold to their current bandaged course for six months more. Get the collateral needed to stay afloat, then once more enjoy the long-term gains Pace had established a decade ago. Their products continued to be unparalleled. Pace carriages were legendary in their quality.

Andreas owned five of them.

It was the financial speculation that was the problem. Whatever had beset Pace's financial sense in the previous year had doomed the company.

Though Pace had retreated from the public eye six months ago, and had begun making safer, wiser decisions once more through correspondence and courier, sources suspected the son was behind much of it.

It had been enough to keep the company afloat and the rumors from fully blooming. But the sharks were circling—with Viscount Garrett at the front,

angling to become a controlling shareholder in the
carriage company that helmed Pace's businesses.
Andreas could almost commend the viscount, and
his conspirators, for the painstaking way they had
engineered the entire scenario. Getting Pace right
where they wanted him.

Desperation sometimes bred cleverness after all,
it seemed. Andreas would never have linked intelligent creativity to the viscountcy. Ruthlessness and
cruelty were the traits bred into the Garrett coat
of arms.

"And we are determined to steer our own
course," she said. "It will be a profitable one for
you, I assure you. The company will bounce back
stronger than ever."

The Paces had somehow kept Garrett just out
of reach of the company for months. It had been
the only reason that Andreas hadn't crushed them
yet—for he wouldn't let Garrett get his hands on
a roughened gem like that, then leave the gem unbroken. Wouldn't let Garrett rebuild his finances
like he'd be able to do should he land the Paces free
and clear. Andreas had been steadily draining the
man for far too many years to simply let him have
such a ripe plum.

One all the riper once Andreas had seen . . .
her.

The plum had stayed out of Garrett's reach,
though. And Andreas had wondered if it might
stay . . . unsqueezed.

Then Christian Pace had poked his head out too
far and been *taken care of*, throwing everything
into turmoil.

"There is just the matter of payments," she said, seemingly having no problem with his continued silences.

Yes, payments. The son's . . . disappearance . . . had changed matters, and Andreas had covertly purchased and consolidated Pace's debts so that he could pull the company and family under his control at any time. If Garrett got ahold of the company, Andreas would crush him in one final fell swoop.

He examined the woman across from him. Andreas should have given Garrett the opportunity, then done it already. That he had *not* yet taken that path irritated him on a fundamental level that he did not wish to examine.

He shook the dark thoughts away. The Pace fund numbers would be out in a month. Once they became public knowledge, events would explode. Andreas was already anticipating the direction of the eruption and had his pieces in place.

"I have a payment schedule plotted out here. You will make less in the short term, but I have"— she coughed and he narrowed his eyes—"it will benefit you greatly. My father has put quite a bit of thought into this and believes that the increased payments on the back end will repay you fully with significant interest. Our company will be fully solvent in a year."

It would fit Andreas's plans for the company to be dead in a year and to take Garrett to the grave with them. *He could still do it.* He had their debts.

"In a year?" he asked, watching her expression.

He found himself unaccountably interested in the thoughts of someone else for once. "How?"

Brilliant, upward turn of lips, eyes open and expressive. "The fund needs to be diverted and divested, of course. Then the books need to be updated and our expenses better tracked. All of which Christian was doing, and now Father is completing. We need to show that the structure is sound and future growth is inevitable. Sound enough to remove us from the danger of Lord Garrett's machinations."

Lies mixed with honesty. Not interesting usually. From this woman, *very* interesting.

"Lord Garrett's machinations?" He watched her closely. "Do you have proof of such?"

"I have a sound feeling on the matter."

"Feeling? Feelings have no place in business."

"No? Then when one man throws a punch at White's because of business dealings, there is no emotion involved?" She looked at something in the corner behind him. "Or revenge? Does that not spring from emotion?"

He stiffened. He couldn't help it.

"Does it?" He tapped a finger, then stopped the telltale sign, focusing the darkness. "And in addition to a piece of these *potential* future profits I will get—you?"

"Yes." She gave him a soft smile.

"You propose to whore for me?"

He had chosen the words deliberately. Her smile slipped, and she looked at him for a long moment, and for the first time he had no idea what was going through her head.

"No. I did not mean it in that manner, though I see now how you might have interpreted such a thing from my words." Bloody head tilt. "Is that what you require? I don't know that I'd be very good at it, as I lack the necessary experience."

"Then why would I want you?"

"You have no love for Lord Garrett. I am willing to share information with you. I kn—" She smiled suddenly. "That is, we would like immunity for his sons but will help you with the viscount himself."

Coldness swept him. The beautiful curve of her lips was almost enough to make him miss the slip. But that hadn't been what she had been about to say. It was the part of her answer he most needed to address. But saying anything further would only bring attention to it.

It looked like he'd finally need to send in some cleaners to the Pace household.

"And I can offer other services," she said. "I have a good head for when to make deals, for instance. For discovering the intentions of others."

He couldn't help himself, the overwhelming darkness breaking to shards for a moment. "You? You are good at discovering the intentions of others?" He laughed. Hard. He was so unused to the action, that it hurt.

"I am." She watched him calmly. "For instance, I know that you are interested in the company for reasons other than ones you would presently state. You not only have helped to consolidate our debt, you have heavily invested in both the company and fund through single share buys, though I"—there was an odd pause he could barely pay attention to over the sudden sharpness in his gut—"I, I know my father has managed to keep you from obtaining a controlling interest in either, despite your words on our company's and fund's investment risk."

The shards sealed back together—thicker than before. He watched her for twitches. She stayed still, watching him back.

She knew.

She knew *something*. Knowledge that could be gleaned from a note from her brother or from observing part of her father's correspondence. Something entirely innocuous, connecting his name with other information. He had been very, very careful to cover his tracks.

"You only invest in ventures you feel wise, with future profits on a scalable range," she said, fingers clasping more securely.

Her problem was that she seemed unable to stop speaking when she truly wanted something. She lacked that cue of social control that dictated silence in variable negotiating conditions. That lack, along with her extensive and knowledgeable verbiage, allowed him to fit pieces together into an interesting picture. He remembered everything he read. And she had paused far too suspiciously on multiple pronouns.

"You have been writing to me in lieu of your father."

It was her turn to freeze, eyes wide. About goddamn time too.

She could have argued that she simply read all of her father's correspondence before he sent it, but her reaction killed any refutation.

"*You* are James Pace. Others have speculated that your brother was leading things. But it was *you* all along." Handwriting, timing, need. "At least for the last six months, you have been acting as your father."

His reevaluation of her was quick, but not as sharp as it would be in other circumstances. Blunted edges and a trace of uncertainty would need to be ruthlessly squashed later, but he had enough to work with for the moment. No one but Roman had ever survived against him.

His laughter emerged darker and far more familiar this time. Dark silk wove from his tongue. "Forgery and impersonation." He leaned forward, letting the dark smile curve. "I could have you or your father arrested or ruined for worse."

She pulled herself together more quickly than he was used to with opponents. She didn't confirm or deny it. Her eyes simply held his. "You could, but I do not believe that will serve you best."

"You don't know *what* would serve me."

"Me." She folded her hands together, her eyes still meeting his. They were outwardly calm, but there was a vibrating energy underneath. The damn woman didn't follow any sort of normal script, but she wasn't unaffected. "I . . ."

She hesitated for a moment then her whole body seemed to push forth. "*I* have reached a mutually agreeable business correspondence and relationship with you in the last few months, even if under a somewhat cloudy guise. And I hope that knowledge will make it apparent that I can and will serve you. Well."

He pressed down on the automatic reaction of his body. He had gotten rid of people for decades without trouble. One wisp of a girl would be no different, no matter the underlying grit she continued to show. "You have obviously not thought through ways I might require you to serve."

He let his eyes drift over her. "And without your consent on the matter. I could extinguish your life this instant should I choose. With one flick of a switch. Or I could push you against this desk right now, strip your virtue, make you unmarriageable for anyone. You could scream and scream, and no one would come to save you. Not from me. Not here. Here, where you've so willingly offered yourself. Where I could so easily use you, then toss you away."

She twitched. *Good.*

"My brother's language is . . . was . . . foul at times, but yours, sir, contains a new level of filth for me."

The clock in the corner issued its first chime. He stiffened. Had she been in his office that long? What was he doing? Goddamn woman and his goddamn *issues.*

"*I* am foul. *Now get out.*"

She gaped at his tone, and the first inklings of true uncertainty gleamed in her eyes. For some reason it angered him as much as it darkly pleased him to finally see it there. "I . . ."

A rustle of sound at the door extinguished all emotion, smothering it by a solid wall, pulling his senses around it and into sharp, pointed focus. Too late for her to leave.

"Do you know why I have been keeping to shadow, Miss Pace?" he asked, almost conversationally, as he extended his right hand toward the candle's flame and slid the blade down his left wrist and into the belly of his palm, fingers curling around the tip.

The uncertainty in her eyes grew at the abrupt change in tone. He would have reveled in it a moment ago. "I had a thought that perhaps you were either overly dramatic or physically scarred somewhere I can't immediately see, Mr. Merrick. Either is a possibil—"

The gaslights near the door shattered. He flicked his fingers forward, the blade slicing through the air, and the man who broke the lights hit the floor amidst the glass. Andreas was around the desk and pushing Phoebe Pace from her chair before she fully knew what was happening. Before the reflection of light extinguished completely from widened eyes as he snuffed the candles on his desk.

The back section of the room was cast into darkness as he pulled back quickly into the shadows, away from her. Pushing her to the floor had cost him the view of the door and the easy answer as to how many people were now in the room. The air near his uncovered throat rippled, the bullet passing within an inch, as he stepped through the smoke produced by the retort of the first shot, then the second. A darker pillar of shadow broke the wall of midnight. A quick flick of his wrist, and it folded into the dark of the floor.

The board three over from his right foot creaked. He threw out the heel of his hand and snapped the neck of the second man and gutted the third who had crept behind—the man shouldn't have taken such a job with a wheeze in his chest. Andreas flattened himself against the wall, flipped his last knife, and listened.

Too easily dispatched. The thrill of the hunt pressed, as expected, but something tightened underneath his deadened feelings.

The whimper was loud. The scrape of the edge of her slippers as she was pulled upright.

"Show yourself, Merrick, or I'll gut her."

He knew that voice. A head shorter than himself, he'd be three inches taller than Phoebe Pace.

"I care nothing"—he threw the knife as hard as he was capable—"for her."

A body hit his desk. He waited until he heard the quick intake of soft air. He moved to the desk, relit the first candle, then pushed the body to the floor. Normally, he would retrieve his blade, but he watched her instead. That insect had looked that way, eyes so wide, as he'd raised a hand to squash it.

He motioned to the door. "Get out." The familiar smell of gunpowder finally penetrated his senses fully. He lit the other two candles. The wax hissed faintly.

"You saved my life."

He reached for the bellpull and gave it a yank.

"What are you doing?"

"I don't clean." He didn't know why he answered. But the statement was true. He didn't, not anymore.

He didn't need to look at her to know what she was doing. Everyone who wasn't used to it stared at the bodies. Sometimes they had to be pulled away, eyes unmoving.

"They are dead. You killed them."

"Get out."

"You saved my life." He could hear her step closer, her voice uncertain. "I owe you my life."

He liked neither the wonder nor blankness he heard mixed in her voice.

"Doubtful." He sneered at her and saw the reflection of the mixture on her face, eyes and lips wide. "Perhaps your virginity. They would have likely found that a good reason to leave you alive. Are you going to owe me that?" He let his lips twist, heavy and sardonic, watching her. "No? Then get out."

"That is awful." There was still a tinge of awe present, though.

His palms flattened on the desk, and he leaned forward into her space, wanting, needing to wipe away any good feeling she might have concerning him. "And it is the only sentiment of which I'm capable. I never invited you into *my* room. *Leave*."

"Someone tried to *kill* you. Your wrist!" She touched his hand, and he went stock-still. She leaned over to examine it, the top of her head brushing beneath his nose. Only his sudden immobility stopped him from violently pulling away. "From the candles?" Had she *bathed* in bloody honey? "How did you get this burn?" Her gloved finger pulled along the flesh beneath, carefully not touching the burned skin.

He abruptly pulled back. "Leave."

"You need help." She grabbed her bag. "I have liniment at ho—"

"Leave."

More digging. "I can help you."

"I don't *need* help."

She paused and looked up. "Someone just tried to kill you. Five—*five*—men tried to kill you."

"And six will tomorrow. Now *get out*."

"Even if you won't accept aid, I still need to speak with—"

"Your debts are resolved."

"What?" Her eyes went wider than they had when seeing the bodies.

He grabbed the folder from his desk—for the past few weeks he had always had it near, tempting him—and thrust it toward her. "Here are the majority of your markers, now *leave*."

She stared at the folder, not touching it. "You accept the terms? But I haven't even shown you—"

"Forget the terms." He thrust forward the last few inches and shoved the folder into her delicately gloved hands. "I'm not interested. Leave London and take your parents with you, or you will regret it."

"But"—she looked up at him with those wide eyes—"what do you want in return?"

"I want you to *leave*."

"I can't just take these. They are worth far too much—"

He walked around the desk and took her satin-covered arm in his hand. Soft under his bare fingertips. He had no use for gloves unless he needed to hide himself. They hindered his aim.

And he never touched people unless it was to harm them. Nobody except Roman and Nana.

He could feel the heat of her beneath his fingers, warm and real.

He picked up his pace, opened the door, and thrust her into the hall. Two men were running down the corridor, and he gave a jerk of his head to the interior of the room. They slipped inside.

Her solicitor was groaning against the wall of the hall as if he'd been attacked too, but Andreas didn't spare him another look. He pulled the door shut.

He stared at the wood as the sounds of the men moving bodies echoed behind him. He knew she was still standing there on the other side, unmoving, folder in hand.

He could still *smell* her there, standing on the same boards.

He had given her most of her family's debts back. Ripping his plans to tatters. A variety of horrible outcomes could now commence.

It didn't matter. He never relied solely on one course of action. He could complete his revenge in a variety of ways.

And he could still feel the heat of her in his usually rock-steady fingers. If any of the men behind him were stupid enough to comment upon the twitching, they would join the bodies already on the floor.

Better to get *her* out of his office and life. That way he'd never see her again.

Chapter 3

"**W**hat?" he barked at the knock. He had gotten a sum total of two hours' sleep. Though dealing with the perpetrators who had burned Building Twelve in their search for the Exchange records had relieved some of the tension *she* had created.

A head peered around the edge, a very nervous look upon young features. "Sir, there is a woman here. She, um, she is making trouble downstairs."

He very carefully laid down his pen. Stupid tilting-headed nightmares. "Describe. Her."

The boy's eyes widened. "Gray hair and brown eyes, smartly dressed."

Something loosened. "Gray hair?"

"Well, not really. It's brown—she didn't get the wig all the way on, you see." The boy tripped over the words at Andreas's expression, displeasure assuredly tightening it. "My sister's an actress and she always complains about the sides, so I know what ter look for, especially when I see a pretty face," he squeaked in a half-broken voice. "She brought biscuits!"

Andreas stared, sure that he had incorrectly heard the boy's terror-filled last words. "She brought biscuits."

"Yes." The boy perked up, terror receding for a moment. "And they are quite tasty, fluffy centers and butter-crisped crus . . ." The boy physically shrank back. Good. "Yes, um, well, but, she delivered four baskets and is asking for requests for the morrow. It's pandy-, pander-, pandetmonitum," he said faintly. "That's what Mr. Fox called it."

Andreas tapped his finger on the desk, staring hard at the messenger.

"They said to tell you." He could barely hear the words, so faint as they were.

"Then Mr. Fox should fix it, shouldn't he?"

The boy ran to the door, hell's hounds on his heels.

As irreplaceable as Milton Fox was, if he didn't take care of the problem, he would *be* replaced.

Milton could deal with her smile. It was like the plague, creeping in on little rat feet, reaching to infect him. He wasn't going near her.

The next day he was interrupted by another knock.

A slightly older voice spoke this time. "Sir, Mr. Fox thought you should be informed that there is a woman downstairs—"

"Describe her." He didn't lift his head, his voice harsh and partly directed at himself.

"Prettier than street Sarah, uglier than floor Sarah." When Andreas didn't look up or respond to that absurd description, the lackey hurried on. "Floor Sarah has bigger ti . . . er, um . . . the woman downstairs is handing out pamphlets."

Andreas counted to ten. Roman always wanted him to do that when he contemplated murder.

He wanted to know if Phoebe Pace was still in disguise and what impression she was giving. His vague question asking for a description served that purpose well. This was by far the stupidest answer he had received in the flurry of visits in the past two days.

He finally looked at the boy, who shifted under his black gaze. "Pamphlets?"

Andreas recognized him as one of the leaders of the twelve to eighteen crowd. That explained the pubescent response to her description. The boy shifted at whatever showed on Andreas's face. "Yes. She got into a right state when she realized no one could read them, though. She's setting up some sort of litacerary curse. Some of the boys want to know—is that like gypsy magic? Can you curse someone to read?"

"*Leave.*"

It was good to know that people still promptly followed darkly hissed commands.

"Sir, we have a problem."

"Describe the woman."

" . . . how did you know it was a woman?"

"Describe. Her."

"Reminds me of my aunt Patty. She always

smelled like baked goods and hugs. I like her." This was said somewhat defensively.

Andreas rubbed his eyes, figures blurring on the page. The responses were growing worse. He should do something about it. But it meant acknowledging the problem. He didn't want to acknowledge her existence at all.

"But, see the thing is, sir, we don't know what to do with a hundred chickens."

He didn't take his eyes off the paper the fourth day as the first knock came. "Describe her."

"Oh. How—" Whoever it was cut off abruptly at Andreas's hand gesture. "Nice? Kind of strange for the Quality though. Even the men get their noses upturned. But she didn't blink at the smell in the alley at all."

Andreas paused. "The alley?"

"Well, she must have smelled it, as she is having people clean it. But she didn't get high-and-mighty about it, and she's chipping in herself too. Got all of the boys to help even. Helps that their bellies are full of biscuits each day. Right good, they are. Think she even bakes them herself. A woman of *quality* baking for us, can you run your head around it?"

Andreas lifted his head, sheer rage—mostly directed internally—searing him. The boy suddenly seemed to remember to whom he was speaking.

"I'll, I'll just be going," he squeaked. "Have it under control, of course. Mr. Fox just thought—"

"If anyone comes up here again to inform me of something *she* is doing, I will shoot him." He thought that was said quite pleasantly too, and it bore forth when the boy tripped running out. He should have issued the threat on the second occasion of disturbance. He would have had peace and quiet since—no one would be fooled into thinking it an empty threat.

Andreas waited for the door to slam before pushing away from the desk. He whirled around and walked to the window, then edged the drape and sheer away to peer through the slit. Sure enough, there was a strange gray-haired head—a ridiculous wig mussed from activity and sticking up in some spots—directing mismatched street rats in the back alley.

He could even hear some of her words, now that he allowed himself to think it not just a crazed remnant of an overactive imagination.

"We'll get this done quickly, working together! There is some nice architecture here to admire too. Perhaps we will tackle the front next week?"

Andreas let the sheer fall back into place with the drape, his fingers still touching the material. Perhaps he would wake tomorrow and find it just another in a string of nightmares.

No one knocked on his door the next day. Nor the day after. Nor the one after that. But that didn't mean he was unaware of what was happening. Someone had carried a plate of those fucking biscuits past his room, and even the oak door had provided no barrier for the smell. Not for anything of *hers*.

After someone had put one on his lunch tray

the first day, he had . . . discouraged . . . such a future action. Not that he ate most things that were brought anyway, but the biscuit had sat there, looking fluffy and happy and innocent, and smelling of the same, and he'd wanted to squash it beneath his bootheel.

The boy who had retrieved the tray had been the recipient of his ire instead. He hadn't had one on his tray since. And he'd heard the little shits whining ad nauseum in the kitchens later asking when Mr. Roman would return.

Work again commenced on the alley in the back for the fourth afternoon. With a cheerful voice leading the damned.

A cheerful voice emerging from lush, curved lips, no doubt.

"You are doing a great job. We will have this space looking like Berkeley Square in no time."

He rhythmically tapped his pen against his paper. Tap, tap, bloody tap.

"Great effort, Fred. And Johnny, you are giving it your all. The pride in your work is really showing. You said you were a crossing sweeper? I can tell. I'll bet you earned at least a pound a week." Pause. "Ten pence? Really? Well, I'll be sure to tip Smitty—he's the boy on my corner—extra tomorrow."

Andreas pulled his hand over his face and stared at the heavy oak of the door. It was just this side of stifling in the early July heat, but he couldn't risk opening the window for a breeze. He'd done that the day before yesterday and had accomplished not a single thing as a result.

He should just open it. It's not like he couldn't hear everything she said anyway. His ears seemed specifically attuned to the sound of her voice, like a faulty violin in an otherwise seamless orchestra.

Or more realistically, the perfect violin in their disreputable symphony.

Why wouldn't she just *go away*?

"Of course, I will keep bringing biscuits." Pause. "Do you think so? I will definitely do that."

A flurry of voices melded together, then stopped talking abruptly. As soon as she probably opened her raspberry bloody lips.

"Oh, yes, I plan to be here for months."

His hand jerked forward, and his quill broke against the spine of a book on his desk.

Three more days. Two sets of footsteps. One hesitant knock on the door. So it had come to this. Someone had bent under the pressure, acquiescing to large, liquid eyes and succulent lips. Risking death to bring her here. He squeezed his seventh quill in as many days between his fingers. It squeaked under the compression, knowing its life too was close to an end.

He would say nothing. And she would go away.

A knock sounded again. This time he knew it was hers, soft gloves rapping the hard wood.

"Enter." The damning word slipped from his lips.

He couldn't even swear profusely at himself, so tight did he grip his physical and emotional responses immediately following the escaped word.

He could smell her as soon as she entered. Ten

long paces away, and, without looking, he could pinpoint the exact spot on which she stood by smell alone. Goddamn honey and biscuits.

"Good afternoon, Mr. Merrick." Her voice was happy and warm. "I've been looking forward to speaking with you again."

He didn't look up. He refused to do so. If she had a pistol, he would just have to die, triumphantly oblivious to a last sight of her. "I don't believe I invited you back," he replied.

"No, and I waited a period of time for you to do so, but I have come to the conclusion that it is not a good idea to await an invitation from you," she said cheerfully. He stiffened as she padded over on her slippers and sat in the chair across from his desk. Thick wood threaded with impenetrable steel stood between them, but he would have been more comfortable with half of London betwixt instead. "I have a status report for you if you have a moment."

He forced himself to keep writing. Long scratches that would likely make as little sense later as the woman seated across from him. "A status report?"

She rustled her bag, and the sound made him stiffen automatically, but he forced his shoulders to relax.

"Yes, I am noting everything here."

He peered through his lashes just enough to see a large ledger open on her lap.

He said nothing, and as expected, she filled the silence.

"It will take quite a bit, but I believe I will have our debt repaid even sooner than calculated."

He stopped writing and looked up sharply at those words. The wig looked as ridiculous up close as he'd figured it would, blocking her rich brown hair. How anyone would be taken in by . . .

People were stupid.

She kept speaking. "I have many plans, though I invite you to help me by making requests. I will see what we can accommodate. Working together on this will be nice, don't you think?"

"What are you babbling about?"

His harsh response didn't diminish her smile one bit. "Well, we have currently repaid eighty-four pounds, Mr. Merrick. And by the week's end, I believe that number will be ninety-two."

He stared at her. "What?"

"The biscuits and treats I make are gifts, of course. But the chickens constituted the bulk of one debt itself."

"Chickens?"

Of course, he knew they were overrun with fowl now, as even though he had patently defied asking questions about her visits, he had been informed of the chickens' presence and had heard the birds squawking—who in the neighborhood hadn't?

"Yes, I thought they would be quite useful as you have many mouths to feed. Your kitchen staff seemed most pleased."

He stared at her. "You thought chickens would be useful to us, so you brought us enough to feed the entire East End of London?"

She nodded. "Twenty sterlings' worth."

"One hundred chickens equals twenty pounds?"

"You do not agree?" She nodded and made a

notation. "Fifteen then, and I will do a personal favor for you."

Dear God. "No, twenty sounds appropriate," he said, a touch of horror creeping into his voice.

He pinned his darkest look on the large man hovering at the door, who flinched away. After defying a direct order already, the man's ability to breathe depended solely on his silence concerning this conversation. And they would be having . . . words . . . later. The man vigorously nodded his understanding. Andreas turned his attention back to the current bane of his existence as she continued to speak.

"I scrubbed the alley." She made a check mark. "That is worth three pounds four pence a day for a total of thirteen-"

"You used *my* labor."

What was he doing? *Shut up.*

She looked up. "I paid them."

Don't say a word. "With what?" *Goddammit!*

"Food."

"You can't pay them with food."

"Don't be silly."

He stared at her.

"You look struck by the notion, but of course I can, let me explain," she continued. "You pay for a meal at an inn or dining hall, do you not?"

Silly?

She tilted her head. "Or do you not pay? Do they let you bribe them?" This was said somewhat cheerfully.

The words of the query were on his tongue, but he swallowed them. He already knew the answer. Her instability was obvious.

"I am sure you then forgive one of their debts," she said in that perpetually warm voice.

He had seen desperate, starving men eat rat shit on the streets. They usually foamed at the mouth within a week, crazed and infected. That had to be why he was staring at her lips so hard. For evidence.

She leaned forward, conspiratorially, and winked. "I won't tell."

Rat-shit-eating insane.

He flicked a finger at the man by the door without looking away from her. "Leave."

She raised a brow as she turned to watch the man flee, his large frame not hindering his flight, the door slamming behind him. "I say, you are most abusive with that word, Mr. Merrick. Poor Bertrand. Do most people hop to do your bidding?"

"Yes."

"Well, that is not good. It builds character to be told no."

"You must have a lot of character then."

"That is kind of you." Warm smile.

"I was being rude."

"Well, then at least I can say you are an honest man."

He stared at her. She smiled back.

He felt like a bow, strung taut in the hands of a warrior who had been holding it in position far too long. "What do you want, Miss Pace?"

What do you want from me? It was the question that had been plaguing him day and night for a quarter cycle of the moon now.

"I aspire to fairness, Mr. Merrick. I appreciate

your relief of our debts last week, but truly cannot in good conscience just accept such abject generosity. The Paces are good for their words and debts."

There was a slight buzzing in his ears. "You are going to deliver chickens and clean alleys for the next decade?"

"Oh, no. Those are just small things. Things I thought would be nice to trade for. It hasn't fully trickled through the business vines yet that most of our debts have been cleared, so I am still forced to negotiate for things without true wherewithal. That will change soon though, thanks to you."

Roman would love her. They were both foolishly chipper people. Especially in the face of dire circumstance.

If only Roman were here, Andreas wouldn't be dealing with this. *No one* dealt with Andreas when they could deal with Roman. Which was *exactly* the way he liked it.

"In the meantime, Mr. Merrick, I have begun to list all of the ways that I can help through means other than using currency. For instance, I am quite a good matchmaker. I have a few possibilities for you already in mind. You could certainly use a woman's sensibilities around here. The boys downstairs are desperate for a mothering influence."

He couldn't even credit of what she was speaking. She thought he'd care about a mothering influence for the boys who worked for them? They were Roman's responsibility. Everyone employed here was. Everyone knew that. And yet with those wide eyes staring at him, he almost felt an . . . an urge to nod.

Perhaps shooting *himself* was the answer.

"The prospects must be of hardy temperament, of course. You seem to terrify the daylights out of nearly everyone."

"I've always found the *nearly* to be a pity."

She clapped her hands together, leaning forward, *inviting him in.* "If you show that humor more often, it will make things infinitely easier."

"I wasn't being humorous," he said stonily. This was just like the first night she had shown up. A pit of terror he hadn't felt since he was ten years old was creeping up on him. Self-preservation telling him he had to get rid of her any way he could.

"There are a number of—"

He leaned forward, and she stopped talking, leaning farther toward him as well, watching him with interest. She had freckles on the bridge of her nose. He could picture her lifting her face to the sun. "Do you know what I would do to a woman who married me?" he said softly.

She quickly turned a few pages and poised her hand to make a notation. "Do tell me. The more details I have, the better I can help."

"I'd likely kill her within the first week. With my bare hands, so I didn't have to dirty anything else."

She blinked, then carefully turned the pages back, sitting upright again. "We'll revisit that subject in the future then, shall we? For now, there are a few personal tasks that I would like to undertake for—"

"*No.*"

"—you. They won't cancel any other debt, but you saved me from—"

"*No.*"

"—certain death. It was beyond noble. And I would be recalcitrant to simply ignore your gesture."

He *tapped* his quill, and felt the give and heard the soft thwump to know it was broken, the top half hanging by a thread. He glared at her as ferociously as he was able.

She smiled back. "I imagined you would be lovely, but you increasingly show your generous spirit."

He tapped his broken quill ten more times, just to pretend he still had control, and ignored the thwumps that should have been sharp raps.

She tilted her head at him. "You are quite handsome, Mr. Merrick. In a very striking and severe way, of course. But it is undeniable. Like a harsh thunderstorm, beautiful lightning cutting and flashing. Did you know?"

Not even the gloriously colored insect had been this repellent and astonishing. He felt an overwhelming urge pulling him to capture such a unique specimen in a jar, so he'd be able to study it forever. But the equally powerful urge to push it as far from him as possible pressed.

"Is that all, Miss Pace?"

"Oh, no, of course not. You have quite a powerful and mysterious way about you as well. It goes with the thunderstorm analogy really. You're quite, well, magnetic. I'd say that—"

He dropped the broken quill and held up one hand. The other pressed against his forehead. He *never* gave in to such urges. He would have had to kill Bertrand if he'd still been in the room.

"Is that all you have to *report*?"

"Yes, for now," she said cheerfully. "Though I will be around quite a bit more in the coming weeks."

He couldn't contain the horror that caused within him.

"Doing a bit of extra work, nothing to be concerned about." She waved her hand as if those words could be any further from the truth.

"Concern doesn't reflect my feeling on the matter."

"And they say you don't have feelings." She winked at him.

Winked. Then pushed at a stiff side section of wig.

"Why are you wearing that ridiculous thing?" he demanded.

She didn't seem to find the sudden conversational change strange. He wondered if she found anything strange.

"No one pays attention to the elderly on the street. And your men seem quite loyal to you. Do you think they will give me away if they discover my true name? I figured that you would know who I was, and that that would be enough for our debt situation."

His men knew who she was without his having to say a word. He had a retinue following her at all times. And a girl from Mayfair wouldn't be able to give hardened street rats the slip. The gossip would have spread quickly from the men who followed her to the men she interacted with at the hell.

Kitchen conversations had probably been vastly

amusing concerning the strange, bewigged society girl.

The wig was truly awful.

"Don't wear it when you are in here." Coldness spread, and he willed the words back. What the hell was she doing to him? "*Don't come here at all.*"

She smiled oddly at him, then carefully removed a few pins and shook her head, freeing her real hair from beneath the dowager helmet. Brown hair tumbled messily around her shoulders and down her back.

He could feel the already broken quill break into another piece under his clenched fist but couldn't bring himself to care. "Your reputation will be stripped if you are found here, yet you reappear every day. Which is much to my displeasure, Miss Pace."

She pulled fingers through the hair at her temple, looking at his desk as she did so, thank God. "My family's reputation is the one I am currently trying to rebuild, Mr. Merrick, as I told you previously. It is that which I am concerned with at the moment. I need hardly worry about my own reputation if I cannot fix my family's."

Her eyes met his for a moment, piercing, then she smiled softly. The hair on his neck rose. "I am quite pleased with my progress, though. And as a particularly valued investor in our company and fund, I will keep you apprised of all transactions, of course. And—"

He held up his hand again and narrowed his eyes, watching everything about her. She waited patiently, expression bright. As if she were perfectly innocent and naïve. Sparkling like fresh morning dew. Only occasionally slipping to show the workings of a keen mind behind the daftness. Sitting there thrusting that *something* at him, drawing his interest.

He didn't think she was acting. She was innocent and naïve, *and* sharp and clever. It was irritating. Repulsive. Captivating.

The sudden financial silence of the Pace affairs in London had seemed a godsend for the past week— the only bright spot. Since with her hassling them in the East End, when would she have time to do other things?

But if he forced himself to think on it—and her—the silence meant someone in James Pace's company was extensively plotting.

And that person was very likely seated across from him.

He studied her. There was a twinkle in her eye. It was nauseating even to recognize such a gleam. She was up to something. She had taken great care, but though well covered, there were smudges under her eyes that bespoke of long nights and too much responsibility.

Plans swirled—strategies formed—vines of ideas and alternatives twirled around and gripped possibilities. Dissonance and dread.

"Very well, Miss Pace. You will give me a weekly report on the fund *and* your company. When you gather details, bring them directly to me before speaking to others."

Once a week. He could do it. Better to see her

once a week and be on top of any possible machinations.

He turned back to the papers on his desk and
searched until he found an unbroken pen. And if
she wasn't going to worry about her reputation,
he sure as hell wasn't. She could damn well bring
him information directly. She was going to come
anyway, obviously. And better than dealing with a
half-wit, gibbering accountant. "But I don't want
to see that wig once you enter."

Shit, damn, cock, fucker.

The silence grew on the other side of his desk.
He kept his gaze on the ink stuttering from his new
pen as he moved it in what he hoped was the start
of an actual number.

"You are *dismissed*, Miss Pace," he said without
looking up.

"Very well." Her voice was full of verve. *Of
course it was*. He could hear her reattaching that
ridiculous thing to her hair and gathering her
things. "I'll see you by the week's end. I wish you a
wonderful afternoon, Mr. Merrick!"

He peered up as she walked to the door with
soft, swaying movements. She turned at the door,
catching him staring, and gave him a bright, soft
smile, then shut the door behind her.

He stared at the door for a long, long time, ink
pooling around the nib stuck to his page.

Chapter 4

There was a small woven basket waiting on his desk the next day, still smelling like warmed-from-the-oven sin. A note was attached written with the words "Have a good day!" A drawing of a tiny dog chasing a butterfly completed the absurdity.

He stood in front of his desk, just staring at it and the basket for a full minute. Asps didn't smell like baked items, but the latter were no less dangerous. He tented the edge of the cloth cover with his smallest finger. Three fruit tarts lay inside.

Poisoned most likely.

He never ate anything that was delivered. Sometimes he didn't even eat the items brought from the kitchen downstairs. It depended on who cooked and who delivered. He had plenty of experience with an empty belly both before and after he had been dumped on the streets, so it mattered little most days if he survived on salt and water.

The basket sat untouched on the far corner of his desk until one of the boys swept it away at midday. He felt an absurd amount of relief when it was gone.

The next day the note said, "Wishing you good luck with your day's agenda!" and the drawing showed a man playing chess. There was a dog in that one too. Cinnamon and honey wafted through the room.

The third day it said, "Hard work is beautiful, and you work hard!" with a picture of a grinning dog, tongue out. Andreas's lips twisted in distaste, and he gingerly pushed the note away from him, so it was facing the other direction from his chair.

And still he could see the curves of the letters in his head. The hand-drawn figures made for him.

He was slowly going insane.

On the fourth day, he drummed his fingers looking at the top of the newest basket on his desk. At the linen covering the rich-smelling bread beneath.

Sticky, honey-fingered scent trails finding cracks in the barrier, drifting upward, straight to his brain.

Each day the baked goods smelled *better* than the day before. Like she was putting in extra effort each day. Trying to break down a wall that was unassailable.

He pushed it away.

Five minutes later, he pushed it farther away.

Ten minutes later he threw his pen across the room, grabbed the handle of the basket, and strode toward the door. He swung it back in order to chuck it down the hall. Even as it swung past him, the scent trail lifted, and his arm stopped the forward momentum.

He hadn't screamed in a very, very long time. But his throat tightened, remembering how.

He took a deep breath, eyes closed, then triple-locked his door and strode downstairs.

He tossed the basket to a boy at the door, who barely caught it, stupid surprise painting his features. If the boy was smart, he would get rid of the basket and not open it to find the savory cobras inside. Andreas brushed past him roughly and walked down the alley. The *clean* alley. Hell, a prostitute would be hard-pressed to choose between the street and her sheets at the moment.

And he could still smell those fucking biscuits, like they had lodged themselves permanently into the space between his lips and nose. Into his consciousness.

Standing near a three-day-old hanged man would be preferable, if only to freshen the tainted air.

Three streets over the shadows behind him grew longer. Fine. Perfect. Whatever it took. He turned into the main thoroughfare. Citizens enveloped him on all sides, and he grimaced in distaste. It was always such when he first entered a crowd. But bodies automatically began shifting to the perimeter of the walk, and he strode through the middle with ease. People could feel the devil in their wake.

He avoided looking at the faces of the hoi polloi around him. People going about their business. Some bemoaning their lot in life, others celebrating their good fortune. Watching them stare or flinch was always irritating, so he avoided making direct eye contact.

But that didn't mean he wasn't aware of them, as a body, a unit, individuals making up a sweeping tide. When someone wasn't a part of that crowd, they stuck out. Eyes told much about a person, but in a crowd it was too easy to become distracted by the extra thoughts inevitably caused by meeting a person's eyes. The way a body shifted never lied.

And the man striding toward him, twitching just a few inches inside the vee of the crowd line that spread in front, might as well have been waving a red flag. The movements of the crowd slowed in Andreas's view. Two steps away, the man's arm moved out in a diminished line. One pace away, Andreas stepped into the man, caught his wrist and twisted it, embedding the man's blade into the man's own stomach using his forward momentum. Andreas let go, shifting his body forward again, and continued walking, the crowd closing behind.

The screams didn't start for another six seconds.

It had been a short knife. The kind favored on the streets of York. One of Cornelius's men most likely. And Cornelius, who ran the underworld of the northern countryside, wasn't stupid. Which meant—

Andreas pulled his head back just in time and grabbed the arm thrust in front of his neck. Thrust from the alley to the right. The fist glittered. He gripped the exposed wrist and pulled at the same time he thrust a palm against the man's shoulder. A loud crack sounded. Pushing the openmouthed man away—no one could hear him scream over the racket of the crowd gathered back around the first fallen man—Andreas whirled into the alley and caught the arm of one of the men who approached from behind—shadows snapping back into the darkness.

A quick move sent the man's head into the wall. He fell to the ground without comment. Another man rushed in, trying to capitalize, *sword* thrusting forth. *Sword?* What the—

He dodged and twisted his body, flat steel sliding along the fabric over his midsection. He grabbed the man's wrist and cracked a bone there. The man screamed, and the sword released. Andreas pulled his fingers up, smoothly removing it, and stepped back as the man fell to his knees.

"I know who you are," the man said hoarsely, clutching his broken wrist.

Andreas didn't show his tension, but he watched the man more carefully.

"People call you the mastermind, the *unnatural*."

Relief mixed with irritation. Andreas slid forward a step, knowing what the partial afternoon shadows would do to his particular features. Sharp and dark and strangely regal. *Unnatural.*

"Am I?"

The man hissed in a breath. "You have at least ten targets on your back. You won't survive the day."

"And yet I've survived all the days thus far."

"You control the devil's machine. And you will be destroyed along with it."

Ah, a zealot. With a sword. A *sword*. It was like rolling a cannon into a tavern fight.

Though there were some of the Quality who still favored the weapon. For *honor*.

Phoebe Pace's world.

It was a moment's hesitation on top of his arrogance, but it was enough.

The man lunged forward, and with his functioning hand, he thrust a knife into Andreas's right leg. A final, desperate effort. Andreas looked down at the knife oddly sticking out, then looked at the man and smiled.

The complete terror that action inspired was . . . always welcome. And worth a few scratches.

He kicked the man in the teeth with his left boot, then reached down and slowly pulled the knife free. The man scrambled back against the wall, the back of one hand clutching his broken wrist over his bloodied mouth, complete terror in his gaze.

Andreas cast a look around the alley. Eyed shadows drew back, disappearing into rock-faced holes and doorways.

Satisfied, he moved forward, towering over the man, weaving the flat handle of the knife through the knuckles of his right hand, blade flashing as it turned. A cute trick he had practiced during the long months he had been bedridden so long ago. "Now then, let's get to business, shall we?"

He had approximately five minutes before reinforcements or the Watch arrived.

He wistfully pushed aside the thought to crouch at the man's level, all bare-toothed smile in place. But if he crouched on the ground right now, he'd never get back up.

"You, you . . ." The man was staring in abject horror at Andreas's trousered leg. There was a thin stream of darkness there—he could feel the trickle of blood. But it was nowhere near the bloodletting the man would imagine from an embedded knife wound.

It was luck or a curse that everyone went for his right leg.

Andreas smiled coldly, eyes never leaving the man's, and tested the sword in his left hand, getting a feel for it. It had been a while, but he had been raised to handle one, and he'd practiced fiercely years later, hoping that someday he'd use one to kill those who had insisted he be taught in the first place.

"You are wasting your time," the man croaked. "It doesn't matter what you do to me."

"No? I would think it would matter quite a bit to you," Andreas said. He lifted the man's chin with the long steel, wryly grateful for it, as he didn't have to bend to the man's level. "You can make this as easy or as difficult as you want it to be."

"Whatever you do to me, twelve men will replace me, just like the Hydra."

"Twelve." Andreas eyed the man's limp and broken hand. He would give him credit for that last strike, but little more. "Each time I speak to one of you, I grow dimmer."

"Gone will be the slavers of old, of all that is decent. I fight under the banner of revolution."

Andreas ran the tip of the blade under the man's jaw, stroking. These *interviews* always worked best when he and Roman worked in tandem, so different from each other in some ways, so similar in others that it was disconcerting. His brother made it a game to extract information easily with his glib smile, but Andreas could inspire terror without help just fine.

"You will fight under a gravestone," he said, his normal bored tone edged with silk. "And doubtfully a decent one."

There was a twitch to the man's puffed eyes. Tiny, but perceptible. Good.

"Or with no marker at all to show you were even of this earth once." He forced the man to tip his head to the side and saw the diamond mark beneath the starched collar on the back of his neck, the brand. Certainty burned coldly. "No. Straight through to hell. I'll be waiting for you there too. And your revolution will be snuffed as easily as you extinguished the lives of six men." He might not keep track of their names from day to day, but the Merricks took care of their own.

And Andreas was *very* good at revenge.

The twitch became a swollen lurch. "I, I don't know about any dead men. But, but . . . sometimes losses occur. For the greater good. Any who die will die in glory. And their families will be provided for in the new world."

"Is that what Cornelius told you?" Andreas smiled at the man's jerk. He hated the bastard who ruled the north, but he had to be admired for the way he ruthlessly used people while at the same time making those people think plans were of their own design. "Did he also tell you that if by some remote chance I decide to turn you over, you will be sentenced to hang? That you are being held responsible by the Crown for last week's events?"

He put pressure on the blade. "Lucky I got to you first," he whispered.

The man gave a choked sound, eyes wide.

"All debts will be wiped free." Words spilled like the trickle of blood down his neck. "Everyone starting fresh."

Andreas watched the way the man tried to hide the shaking of his limbs, the cold sweat dripping down his face from the pain of his wrist and his fear. "You want the Collateral Exchange burned, hmmm?"

"It is *evil*. It preys on vulnerable, desperate people."

Personal feeling. Andreas examined the hilt of the man's sword before the link slotted into place. "You are Barton's fourth son, who lost forty thousand last year."

The man's eyes widened. Andreas gave a cold laugh. "Of course you would want the Exchange burned."

He rarely played with the *ton*. That was Roman's game. But he had met the senior Barton once when Roman had called him over in the middle of a hand. And Andreas knew everyone, down to their last groat, on paper.

"Forty thousand, seven hundred and forty-two, with seven darlings to spare, as of last week, wasn't it?" Andreas said, almost lazily. "Gregory Daniels forgave you the two markers for fifteen pounds, twelve pence though. I wouldn't have. That was a stupid bet to make on O'Leary's daughter."

"How—"

Andreas leaned forward, tip pressing and drawing more blood. "I want to know where Cornelius is," he said harshly.

The man usually stayed holed up in the north, where he held power, but he had been expanding his territory, creeping south more and more over the past year. Trying to make deals and sway those in the middle to his side. Making a play for a piece of the capital. London was the jewel of England, and the Merricks had held that jewel tightly and completely without challenge for the last decade.

Cornelius had smartly latched upon Viscount Garrett as a pawn. Which meant that he knew something of Andreas's past.

"I don't know." The man's words came faster, as if by doing so it would wipe out the rest of the conversation. "Our revolution's glorious beginnings will help all." But the desperation was leaking from his lips like the drops of sweat from his chin.

Raised in the lap of luxury, likely with two nursemaids to wait upon him. Andreas watched him coldly. "Strange how one always wants to destroy for others that which he has taken for granted and destroyed himself."

"I have seen the glorious light."

"Doubtful."

"Debt is evil. You are evil."

Andreas pricked the other side of his neck, causing a line of warm liquid to course there as well. "And Cornelius is the Redeemer," he said silkily. "He will burn off the sins of everything foul. He will return you to a life filled with golden light."

"*Yes.*"

"Don't you know it is foolish to trust in angels?"

Andreas smiled. "He will pretend to burn the papers, then kill the lot of you and take over the Exchange himself."

"No—"

Andreas pressed the tip into the underside of the man's jawbone. "You are annoying me now. You have five seconds before I tilt the blade and let it slide."

"We always meet somewhere different! And never in London! I can help you in other ways. I have information," he said desperately.

Of course he did. Should have started right away with this course of action. Phoebe Pace's bloody penchant for commentary was rubbing off on him and ruining his peace.

"Do you?"

"I can tell you schedules and plans and players."

He smiled darkly. "Good. Make it quick and concise, for my hand grows weary." He leaned forward an inch. "And don't lie."

"I won't. I know what happened to Christian Pace too," the fourth spawn of Barton babbled almost incoherently.

Andreas froze but kept the blade steady. "Do you now?" He shifted and scanned the alley, looking for a pair of eyes and arms he could use. The man would need to be moved so Andreas could question him further later.

He forced his voice to stay neutral. A feeling coursed through his body—one he hadn't had in a long time. That pause before his heart stuttered faster. "What exactly do you know? And whom else have you told?"

* * *

Three minutes later, he brushed off his hands, content that his directions would be followed, and shifted his long-term plans once again. He would bring all of them to fruition regardless of Phoebe Pace.

Chapter 5

Fruition was the fruit that realized its own rotting carcass.

He stared at the devil's basket in front of him from under the shade of his fingers, which were pressed to his brow, hair falling too long over the top. Hell's mistress whistled a tune full of seductive entreaty that pierced right through the glass and drapes.

All it had taken was one whiff of the fresh, new damn basket, and one glance at her overly cheerful note the day after apprehending Barton's son, to make him promptly . . . implement none of those new plans.

He didn't sleep or eat well on the best of days, but the last week had been worse than most. He violently suppressed any of the dreams that slipped around his nightmares, dreams that all carried the same face. He had woken in a cold sweat from both the dreams and nightmares.

And still, he had . . . done nothing. He had invoked none of the plans that he could have, instead continuing on in a sort of half-witted daze. Listening. Inhaling. Pushing away every damn morsel of sweetness that he could. Who the hell knew what would happen if he *ate* one?

He could hear her again. He heard her every damn day. In the halls, outside, in the kitchens downstairs when he slipped inside to grab something to eat, in the dead of night in bed—her voice overlapping all of his thoughts of the day.

And the smell of honey had overtaken every other sense he possessed. Honeyed biscuits wrapping her scent firmly in a knot around his neck.

He had lived a wretched life. He was an all-around bad person. He both acknowledged and had never cared about these facts. That Phoebe Pace might be some type of hell-spawned punishment was not out of the realm of possibility. He wondered if the end of twenty years of vengeance and street life had finally marked him for justice. If it had, he would face it like the blackened soul he was and stride home to hell. After his revenge was complete.

Twice he had opened his mouth to tell Milton Fox to get rid of her. To turn her out, to chase her away, to threaten her, *to do whatever he had to.*

Milton had stood there waiting on the other side of the desk, with a suspicious glint in his eyes. The edge of humor.

And Andreas had said nothing. What was he going to say? That he was scared of a lady? A little girl?

Of course, that just brought to mind that she wasn't, nor did she *look*, like a little girl at all. And

he'd angrily dismissed Milton, who should have
known what to do without being told.

"Oh, Mr. Fox, that is very sweet of you," that
damned voice in the alley said as she did the weekly
sweep she had set up.

It was obvious, when it came to it. Milton had
to die.

He struggled with the thought for a minute.
They needed Milton. And Roman would be upset.
Their weekly card games—*family* card games,
Roman called them—would be one short. Roman
would probably invite *Charlotte* then, and Andreas
would have to shoot himself.

"I would be honored."

His pen slipped and dragged a line on the page.
Honored to do what?

"Yes, ten tomorrow is fine. I will be there." The
ever-present warmth in her voice hinted at an unfettered smile as well. One given to Milton.

Andreas carefully blotted the trail of ink.

Charlotte was not the worst addition to the card
games. And Roman always understood.

Morning shadows were replaced by the sun's
rays as it rose toward midday. Andreas could tell
by the sliver of light that slipped its way around the
eternally closed drapes.

Soft slippers and the cracking of the door didn't
surprise him in the least. Not today. "Good morning, Mr. Merrick. I am sorry to bother you, but I'm
looking for Mr. Fox. Do you know where I might
find him?"

The soft voice curled around him. He motioned

to the boy who was waiting for the note he had been penning. The boy snatched the paper, relieved.

"Mr. Merrick?" she questioned again from the door, slipping fully inside as the boy quickly exited.

He looked back down at the page and continued writing. "No, I do not know where you might find him."

"Will he be here later?"

"No."

"Oh. I was supposed to meet with him at ten." He could hear her chewing her lip.

"That is unfortunate."

"Yes. I had an . . . issue . . . I needed to discuss with him. Well, I suppose I will need to deal with it on my own. And I don't regret finding myself here—a visit with you is always welcome."

He stiffened as she walked toward him. "You have a report for me?" he asked, his voice even.

"Oh, yes. Plenty of items to report."

"I have little time."

"I'll make my words quick then. I have been working to edge Lord Garrett out of the Pace shares he has been requesting for months. I have constructed careful legal maneuvers in order to do so." She set a sheaf of papers in front of him. He scanned the first few. He had to admit, the woman knew what she was doing. It would not do to forget that she was intelligent and clever. It should be *further* impetus to get rid of her.

"We had no cause to deny Lord Garrett the purchase before, as the company was hanging by a thread. But you came in and saved us." Large smile. "Gave us back our debts and options."

He tried never to think on those actions too hard. Nor to reflect on the fact that he was still operating under the same conflicted absurdity whenever dealing with her.

"Lord Garrett will not be pleased," he said. Normally, that would make Andreas very, very pleased. But . . . these maneuvers would make Garrett desperate. It would make him operate out of the construct Andreas had initially placed him in—one of overconfidence.

The original plan had been to have Garrett fully invest his remaining groats with the Paces, then Andreas would crush their company all around him.

"No. I expect him to attempt negotiations."

Garrett, and the man pulling Garrett's strings now, would negotiate her death if they grew desperate enough and realized that she was the one making the decisions. At the very least, they would try to eliminate James Pace and buy the shares in the resulting chaos. Garrett would be able to do so if he had bribed the right people.

Andreas made a notation on the edge of his page.

"And the viscount's sons?"

"They will keep their shares. I cannot in good conscience hurt friends just because their father is an . . . unkind person."

"You will fail at business with that philosophy, Miss Pace."

"Then I will fail with my head held high, Mr. Merrick."

"Even if it dissolves your father's company?"

"I would like to think that I could do both, Mr.

Merrick. And there is no need for such a scowl. I know I dream in purple."

There was something very calm and even about her that he appreciated in an associate. Even though she was greener than green about the way the business world truly worked—which was dark and vicious to the bitter end. Still, she projected a quiet fortitude that would always be respected. Her brother had possessed that trait as well.

Right up until he had been betrayed.

Andreas could picture Christian Pace's expression overlaid on Phoebe's face. It made him edgy.

"I set a few plans in motion this morning. Small things. And I have a few resulting issues already that I need to work through, of course." She waved a hand and stood. "I will be by tomorrow."

She gave him a sunny smile and slipped from the room before he could say anything else or ask what she meant.

Dammit. He considered sending someone after her to drag her back.

She had been keeping things close to her chest—within her immediate sphere—or else he would have heard the whispers. He needed to lean on her harder and make her tell him everything. It just meant that he had to spend more time with her, though.

He looked at the notation on his page. If he didn't crawl on top of her actions though, Garrett or Cornelius would.

A thread of uncertainty coiled. He crushed it quickly and decisively. He had made the mistake. He would rectify that mistake. Garrett would not escape his fate; nor would he be allowed to hurt the Pace family.

But Andreas would have to maneuver Phoebe Pace out of the situation without her realizing it.

He fisted his fingers. From that first smile in a darkened theater . . . he had known from that smile. He should have changed all his plans then and there, cut the Paces completely out of the picture instead of weaving them in more tightly, binding their fate to his.

Something about that damn smile had hooked its claws into him.

He refused to do anything more idiotic because of it.

Like the idiot he was, Andreas looked at the three-story Georgian house across the street from his hiding spot in the darkened park bushes. Groomed gardens and overly colorful plants disregarded, it was a sound stone structure in a fine location overlooking the park square. A good land asset.

I set a few things in motion, she had said. *Small things.*

Why the qualifier made him more nervous, he didn't know. But here he was.

He assessed the home's defenses. The park allowed for a stealth offensive—since it was far harder to sneak through streets lined by row houses on both sides. But it also made escaping easier, should it be needed, for one could also shake off pursuers in the greenery.

There were two exits to the house, one in front,

one in the rear. A garden wall low enough to scale bordered the neighbor's yard on the back side. That house had an easy ingress and egress as well. If one needed to escape over the wall and through to the other street, the locks on the other property were barely fit for a child to pick. And the wood around the doors had mites. Two good kicks, and he could be through.

He had also analyzed the houses on either side of the Paces' property and the ones to the sides of the neighbor's property behind. Those were less effective exits. Still, he knew those layouts as well, just in case.

Exits scoped out, he examined the windows. Two could be used as entering points, though someone had been smart enough to plant thorny bushes below. The swearing that would accompany that method of entrance would negate any stealth gained. There was a window in the back that was unsecured, and it was the main security weakness. One of the boys would shore it up later. The occupants would never be able to open the window again, but that wasn't his concern.

There were three servants. A housekeeper, a maid, and a footman. They had lived on what appeared to be goodwill for the last few months, as there were no increases at all in their accounts, and their expenditures had dwindled considerably.

They had remained tight-lipped as ever though.

Again, Andreas was struck with the same uncomfortable notion that had led him to that damn theater. Sure, he had lived for twenty-odd years with someone inhuman enough to provoke uncompromising loyalty. But Roman was Herculean. He existed on a pedestal Andreas was loath to touch. But the rest of the populace was broken and shattered on the floor, beneath Andreas's regard. Normal souls just didn't instill such devotion. What had made the Pace servants so loyal? Loyal enough to follow the Paces into near bankruptcy.

It was unnerving. Just like everything surrounding her.

And here he was, lurking outside her house himself instead of letting his very qualified men do it. He had grabbed two of his most capable to stay here for the night. There was no need for him to do sweeps and reconnaissance like some lackey.

He would get a royal amount of shit from his brother upon his return to town. Andreas automatically started planning his responses.

. . . the Paces were now working for him as a result of Phoebe Pace's promises.

. . . he was enveloping the family further into his plans for revenge.

. . . they had already been enveloped.

. . . he had already deployed men to watch them. This added protection was to ensure everyone's safety.

Mocking laughter echoed in his mind.

His fingers tightened into a fist. He stared up at the one window where the drape was parted just an inch. It had been thus since he'd been there, no cause for alarm. Still, he pictured her peeking through, a smile pulling red lips.

His attention immediately pulled back to his surroundings when he saw the edges of the shapes moving down the street. His instincts had been correct. He wondered what had tipped off his enemies—*their* enemies, since the Merricks and Paces were now linked—*their* enemies, *and wasn't that just irony.*

Twenty minutes later, he and his men finished incapacitating the last of the moving shadows outside of Phoebe Pace's house. For a moment he thought he saw that same damn drape move. Pulling into the absolute darkness, he kept his gaze narrowed on the window for long minutes, but nothing happened.

A trick of the moon? The attacks had been noiseless. The torches had been easily snuffed before the attackers' intentions had become obvious. And he never made the mistake of letting anyone see him.

Still, his gaze rested upon the window for far longer than necessary, once again.

He didn't know what he expected. For the foolish woman to peer through? For her to lift up the pane and wave?

Tension thrummed through him, unabated by the fight. The extinguished torches at his feet smelled of oil and snuffed flame, curling through the air, making his eyes close for a moment.

When he opened them, he swore the drape had moved once more.

He cursed himself and whipped through the shadows, back to the East End of town. The house was safeguarded and *would* be safeguarded—a continual exchange of men to guard it—and so maybe now he could purge the damn woman and her damn smile from his mind.

Chapter 6

She was sitting in the seat on the other side of his desk the next morning, tilted toward the door, with the damn basket on her lap. The same one he had been haunted by for a week. Wearing the same smile he had been haunted by for months. He entered the room and quickly averted his gaze.

"Good morning, Mr. Merrick. You are looking fine this morning."

He had passed the looking glass on the way here. He looked like the back alley—before it had been scrubbed. He had grabbed three hours of sleep after another assassination attempt, the burning of Building Seven at the docks, where his enemies had thought the Exchange records had been transferred, and the *amusement* outside her home. Last night's assailants were down the street in one of his secure facilities, waiting for him to do with them as he willed.

Having in custody the men from her attack meant he had to do more questioning. He hated questioning. It meant speaking, and possibly having to change his clothes afterward. But he wasn't going to trust the questioning to someone else—not on this.

And here Miss Bleeding Sunshine sat, looking as if just this morning she'd been attended by fairies, baked with elves, and had tea with a unicorn.

"What do you want?" he asked brusquely.

"I am here to offer my report and to share what I've been up to." She extended the basket across his desk as he sat in his chair. "And to bring you these. The basket has been empty each night, so I hope you have been enjoying them."

Of course the boys would have finished the treats after removing them. It was always their own choice whether to eat Andreas's food.

He flipped open his ledger and looked at the tasks for the day. He wanted to scrub a hand over his face, but he pinned her with a dark look instead. "Well?"

"I am well, yes. Though we had a tough night. Fires, you know. And scuffles. And gunshots. All of London is on edge these days."

He tried to keep loose. He narrowed his eyes. "What?"

She waved a hand. "Nothing of consequence."

Fires, as in plural? He drummed his fingers on his desk. *Don't ask.* "Fires?" *Ass, cow, lips, shit.*

"Yes." She looked up and to the left. "I think there were three. One was quite concerning. The other two were fairly small."

He usually left the discipline to Roman or Milton or One-eye, but all of the men who had watched her house last night after he'd left would be in for a trouser change at the very least.

She leaned toward him conspiratorially. "Our maid is interested in the neighbor's footman. Quite a nice-looking fellow who has solid goals."

Andreas stared at her wondering, not for the first time, what in the hell she was talking about.

And . . . she was still sitting across from him. He didn't have any new scowls left. He had used up all of his fiercest ones with her, ones he hadn't even had to use on his bitterest enemies, and to no avail. He was becoming a little concerned actually that he was . . . stuck with her. There was something about the set of her body that said she might be . . . permanent.

She nodded back sagely at whatever she read in his face. "She was watching him, dreaming, and she lit one of the drapes on fire with a collected candle that was not yet extinguished."

It was as if she were encouraged by his responses, his general state of breathing. Because . . . when the hell had he ever been encouraging . . . *ever*? Getting rid of people had always been easy. A flick of a wrist or a dark scowl, and most people ran in the opposite direction.

"I see." He wished he did.

She waved a hand. "The gunshots were farther away, thank goodness. The papers were full this morning of the events. Would you like me to summarize them?" She leaned forward, smiling, intent. Turning the full force of her bright gaze against him.

He concentrated on his desk for a moment and took a deep breath. He needed one in order to deal with the . . . disturbance . . . that was Phoebe Pace.

"No." He didn't need to read the papers to know what had happened last night. "What do you have to report, Miss Pace, about the company and your maneuvers? That is why you are here."

She seemed unfazed by his tone and change of topic. "Well, I wanted to stop by to see you too, of course." That disturbance—located somewhere in his midsection—disturbed more. "But I do have events to report. I am meeting with a few investors and Lord Garrett's assistant this afternoon. I will further negotiate with his assistant to withdraw his interest."

It was what he had expected. Garrett was obviously expecting it as well, given the activities of the previous night. How had Garrett known, though? Was she naïve enough to have corresponded with him too? It had to have been in secret because otherwise his spies would have known.

That she might be secretly corresponding with Garrett disturbed him far more than it should. *Further* negotiate . . .

He narrowed his eyes at the tangent his brain had started to traverse. She had avoided talking about the fires quite skillfully. Planting little seedlings to lure his mind in other directions.

"You are meeting with Garrett's lackey alone?"

"Lord Garrett, and no. Mr. Harris will be there, of course."

"Your esteemed man of business."

"You don't approve."

"Of spineless fools, who faint at the first sign of trouble? No."

"Mr. Harris is quite quick with figures and—"

"And he knows you are fully running things and will accede to your wishes."

Silence. "Don't be silly. Of course I am not fully running things," she said carefully.

"You should get another man of business."

"Well, you see . . ." She trailed off as he pinned her with a dark look, coiled darkness easily gathering at the hesitation in her voice. Hesitation inconsistent with her previously displayed personality.

"He's blackmailing you." His response was flat.

"Oh, no," she said quickly. "Of course he is not. Mr. Harris just made a sensible suggestion yesterday that we have done well together so far, and talk would be to no one's advantage." Her shoulders gave a little droop under his steady gaze. "He is blackmailing us a bit, yes."

One of the curls around her face seemed to droop along with her body. He looked down at his desk, unwilling to watch her. He was feeling quite violent. He had expected to put on a show for the captured arsonists down the street, but the rage was exceedingly fresh all of a sudden.

He kept his gaze fixed on the papers on his desk. "Put off Garrett. Reschedule for tomorrow. I will take care of Mr. Harris."

He should have gotten rid of the man already—he hadn't trusted him on sight. Harris was undoubtedly the cause of the move last night. But Harris couldn't have given away the ties between the Paces and Andreas yet—nor her visits here—or else other dominoes would have fallen on Andreas.

But the man would. It would be only a matter of hours probably.

"Oh, no, I couldn't. You've done so much to help already—"

"I dislike your Mr. Harris. I will take care of him one way or another. If you don't want blood marring your front rug, you will put off the meeting until tomorrow."

Silence. "You are quite unsettling at times, Mr. Merrick."

"Good."

"I do not wish Mr. Harris ill, despite his recent behavior. I will dismiss him myself."

"Fine." The man would be easy to find. He made a note in his margin.

"I will need a new man of business."

"Undoubtedly."

"I had hoped to discuss these issues with Mr. Fox. To see if he might help me locate a suitable replacement for a few weeks."

Andreas single-mindedly concentrated on his papers and tried to blank his thoughts.

" . . . yes . . ." she murmured. "That might work . . . just for today." The baubles in her hair jingled, indicating a nod. "Very well. I believe I have the perfect man. You have helped me greatly."

"Who—"

But she had risen already, baubles jingling merrily, causing him to look up to see her sunny smile blazing at him. "Thank you, Mr. Merrick." She was out the door, wig in hand, before he could finish the question.

He wondered what she would do if he attached a leash to her collar next time she entered the room. No, he wanted her far away, not at his feet. *Dammit.*

He tapped his finger against the desk and looked at the basket sitting innocuously on his desk. "Hope you enjoy!" Another damn dog image alongside a waving girl.

What was with the dogs? And the merriment? And the smell of bloody biscuits haunting him all the damn time?

He stared at the basket.

He was hungry.

He drummed his fingers harder.

She had delivered them herself. And she was obviously trying to kill him in other ways. This way likely wasn't quite twisted enough.

And they smelled . . . really good.

He tented the cover, long fingers slipping under the cloth and over a still-warm biscuit.

The fragrance emerged more strongly, now that it was freed from its binding. Smelling like her really, of warmth and honey and home. And secrets. Thrusting out, tugging one's desire.

No. *No.*

He pulled his fingers back, empty, and forcefully pushed the basket away.

No bloody way was he eating one.

He pushed himself away from the desk and honeyed temptation. He needed to figure out what that blasted woman was planning.

Everything about her was driving him insane.

Chapter 7

Andreas watched from the shadows on the side of the house that belonged to Garrett's solicitor. The windows were open, due to the heat, but he didn't need to hear the overly husky voice to be fooled by the picture inside, no matter how unbelievable it was.

Good Lord, she was dangerous. And she didn't dillydally. He would remember that for the future. He should have been a step ahead of this insanity instead of simply covering it as it happened, but it had only been three hours since she had been in his office. Not enough time for the men watching her to report back that she needed to be *shot* for her own good.

Rat shit. Had to be.

"Good afternoon, Mr. Johnson." A short bow from the man who had entered the room. "I'm Mr. Harris."

Johnson, Garrett's assistant, arched a brow at the man, examining him from top to bottom, lingering on the thick glasses, the bushy mustache, and the traces of fallen powder on his shoulders. "Pardon me?"

"Mr. George Harris." The man tapped his hand against the case he was carrying. "Mr. Thomas Harris's brother, of course. He is indisposed and asked me to attend instead."

"I see." Johnson looked beyond irritated at the change.

"I will be replacing the other Mr. Harris as the Paces' man of business, at least temporarily." The new Mr. Harris waited patiently for Johnson to ask him to sit.

Johnson's eyes narrowed. "Why?"

"Mr. Harris's indisposition is a matter of some delicacy. He required some time off to think over his future engagements." The new Harris waved a hand in a far-too-feminine fashion. "He's taking a respite in the country."

Andreas had wondered. Obviously, Miss Pace had been intelligent enough—and far too compassionate—to warn the cretin. According to the original Harris's neighbors, the man had sprinted from his house two hours ago carrying two bags only half an hour before Andreas's men had arrived on his doorstep.

"I have a letter here from Mr. James Pace that gives me action on his account. Forgive me—I just left chambers and came directly here. I received a distressed note about the matter this morning, so it was a sudden change of appointment."

Andreas wanted to see the new Mr. Harris write in a different script than James Pace. And he wanted to see James Pace write in a different script than Phoebe Pace.

Johnson was still too obviously irritated by the change though—a change that removed the old Harris, a player who had just been culled to Garrett's court. Johnson was too irritated and thinking too hard about how to salvage matters to realize what was in front of him.

Johnson gave the new Harris an ingratiating smile. "Of course. But I'm a traditionalist and appreciate the old ways. Please, sit." He looked at the paper Harris held. "Though I admit surprise that Miss Pace did not accompany you."

"Yes. Had to convince her this was better." Harris leaned forward. "Better off without the womenfolk." He laughed heartily.

"Agreed," Johnson answered, some of the tension leaving him as he spotted an opportunity. He gave Harris a meaningful look. "Going to have to nip that one in the bud."

"Damn bluestockings. Just between us, I'm a bit concerned by the amount of leeway that female gets."

Johnson relaxed further. "Too true, Mr. Harris. But Lord Garrett will bring her to heel."

Harris raised a manly brow.

"Or his heir will. A good match there." Johnson sneered.

Andreas's fingers twisted around the branch. Johnson would require further watching.

Mr. Harris nodded briskly. "The young ones never know what's best for them though."

"Perhaps you might help her see the benefits of such an alliance. Miss Pace has been . . . rather dismissive of any marriage offers."

"Rather silly of her." Mr. Harris shook his head. "Everyone knows a woman requires a man to steer her on the correct path. That woman keenly needs a husband."

Though shrouded in words that seemed serious, but were undoubtedly sarcastic, they underlined a mystery of the situation right from the horse's mouth.

Phoebe Pace wasn't stupid. Far from it, if rather unconventional. The matter of her motivation was key. The forgiveness of their debts had opened up a number of opportunities for her, not least of which was an increased opportunity to find a decent husband to help her.

One who would deal with the company's issues and gain them a solvent path. A path that could be free from Garrett's manipulations. But yet, was she out in the country trying? No, she was sitting in the room before him hidden behind a ridiculous amount of wig, overly bushy brows, and mustache. Powder and affect.

Another good question was why the clothes fit so well.

"Perhaps you can guide her." Johnson was obviously feeling good about the new Mr. Harris. Andreas narrowed his eyes on her. She spun tales and made people see what she wanted them to.

"Perhaps. Shall we proceed?" she said, trouser-clad legs spread at a ninety-degree angle. He stared for a moment, unable to help himself. "Pace & Co.

of London finds itself with an influx of new capital."

Johnson's eye twitched. "And?"

She needed to be locked into a room. The key thrown away. If Johnson figured out who this Mr. Harris really was, Garrett would use the knowledge and ruin her without any effort.

Only a woman possessed of insanity or desperation took such risks. He wasn't willing to let go of either explanation at the moment.

"The Paces have come up with some disturbing ideas of what to do with it. Unfortunately, I have little say in the matter as of yet."

A gambit to keep the interaction between them friendly and turn the blame on the absent Miss Pace while hinting at the possibility that Mr. Harris might be able to help.

She was playing a deadly game, and he was again struck with the question—*what did she know?*

She put her hands on her thighs, elbows out.

Too forthright to be an actress, though someone had obviously schooled her. All of the reports of her lengthy visits to actresses at the Claremont Theatre and Covent Garden suddenly took on a new meaning that was *not* philanthropic in nature. Still, she was trying to display too many male mannerisms. Luckily for her, Johnson was too concerned with saving his own ass at the moment to notice.

"The Paces are decreasing outside investment to twenty percent. They plan to invest twenty thousand buying back shares."

He could have shot himself in that moment— right after he shot her first. That moment of insanity—giving her those debts back—had allowed this to happen.

Garrett wanted that twenty thousand. It was evident in Johnson's movements. They needed the Paces under their thumb. Andreas didn't think Phoebe Pace knew quite how much. "How do the Paces find themselves with such capital? I had understood that they had gotten themselves too far in debt to do such a thing."

"Harris" waved a hand. "Mr. Thomas Harris didn't tell me. And that is not my concern at the moment. What is is your master's interest in buying shares, which will be unavailable for a time." She held up a piece of paper. "A joint meeting is to be held Friday a month from now, though. If you are interested in joining, all parties will be gathering. I have a feeling that you might be able to accomplish much at that meeting, given what I know from my brother, who informed me of much before his departure." The last was said quite mildly.

She was very clever, he'd give her that. She was only pulling back just enough to keep the company and fund out of their claws but yet continued to keep the promise of the bait dangling. Along with the promise of an ally.

She was buying time.

Johnson stared at the paper, eyes narrowed, then looked at something to the side that Andreas couldn't see. "Twenty thousand is nothing to scoff at. They could do much with that. I will speak to Lord Garrett, but"—Johnson looked the man over very carefully—"I think we will be willing to agree with your analysis."

She had just agreed to become a snitch on herself under the guise of a bushy old man. Andreas pressed the heel of his palm against his temple. She gave him a headache.

"Excellent." She gathered up her satchel and extended a card. "If you need further information or would like to discuss specifics, please send requests to this address."

"Why don't you return tomorrow," he said easily.

"Because of my overworked schedule, I'm more of a written correspondence man myself. I'd rather do the bulk of our business by courier. Less suspicious. And easier, don't you think?"

"No."

She nodded firmly. "Yes." Andreas felt a strange urge to laugh at Johnson's expression. "Good day, sir."

And with that she walked from the room. Andreas weighed his options. He could follow her or stay and watch Johnson.

"I think we need to discuss our other possibilities, Johnson." The voice came from the other side of the room. Andreas stiffened, and hate curled. He had deduced the man would be listening.

Watching the whole thing through a peep, the mirror of his own eavesdropping.

"Yes. Twenty thousand, my lord."

"I want to know everything. If they have money stashed away, I want to know it. Twenty thousand and with the male heir dead . . . she is the heir. Henry finally will be made to see my way. Wives can be disposed of."

Garrett would use anything in his power to manipulate. So would Henry Wilcox, his heir. He had been raised exceptionally well to be a manipulative bastard. It was too bad he lacked the intelligence necessary to be good at it. Andreas smiled cruelly. The Wilcoxes had poorly inherited traits.

"Yes, my lord. I will have everything for you by Friday, along with the other information you requested."

"Good. I'm feeling the need to stop by the club to have a talk with my heir. Another one." His voice was dark, and Andreas got a little vicious pleasure that the two were on the outs. "And perhaps a talk with the other boy too."

Garrett grimaced, obviously displeased with his youngest son, who had been a school friend of Christian Pace. Andreas kept only bare tabs on the youngest boy, as he had never really known him, but Edward Wilcox was by all accounts a disappointment to the man, preferring livestock to finance. Garrett had always been a fool who had turned over the running of his estates to others, considering such endeavors weak.

Such an attitude got him little in the way of affection from other landowners. And Andreas had secretly created many situations over the years that had forced Garrett to reveal that attitude in the presence of others.

"Should I forward your mail to Dover?" Johnson said.

"No. The information is far sharper here. The exodus to the country has culled the herd."

Andreas's smile grew. He'd have to get the couri-

ers moving quickly. Garrett was too self-absorbed
to think himself outflanked.

"What information do you have on the other
. . . *issue?*"

Johnson hesitated. "Alive."

"*I want him dead. Dead.*"

"Yes, my lord. But we are having trouble with—"

"I don't want trouble. I want death. Dug in the
ground, beetle-infested *death.*"

"Yes, my lord."

"That low-born Yorkshire bastard promised
he'd be dead."

"It seems that Mr. Cornelius has recently developed a different opinion on how to accomplish
matters. He wants to wait on Mr. Merrick's death
until he gets his own results accomplished." He
cleared his throat. "And his men are balking. They
will help with the Paces, but they've lost too many
men to Merrick in London."

"Then hire people outside of him. Like before."

"That didn't—"

"I want it done!"

"Very well. But I'll need increased funds to hire
new men."

Silence.

"My lord?"

"We don't have *increased* funds."

"I know, but—"

"But *nothing.* They are all gone. Stripped. And
I'll bet you *he* is responsible."

"Quite possibly, but—"

"Shut up, Johnson. We need that fund and company. Twenty thousand will let the Paces recover.

Unacceptable. I've spent far too long, and everything is resting on this. Men like that Yorkshire cretin don't accept failure either, remember that." His fists curled. "And I want that *bastard* dead. I don't care how it has to be accomplished. Even if I have to do it myself—"

"He rarely leaves his office. There are rumored to be fifty guards inside."

Andreas manipulated his knife through his fingers. He could just end it now. Right this moment. He was *right there* in front of him.

"Don't give me excuses, Johnson. Get my information. Get the Paces under our thumbs. Get *him dead*."

Andreas could kill him. Right here, right now. Revenge curled. Beckoned. Wanting fulfillment. It was broad daylight, and he would most likely be caught and imprisoned. But it would be over.

Roman had a new life. He was happy—Andreas no longer had to worry about him. And he had provisions in place for Nana. He could just end things now.

He fingered the blade, then a vision of Phoebe Pace walking around, exposed and without guard drifted across his vision.

He gave the steel one last gentle, promising stroke and slipped it into his sleeve. Soon. He had been waiting twenty-three years, four months, and twelve days. Cold certainty washed through him. He could wait a while longer.

Andreas lingered until Garrett made to leave the room, then silently headed in the direction of the Paces' house. Harris's going back to give a report to "his employer" would be expected. Then he would see what else she had planned.

Two days later he was still following "Mr. Harris." He had dispatched and discouraged a variety of people who'd followed her over the past fifty hours while she had been out visiting Pace craftsmen and financiers.

She was walking a thin line, but he hadn't confronted her yet. His curiosity burned. She had been meeting with their craftsmen mostly, but there had been some surprising other destinations, and he was starting to realize that she was involved in far more plotting than he had assumed.

He was going to have a little talk with her later. It was time to get her the hell out of this web. He wasn't a guard. And he didn't like surprises. Nor did he like constantly watching the crowd for people who might attempt to harm her. No wonder Roman had gone insane when he had threatened London on Charlotte's behalf.

Andreas fixed a dark look of promise on a man who had been staring too long at "Mr. Harris" while waiting at a street crossing. A dark stain spread down the man's trousers, and he stayed in place instead of following the crowd crossing the road. Just a bystander, good.

Andreas followed the white wig bobbing in a sea of brown. Phoebe Pace would give Roman a run for his money in the crazy department. She was driving Andreas nuts.

He wondered why she wasn't taking a carriage. Concerned about revealing herself if she chose her transportation incorrectly? Or perhaps the heir to the finest carriage company in London liked walking.

He found himself watching her as she moved. She walked with purpose, but sometimes without continual forward progress. She found holes in the crowd and moved into them quickly, sometimes zigzagging, allowing quick movement without either having to stop or being run over by someone else in the crowd.

A man suddenly appeared behind her, but her darting maneuvers forced him farther behind quickly. The man swore as he had to push around a group of women in order to catch up. A poor tail. He was either new, or this was not part of his regular duties.

Andreas had dispatched the more experienced tails in the past two days. Working his way through Cornelius's men, who were obviously working with Garrett, one by one, two by two. Roman was going to tease him mercilessly for doing drudge work. Andreas usually hated to leave his cave for anything other than exceptional events.

Leaving meant he had to pretend other people existed.

Andreas followed Phoebe Pace and her new shadow though, once more, unhindered, pushing his unfriendliness to the front of his features. The crowd parted when he needed it to.

The man started gaining on her, increasing his speed, his frustration overcoming his movements, his motivation to intercept her instead of continuing to trail her suddenly clear. The crowd parted in front of Andreas more rapidly as he quickly advanced, people rubbing their exposed skin, feeling the sudden need to shrink away, to the sides. He made full use of it, caught up to the man, and gripped the back of his neck. "Let's have a conversation," he said in a low voice and thrust him sideways through the crowd and into the alley.

Andreas emerged from the alley with a new low-slung cap to hide the top half of his features. He loosened his knuckles and continued to Phoebe Pace's house. His pace, always quick, was faster than usual.

He rapped the knocker. He should send a courier. He should send an army. There was no reason for him to be standing here as a goddamn messenger.

No one answered the door. He tried again, then just gripped the handle and pushed it open, striding inside, a messenger of death. Phoebe Pace peered around the edge of a doorway to the left, one bushy brow still attached, contrasting sharply with its well-groomed sibling. Both real and fake brows rose in shocked surprise. Her . . . shirt . . . was open two buttons down from the top.

He stared at her for a moment, unable to say anything.

"Mr. Merrick." She started to emerge farther, then caught herself and pulled back, her hand suddenly gripping her shirt together at her throat. "What can I do for you?"

"We need to speak."

She blinked. "It's not a good time. Perhaps I can visit you in an hour?"

"No." He walked forward, looking around the house. It was a standard layout. He headed for where the study was sure to be.

"Mr. Merrick." She hurried after him. "Mr. Merrick, what—"

He looked around the interior. It was cluttered and disorganized. He ignored the mess as best as he could, disorganization always made him feel tense. "Pack and leave for the country, Miss Pace."

"What?"

"Now. Start packing."

"No, I have two more meet . . . I mean, our man of business has two more meetings with—"

"Miss Pace." He thought it was said quite pleasantly. He was quite pleased by the widening of her eyes. "You have forgotten to remove your eyebrow."

Her hand immediately went to her brow, dropping her fisted collar, exposing the skin just enough to see the cleft of a shadowed canyon squished together and bound by tape. "Oh. How . . . how could that have happened?"

It took him a moment to recover from the sight. "How, indeed. Let us just put it down on the register of absurdity that you continue to enact—dressing up in men's clothes in your own home, hmmm? Perhaps Madame Vestris inspired you?"

She brightened, as if it were the perfect excuse. That was not good.

He rushed on, completely against the natural order of things. "However, that is beside the point. Start packing. You have two hours and not one minute more."

"I think we are failing to properly communicate, Mr. Merrick."

"You have one hour and fifty-nine minutes to pack," he enunciated.

She blinked at him. "No I don't."

"Good. You have only fifty-eight minutes then."

She looked flustered for a moment. Her eyes drifted to something in the corner, and she regained a cheerful mien. "I am unable to leave for the country at this time, unfortunately. In a few weeks—"

"The Watch is coming for your father in the morning."

The color left her face abruptly. Rosy cheeks bled to parchment.

"But—"

"Your little antics have forced someone's hand. Your fund's results will be released early and with . . . modifications."

He knew whose hand had been forced. It was better if she just went on her merry, flighty way though.

"You came to warn us." She looked at him through hair mussed and falling over her eyes.

He took a step back. "I was in the neighborhood."

She took a step toward him. "Thank you."

He almost took another step back. He was here . . . because he had helped the situation degenerate. Yes. He had given her those debts back. Enabled her stupidity. A society girl with no claim on real-life matters.

"Don't thank me, just leave."

Her plump lower lip disappeared between her teeth. "I . . . yes. I will have my parents leave immediately. Of course. They can't stay. I will get things settled in the meantime."

He wasn't sure what that cold feeling was in his gut. "*All* of you will leave."

"But I need—"

"To what? Stay here and reap the consequences of whatever mob comes to make the arrest?"

"I . . . no, you make sense. I will go elsewhere for tonight and tomorrow. But I need to—"

"You need to leave *permanently*."

"I can't, I—"

"If you don't leave London in one hour and fifty-six minutes with your parents," he said pleasantly, "I will burn down your house."

Silence. Then—"I think I'm misunderstanding you."

"You are understanding me perfectly well."

"You just threatened to burn down my house. I think that is uncommon enough a response for me to question."

"What do you know about me, Miss Pace?"

It was actually a question that burned deeply and undesirably.

"I know that you are a fair man. And a kind man, when you want to be." Where the hell did she get these notions? "And true to your word . . . oh."

He gave her a thin smile.

Wide eyes stared back. "But I, I mean, I need to coordinate with our man of business. He has all manners of tasks to . . ." She sighed, obviously reading his expressions without trouble. "*I* need to be here for a few more weeks *as* my man of business."

"You can do your business from elsewhere. You have plenty of correspondence capabilities." He motioned toward the doorway.

She stared at him. "And if I say no?"

"Do you really want to say no? To continue whatever idiotic game you are playing? What the hell are you *wearing*?"

She stared down at the eyebrow in her hand. "I'm in too far to be embarrassed at this point," she muttered.

"And why do those trousers fit you?"

My God. He had not just asked that.

She looked down at the article of clothing in question, and he swore for a moment that a smile curved her lips, but when she looked up, that perpetually innocent expression was back in place. A trick of the light . . . maybe. "Took a few goes to get them right. I can give you instructions, though you don't require tailoring." She critically examined his *seams*—where they *met*. "You look quite sleek in—"

"If you haven't moved in two hours, I will guarantee you will." He swiftly walked toward the exit. He had thought to go through the documents on the desk, but frankly, he had to get out of here. The men on duty would take care of things in case the Watch—or anyone else—came early. He didn't need to be here. In fact, he would double the retinue, just to make sure nothing happ—

—to make sure she was gone.

"Have a productive day, Mr. Merrick!"

He hadn't had a productive day since she'd walked through his door.

Chapter 8

Andreas entered the hell a week later. He had chased Cornelius around northern England for a week, always missing the slippery bastard by a few hours. He should have taken lackeys with him to coordinate a trap, but taking others with him meant relying on other people for long periods of time.

He already had someone to rely on. That someone was just taking forever on his goddamn honeymoon.

But at least there was no Phoebe Pace to worry about. He had received a doubly verified report that indeed the Pace family had moved and were safely installed elsewhere. He had almost asked after their new location but denied the impulse.

What Phoebe Pace was, was *gone*.

No more biscuits or trouble or strange pits of thought. Thank God.

He had assigned a set of five men to stay near the Paces, wherever they were. He'd leave the knowledge of where they were to others and just rely on the reports.

People gawked as he walked through the kitchens. He'd been expected back two days from now, not tonight, and he knew he looked like absolute hell. He sneered, and the only boy who had opened his mouth to say something closed it with a snap, backing away.

Useless. He continued up the stairs to the private rooms on the top floor where he and Roman maintained chambers on opposite sides of the hall. No, just his rooms now. The other hall door on the floor was never opened anymore.

He stepped from the landing and walked down the hall. He was going to lock his door and sleep for a week. And anyone who disturbed—

Bark.

He slowed his steps. What the hell—

Yap, yap.

He mentally went through his correspondence. Roman wasn't due back for another three weeks. And Charlotte *would* get some ridiculously yappy dog, but even if she did, it would be taken to the Grosvenor Square house where they lived.

Yap, yap, yap.

If one of the boys had picked up a stray and thought to hide it in Roman's rooms, there would be bloodshed.

A deep voice shouted something, followed by a crash.

Yap!

He narrowed his eyes and put his hand upon the handle to Roman's rooms. It turned beneath his fingers and honey brown hair pushed beneath his nose. He pulled back, nearly stumbling.

"Oh! Mr. Merrick. I didn't see you there."

He stared at her. His living nightmare. Hair unbound and curling around her shoulders.

She wedged her body into the crack of the door, blocking his view behind with her simple dress . . . was that a *nightdress*? "Welcome back. I . . . I thought you would be back two days from now. Perhaps I might speak with you later?"

Something wiggled under her thin skirts, and he could only stare as a scraggly mass of brown fur dove forward, furry paws extended. He reacted instinctively, bending and catching the thing by the scruff of the neck as it tried to surge past him.

"Oh! Mr. Wiggles." She gently extricated the . . . thing trying to bite him . . . from his grip. The ends of her locks brushed his wrist as he rose. He straightened quickly, stepping back, as if bitten after all. "Thank you. He has been into everything. I swear, when we got him we thought he would help with"—she pulled her rosy lips between her teeth— "that is, we thought he'd be better behaved. I must admit I haven't had time to properly train him."

"Why is your . . . dog . . . here?" he asked stiffly. It was far from the most pertinent question, but he thought asking the question of why *she* was here might emerge less . . . evenly.

"Oh, well, when you ordered us out of our house, we needed a safe place to stay, you see, and . . ." She cocked her head. "You look awfully tired. Perhaps we should discuss this in the morning?"

"We will discuss this now."

She shrugged. "I spoke with your men. They

said your brother had abandoned his apartments here."

Abandoned was not the word he would have chosen. He reached down to rub his leg before he realized what he was doing.

"He now resides with his wife," he said tightly.

She nodded. "I wish to rent his rooms."

"*What?*"

"It is perfect. It will better allow me to repay my debt to you, and it is far closer to the financial area in order to complete our transactions."

"No."

"Well, you see, I must admit, we've already moved in." Brilliant smile. "It would make things much simpler if you just agree."

"No."

"It's the perfect solution really. You said I needed to leave to parts unknown. And what's more, I figured you wouldn't burn down your own building." An even more brilliant smile.

He stared at her, opened his mouth to say something extremely cutting, then closed it again.

He wasn't going to continue this conversation in the hall where anyone under either landing could eavesdrop. And definitely not with the light shining behind and through that thin . . . thing she was wearing, silhouetting the lines of her body.

He turned on his heel and walked to his door farther down the hall. He could hear her shuffling around in the doorway—probably with that *dog*—then following him. He paused at his outer door. His personal rooms . . . and Phoebe Pace . . . no.

He swiftly walked to the steps instead, taking the stairs jarringly—going down the stairs was always the toughest action he undertook, and when he was out of sorts, it was worse. He made it down the steps to his office on the floor beneath without mishap, though, thank God.

He hated having anyone in his rooms, so he'd easily separated the spaces right from the beginning. That way anyone reporting to him during the day stayed out of his personal areas.

And he had never had to worry about someone reporting to him like *this*.

He made sure the door was closed behind her and all three locks engaged before moving to his desk.

"Why are you here?" he asked roughly as he sat on the other side, trying not to pay too much attention to her until he realized she had somehow managed to don a dowdy full-length robe. Relief was quickly dashed as he saw the *ledgers* on her lap. How had she managed to grab them so quickly? Perhaps she kept them stuffed under her shift in an invisible pocket. Perfect to extract at any notice.

No. There had been nothing beneath. The image of her silhouette burned into his brain.

"Are you alone?" He didn't know why he asked.

"No."

He fell back quickly to safer questions. "Why are you here?"

"The Watch was coming—"

"Why are you *here*?"

She touched the cover of the top ledger. "Well, we owe—"

He thrust out a hand in the universal motion meant to stop someone from continuing. He had never killed anyone with paper. He briefly contemplated the mechanics of it.

No, paper would be too hard to execute. Besides, she was going to be the end of him, not the other way around, of that he was certain. "That also isn't why you are here."

She studied him, head tilting to do it. "No."

He tapped a finger on the desk. Brilliant or daft. "Why are you here?"

Her eyes met his squarely. "Because no one would think we were staying here."

Not daft.

He narrowed his eyes as his mind connected threads and possibilities. "All of your trips here— your debts to be repaid—you were setting this up. Seeing if the building met whatever criteria and plan you had."

"That would be Machiavellian."

"That is not a denial."

"I am firm in my desire to repay our debts. As to our staying here, we hardly make a ripple. Neither of my parents needs to leave your brother's rooms."

He watched her through narrowed eyes. "Do you hold them hostage in the attic?"

Her mouth parted, bottom lip dropping. "Do I . . . what?"

The drapes were always pulled, the father emerging only six times in the last six months. And no one who worked there could be bribed. That wasn't *normal. She* wasn't normal. He thought of her far too often for her to be normal.

"Of course not." But her expression was off. Way off. "They are just solitary."

Her eyes were too bright. It was unnerving considering the subject she was avoiding.

"You are lying."

"Yes. And you are quite fearsome." She looked quite cheerful again, as if his being fearsome was something of an asset. "I would like to take advantage of that as well."

Being silent around this woman was better than gawking like an idiot.

"Charlotte Chatsworth, I mean, Charlotte Merrick . . . I've seen dangerous-looking men cross the street to the other side when they see her. It is a horribly kept secret that your brother threatened the entirety of London on her behalf."

"That is Roman."

"Yes. But I can't imagine that you do not scare the trousers off London's population as well. More so even." This was said cheerfully. Again. "And so we would like to rent your brother's rooms."

"No."

Head tilt. "Why not? He lives elsewhere."

"Because as much as you would obviously like to think otherwise, it isn't outside of the realm of possibilities to others that you would be here."

Cornelius was not an idiot. He would know who had dispatched his men outside the Paces' home as soon as it was reported. If anyone made it to report.

"Who would think that?" she asked.

But it was an answer he could not, would not, give. For other questions would tumble forth, questions he *also* could not answer. Not without divulging the larger picture. To all the factions that were actually involved in this situation. Who would use her family and her to destroy each other.

People like him.

She cocked her head at him. "Who would think that?" she repeated. "The people you have saved us from each night, and me each day? Those people?"

He stared at her, his heart not beating in his cold, dead chest. "What?"

She stared at him, without answering, her gaze clear, a smile half-lifted upon her lips.

He flattened his hands against the desk instead. "*You* make no sense. Why do you *return* here? What part of 'assassination attempts' that first night did you not understand? The part where there was a knife against your throat?"

"You invited that attempt."

"*What?*"

"You knew it was going to happen," she said calmly. "You tried to *encourage* me, for lack of a better word, to leave. I must tell you that if you had said, 'Five armed men will enter the door to this office in the next five minutes,' I might have been more receptive to your encouragement. You have a problem with communication, did you know?" Head tilt.

"I would be happy to stop communicating altogether," he gritted out.

"Oh, no, but I wouldn't like that at all. I think you are growing remarkably well."

"I would not wager on such a thought. Do you know what I am thinking at the moment, Miss Pace?"

"Something unpleasant concerning my ability to breathe, I'd wager. But I'd also bet you know when most of the attacks on you are going to happen." Head tilt, head tilt, head tilting his world. "Do *you* wish for death, Mr. Merrick? Or do you require the rush that accompanies such attacks?"

"*What?*"

"I've heard of such things, of course. And experienced quite a quickening of the heart myself that night, I must tell you. I'm not sure I would woo a second such event, however."

His knuckles hurt. "Then you would be foolish to stay here."

"Oh, does that mean you are receptive to the request then?"

"Are you mad?"

"I believe that is the first time you've asked me that, Mr. Merrick." This was said cheerfully as well. "I'm quite impressed. Most people give in during the first conversation."

He decided not to respond. He tried to loosen his fingers instead.

"We find ourselves fugitives at the moment, Mr. Merrick."

"You are not. Your father is."

"Yes. But that means we all are. We would not let Father go alone," she said softly.

"You are a fool." Yet something tightened in him. He believed her. The blackness swirled, gasping.

"I believe we have been over this."

"Why didn't you go to the country? Hide somewhere far from London. *This* is where you are in the most danger."

She tilted her head again, and something in her gaze warmed. He hurriedly pushed the emotion away from him, even as it just kept *coming* from her. "Yes, and then what? Wait for someone to save us? For someone to prove that Father is not the guilty party while he rots in jail?"

"If he is not, eventually it will bear out."

"Now who is being the foolish one, Mr. Merrick? You do not believe that."

Of course he didn't. He wanted her twelve counties away, and damn the consequences.

"Someone is trying to kill you, someone is trying to get rid of us." She nodded. "And you have been helping us, all on your own. All in all, it would be easier to join forces in thwarting such attempts." She nodded. "Mutual benefit."

He felt something surprisingly like dread build within him. The tightening of melded circumstance. The smell of home-baked pastries, foul and seductive. "Go to the country. Let events unfold, create new identities, and forget about everything else. Your life will be far lengthier. You have a little over ten thousand pounds from your accounts this week hidden away. Take it and go. Your craftsmen will be hired by others. They are the best. No one will go hungry."

She looked at him, seemingly unsurprised that he knew their financial situation so well. Her gaze moved to something over his shoulder, and she said nothing for long moments. It unnerved him far more than anything else. There was an old spirit there, peeking out behind the normal innocence of her gaze.

She smiled but didn't successfully banish the shadows this time. "But it would be hardly fair to leave in such a way and it would negatively affect our workers. As much as I would like them to be, circumstances aren't quite as simple as you are trying to suggest. And you well know this."

"For you all matters seem simple." She was infecting him. He had just muttered.

"I wish that were true. I wish we could retire to Norfolk, to Essex, to Somerset, and leave the rest behind."

"Go then."

"No. We would eventually be recognized. Word travels fast."

"Go across the ocean. America. Australia."

"No."

"Why?" His voice was harder than he had thought it would be.

She looked at him steadily, with eyes far older than they should be. "In addition to our business concerns, my brother's disappearance was well timed. Though I sometimes play the muggins, Mr. Merrick, I am not one."

He grew cold. One finger twitched toward the mechanisms on his desk. "And you hope to find his killer? You think the events connected."

She looked away. "Yes," she whispered.

"You still hold hope that he is alive."

She looked at her hands, folding them together on top of her books. "I hope, Mr. Merrick. Simple hope. But it has been well over two months, and at this point it would do little good for someone to have held him for that period of time. And . . . and

I hired men. They confirmed that someone matching his description had been shot on Blackfriar's Bridge."

He tapped his finger more violently—in order to keep it above the desk top. "And? That's it? No description of the person who shot him?"

"No. The man who claimed to have known that information disappeared before I could speak with him. The information trail has closed quite tightly."

His finger stopped tapping as hard.

"Though I have been speaking to people again," she said.

Itching twitch. Her actions with his men and helping around the hell suddenly gained subversive meaning. He had concentrated so much on *her* being near him that he hadn't thought enough of *why* she was always around. What had he been *thinking*? That it was his charming personality causing her to seek out the people around him? "You are hoping to find another informant?"

"Or to flush out the guilty."

He picked up his pen and carved a coded message to Roman, who was thankfully far, far away at the moment. "Working the East End of London for information? And you claim not to be the fool."

"Perhaps." He could hear her swallow, her delicate throat working. "Perhaps I am." She leaned forward, her scent growing stronger. "But can you not say the same, that you would not try to find your brother if he went missing? To discover what had happened to him?"

Dark thoughts churned, and he pinned her with his blackest scowl, expecting her to cower. But there was something almost elemental in her that loosened under his look, that caused the hope on her face to lift. What the devil?

"Yes, you would." She nodded and looked *relieved*. Everything in the odd signals she gave, and the antithesis to her words screamed at him. Danger. Everything about her was dangerous. "I see it. And I have to know, Mr. Merrick. I made some . . . hasty inquiries—foolish, as you'd say— in the first weeks after Christian disappeared that lost me a few opportunities I might otherwise have had." She paused and looked down. "It was a loss of innocence I would have rather kept. Not knowing whom I can trust."

"You are a fool if you think to trust *me*," he said coldly. Bright brown eyes full of trust. Words that damned.

"Am I? Perhaps. But I find myself in need of an ally, and despite some of your more beastly tendencies, you have actually been quite accommodating."

His *men* had been accommodating. He was going to have a small talk with the lot of them tomorrow.

She smiled, a small, shadowed smile. "You have, though you might not admit to it."

Something about the shadows bothered him. He was used to seeing them—everyone around him had secrets. But this woman . . . six weeks, no, eight weeks prior, she had been full of life and open desire.

Irritation curled. Or something close enough to it that he identified it as such. "And why should your fate matter to me?"

"Mutual benefit, as I said previously."

"You are going to save me from a knife in the dark?"

"It is my hope to be able to save you," she said quietly.

"No." He physically felt the echo of the word, the recoil.

"I have incentives for you." She opened the top ledger. "It will be profitable for you to allow us to stay. Very profitable. Let me show you how that will be so."

"I am going to burn your ledgers," he said, almost pleasantly.

She paused, then peered up at him. "Truly?"

"Truly."

She carefully replaced the book on the short stack on her lap. "I believe that you will, at that, Mr. Merrick. Well, then I must strictly appeal to your emotions."

"I await with bated breath and heightened suspense."

She smiled at him, face softening further. "You are very amusing when you choose to be, Mr. Merrick. It would benefit us both if you would continue to be more conversant, of course."

He had already spoken more here than he had in the past seven days total.

"No? Pity." She looked at her lap for a moment, then met his eyes again. "What do I need to do in order for you to allow us to stay?"

"There is nothing you can do. And you play a deadly game trying to find out what happened to your brother. You may find everyone around you dead or gone while you are still holding your game pieces."

He saw her breath hitch, a motion that vibrated up from her chest to her chin.

"Your brother Roman—"

The inactive ice in his veins changed to another variety entirely—spiked and deadly. "He has nothing to do with any of this," he said harshly. Considering the consequences and possible pitfalls, he needed to make that very clear.

She stared at him for a long moment, and his feelings overwhelmed him too much to read the expression in her eyes.

Andreas willed the emotion down. Flat. Unemotional. Empty. Flat. Unemotional. Empty.

"I didn't mean to appeal to your emotions in the negative," her soft voice said.

The chant wasn't working. He took to examining her instead, every minute detail of her. "You don't appeal to me at all," he said harshly.

"No?" Phoebe looked at the dangerous man in front of her. The one who had interested her since she'd started corresponding with him. A faceless man on the other end of pressed ink, combined with cautious warnings given by Christian, entreating her to mysterious daydreams and fantastical thoughts.

And then he'd become her link to the world he lived in, and she'd needed to cultivate that daydream into hardened reality. She'd do whatever she had to for her family.

The candlelight flickered across his features. Her fascination with him had not ceased. Had only grown.

He was stripping her bare. Again. He did it so frequently that she wondered if he was even aware of it. Probing her insecurities and flaws. Her weaknesses.

It always made her feel uncomfortable in a way that had nothing to do with fear. Made her wonder about her rationale when it came to anything to do with him.

"Do you plan to seduce me into agreeing?" he asked tightly. "To sell me that innocence, which would still clasp so tightly to you even if you were dressed in the weeds of a whore?"

Beneath the steely, harsh words, he almost sounded disgruntled. But he was on the thin edge of reason, and she needed to choose her words carefully.

"No. I have no illusions about my powers of seduction," she said. He, on the other hand, in his dark way, was the most seductive man she had ever met. "I had thought to appeal to your rational sense instead."

He was the contradiction of rationality and sensuality. This man who sat so still and moved so fluidly when provoked. Power clinging to him, whispering in the air around him. Completely captivating, teasing her senses with visions of grandeur and bargains with the devil. Not a man to flirt with but one to whom you'd have to sell your soul.

Ruthless and fierce. There was something in that ferocity that made her lean closer. Something coiled with it, irreparably bound with that other part of him that he tried to hide, that she was still piecing together. A vulnerability that she *had* to understand. That made every part of her want to reach for him. To fill it, to soothe it, to complete it—that *something* that pulled and pulled and pulled at her, unceasing.

He tensed a fraction at her advance. So small that she wouldn't have noticed if she hadn't been so keenly aware of him.

"Though it seems I do make you nervous," she said softly.

It was as if he was physically unnerved by her at times. Something visceral to his reaction. And she relied far too often on her intuition to discount it.

Christian and Edward always said she gave rationally minded men megrims.

Andreas Merrick's eyes narrowed.

She spoke before he could reply with something cutting that she would need to fend away with humor or innocence. She'd become adept at it in the past few weeks, but doing so was never without peril. "Truly, Mr. Merrick, I desire—need—your help."

When he watched her like he was doing—stripping her—she had to hold herself still. For fear that she would utter something completely past any fair claim of manners.

"I care nothing for your safety or that of your family."

Reason told her to believe those words. The man

in front of her was reported to have but one attachment, his brother, while all others were treated with hostility at best. And yet, Andreas Merrick had pushed her to the floor that night, using precious seconds to do so, then saved her again within a span of half a minute, regardless of his words to the man who held her.

She looked at the floor near her chair, now clean again but for a few darkly stained sections of wood. At the current rate of attacks on him, they would blend with the other spots soon, staining the room's floor a new hue entirely.

Ever since that stain had been made, she'd been hard put to believe his words for truth. Especially with the nights she had peered from her window to see a man parting from the shadows and eliminating any threat that neared their door.

No, there was no question that Andreas Merrick was at least *interested* in their safety.

The question was whether he was complicit in her brother's . . . disappearance. Or knew who was. There was knowledge there. Obvious knowledge hidden behind threatening scowls and dark words. He *knew* something.

"Why should I let any of you stay? Especially with the way you essentially broke in." His eyes narrowed. "Though I'm sure you had plenty of assistance, now that I think on it."

She hurried to respond. "Do not be upset with your men. I convinced them I had your permission. Punish me, if anyone."

"How does one punish you? Take away your ability to speak?"

"No. I would simply use my ledgers more. Writing out anything that came to mind."

She forgave herself for thinking that perhaps a ghost of a smile lifted the left edge of his mouth.

"Perhaps burning your ledgers *is* key then."

She unconsciously hugged them to her chest.

He held out a hand. "Give me your ledgers for the night, and you can stay."

"What?"

He smiled darkly. "You cannot do it, can you?"

There were all manners of things scribbled in her books that he should not be allowed to read. She tended to write her thoughts down as they occurred. Part diary, part business record. Christian had always been appalled by her tendency to add narrative. But she recorded her thoughts as they occurred and somehow, when she looked at them, she could separate the bits and form them into a whole.

She didn't separate her emotions and thoughts on paper or in her head. Personal bled to business and back again.

She couldn't allow him to see what she had written about him.

Yet she needed to stay here. It was the right move, she *felt* it. People—Christian, Henry, Edward—would call her ten times a fool for doing it, but unlike them, she knew there were *two* people Andreas Merrick was attached to, not just the one that everyone knew. That second person was the reason she had dared this move, putting her father within Andreas Merrick's reach. Staking her family's welfare and future on one piece of evidence and a large amount of intuition.

"Perhaps we can compromise."

"Oh?" It was darkly uttered. "What do you offer as your part of such a promise?"

She looked into his eyes. They were a blue so deep that they appeared black on first glance. She had a feeling that most people would say his eyes *were* black, if questioned.

She had noticed their true color in her first close glimpse, though. Like the sky when it deepened to night, midnight with fathomless pinpoints of light streaking through.

The real question was what wouldn't she offer this man?

"I could help with your affairs here."

What wouldn't she offer? It was a question to scare a rationally minded person.

"Doing what? Baking biscuits?"

The man in front of her would never claim to be anything but rational. Yet, he frequently made decisions based on emotion. He just didn't seem to realize that negative emotions counted.

At times she could no more understand him than she could the gargoyles wrapped around the edges of his building. Ferocious creatures snarling above. She'd always found gargoyles interesting and delightfully symbolic creatures, though. Guarding churches and homes, threatening fiercely any force that might oppose that which they loved.

It was something she keenly felt they had in common.

"There are other things I might help with," she said softly.

She looked at his exposed wrist, mostly healed

now. Could still picture it as it had been that first night, singed, dark and raw. It had to have hurt, and yet he had taken care of those five men who had come to murder him and had uttered not a hissed word of pain during the entire ordeal.

He didn't follow her gaze. "I need no help in exacting revenge." There was almost a savored twist to how he said it, as if it was his one true pleasure in life.

Unnerving. And yet like the gargoyles, she felt the draw as if it were a living thing reaching out its tendrils to draw her in.

"Perhaps I can make it so you need never gain revenge again," she said softly.

He was very still for a moment, then suddenly he threw his head back and laughed, the vibrations of it spreading out like he was spreading the nine layers of hell, sin incarnate.

"Will you?"

His eyes traveled over her, a perusal that could not be deemed lazy, as nothing that this man did ever seemed to match that description. It was focused and overwhelming. Intense. Smoking all areas he touched with brimstone fire—the wispy hair framing her face, the curve of her neck, the dips of her body, pulling the feeling over her in a blanket, smothering and tight. A dark, seductive mass of sensation and loss of breath.

"And yet that tells me nothing of what you will actually do for me while you stay here."

"I can help you with your parliamentary procedures, for one. Christian is . . . was . . . somewhat obsessed with politics. I've been handling such matters along with him since Father . . . since Father gave us those concerns."

A true statement, if rather hiding the fact that "gave" was perhaps not the most accurate word.

He watched her for a long moment, and she could barely keep stiff under such a gaze. How did people think this man was made of ice? How did *he* believe it of himself? He all but seethed with heat. Every time that gaze touched upon her, she felt the need to divest herself of any outer garments. To strip bare under the flames.

"And you won't need to leave this building either anymore," she added.

His eyes narrowed suddenly, but the heat kept pressing. "No?"

"There won't be need to seek *outside pursuits*." She hoped that was adequate in telling him that he would no longer need to stand outside to guard their house. They'd be right here.

There was something quite odd about his re- action, though. His muscles tensed as if he were readying for a fight. She had the strange notion that reading wasn't correct though. What made a man react like that?

"Is that right?" Was there something . . . sensual in those words?

"Yes." She cast off the odd notion and nodded instead.

He shook his head suddenly, scowl reappear- ing, the lines around his eyes tightening. She could see her chance slipping through as he opened his mouth.

"I will give you a share of the company," she

blurted out. His gaze went from resistant to unreadable. "And staying here will stop me from doing anything . . . hasty. That has to be a boon, correct?"

It stung her pride, but sacrifices were sometimes necessary.

"And if you need me to stay away from you. I, I can do that. I actually enjoy speaking to you, of course. I find you fascinating, and"—she clamped her lips together, a bit mortified for once—"I will give you thirty percent of the company."

He studied her for long moments, muscles shifting beneath his shirt—it suddenly occurred to her that he was quite underdressed, and that was the reason she could discern the play of the cords at all.

"And I can get Lord Garrett to leave England," she added.

He stilled completely.

"I, I won't do anything to cause Edward or Henry harm, I won't disgrace the family and have one evil set of deeds brought to bear upon the rest. But I can make it so their father *has* to leave. I have Christian's notes."

He was so, so still. Statuesque.

"Very well." His usual surly tone was all but a purr suddenly. "As Roman likes to say, let us see how this plays, Miss Pace. And if you regret it"—he shrugged, but his eyes pinned her, dark and glittering and intense—"don't say I didn't warn you."

"Yes," she responded, though her heart was beating entirely too quickly. Her response anchored to the collection of darkened intentions that stole over his face.

He leaned forward, spreading the path of scorching heat over her, tightening it around her, like the dark manacle on his wrist that was still not fully healed, and her heart hammered, not unlike it had when cool steel had rested against her neck, as he smiled darkly. "Then welcome to hell."

Chapter 9

He tapped.
Taut like the cord of a clock one wind too tight. Watching her disappear again.

Upstairs.

He tapped harder.

Dangerous, dangerous thoughts. Ones that he could not convert to reality. Promises made— promises that she thought something else entirely.

He could call Donald. Donald was in charge, after all, and it was who Roman would have wheedled everything out of if he'd been here. But there were obstacles with whomever Andreas called tonight.

Normally, he would coldly question Donald without fear. Because normally he felt little more than disregard. But Donald, skilled in showing no emotion around anyone other than Roman, would deduce both Andreas's interest and his lack of complete knowledge. Andreas lived by the reputation that he knew everything, all of the time, without having to interact with anyone. It was the gift of his partnership with Roman.

He tapped his finger again on the desk, lips tight at the admission, even to himself, that emotion was involved. He needed someone he could verbally batter and coerce without exposing himself in return.

Andreas eyed the third cord on the wall with something akin to resignation. He loathed that cord. He reached out and yanked three times.

Footsteps pounded up the stairs moments later. Three sets of feet stopped outside his door—two sets quick, the other dragging behind.

"Enter," he barked.

Two boys tumbled into the room, one large and fearful, one reedy and eager. God, he hated that cord. The third stalked in behind, small arms crossed, jagged scar the length of his forehead. Belligerent little fuck. Andreas remembered Roman skirting the boy around him when the boy had first come to their fold.

"Sir, sir, what needs doing?" the eager one asked. He had carrot-top red hair, his skin irreparably spotted from an overabundance of freckles. His eyes held the sort of glazed eagerness of an unintelligent puppy.

Andreas dearly wished for Milton or One-eye at the moment. Someone with proper respect, fear, and intelligence. It seemed like the boys before him comprised only one characteristic each.

But One-eye was with Roman. And Milton was still on assignment. None of this would have happened if he hadn't sent Milton off.

If he had been the type to snort, he would have done so. Milton would have probably carried all of her bags inside himself.

"I want to know about our . . . guests." He let the word roll off his tongue. He could do nothing at this juncture but pretend he had known they would be moving in all along. Anything otherwise would undermine him. Perhaps that was her ultimate goal. She was doing well by it, all in all. "How they arrived, what they've been doing."

"They came in a week ago. They are living in Mr. Roman's old rooms."

Two sentences containing nothing. Eager and blank.

He gave the boy a cold stare. "Do you not know how to report? Or should I dismiss you now for the imbecile you are?"

Carrot-top looked confused.

"Imbecile means *idiot*." Andreas tapped his pen harder.

"Oh!"

Andreas continued the painful tapping on his desk, and he saw the fearful lug of a boy nudge Carrot-top in the side, his pupils nearly overtaking any color surrounding them.

Carrot-top tripped over his words. "Right. Johnny and Tommy helped 'em move out the house, Benny, Trip, and Lefty made sure everythin' got tossed upstairs. We didn't break anything, swears. And we've had fresh baker bread and lil' cakes and—"

The scarred boy elbowed Carrot-top hard.

"Er," Carrot-top continued. "That's it. We did everythin' right, swears."

He wasn't going to pull that cord again. He could bully Donald so hard that he couldn't tell his ass from his judgment center next time. "And the occupants themselves?"

"The lady, course. An older lady too, and . . . another old lady." He nudged the scarred boy, chortling. "Right? Another lady."

The scarred boy kept his gaze straight ahead, eyes narrowed on Andreas. Snotty little shit. "A man dressed as an old lady," the scarred boy corrected crisply. "*Sir.*"

Carrot-top continued, as if the interruption had been part of their act. "Wouldn't believe it at first. Great big side whiskers on a hunched granny." He pulled the hair in front of his ears out. "Me maw would have had a . . ." He trailed off, as he finally looked at Andreas. His face turned an unattractive shade of green. "That is . . . there are three of them, sir. The servants disappeared. Oh, and there's a dog. Tommy's been walking him." He motioned to the scarred boy, then quickly backed away, leaving Tommy to the figurative canines.

Tommy was eyeing him mutinously across the desk. Andreas gave him a black look in return and turned to the third boy, who was quite a bit bigger than the other two. "And what have you observed?"

The boy's mouth worked for a moment with no sound emerging. He was a hulking little beast really. He'd be a force to be reckoned with in a few years. When his mouth kept working, Andreas wondered if perhaps his tongue had been removed. He eyed the boy with anger and distaste. Roman would have taken care of the perpetrators upon being introduced to the boy, but he slashed a quick note to himself to check to make sure. If appropriate measures had not been undertaken, he would do it himself.

He turned to the little shit, Tommy, to continue his questions, but a croak emerged from the hulking boy.

"She said my cooking is good," the low voice whispered, some sort of apology edged with defiance, then wrapped up in a terrified package.

He looked closely at all three faces, eyes narrowed. His lips pressed together hard enough to hurt due to what he read there. They had claimed her as one of their own.

He thought of six ways to insult a man's mother.

But he would bend this, or break it, to his will, just as he did everything. Roman was always trying to coerce him into giving people what they thought they needed while taking everything he wanted, whereas Andreas would rather simply take what he wanted and be on with things.

He addressed Carrot-top. "Send Donald to me. Tell Lefty to put the building on medium lock starting now." They would move the gaming tables on the ground floor to the hell on Third Street. Slowly, night by night. "Start spreading the rumor among the ranks that we are renovating here in order to expand."

He needed to get the building secured. No more invited attempts—his lips thinned further, and the boys across from him shifted at the action—she had been right on that guess.

Now with his new . . . guests . . . he couldn't skirt the edge of death. Not here.

"Who knows our guests are here?" he asked.

"No one, sir." Carrot-top looked eager for redemption. "The lady asked real nice-like."

He simply stared at the boy, tapping again.

"She requested our silence on the matter very politely. *Sir*," came the belligerent addition from Tommy. Andreas shifted his gaze and gave the boy a dark look. Belligerence lifted the small chin, trying vainly to cover all other emotion. "And we've all held true to our word."

Penetrating little gaze as if the bastard were daring him to say otherwise. Roman had been right to keep this boy away from him. It was like staring in a mirror that reflected one's core personality instead of one's face.

"You had better. Tell Lefty. Send Donald." When they seemed to be waiting for additional instructions, he said somewhat more forcefully, "Leave."

They exited the room in much the same ways they had entered. He half expected Tommy to send him a rude farewell gesture as he shut the door.

No one would guess the Paces were here from the procedures he was implementing. This was something most people in his position would have done long before now. Hell knew Cornelius cowered down like the rat he was when his location was known.

His enemies would simply think Andreas was scared. Let them. A cruel smile curved his lips. This would be over soon.

The smile abruptly dropped. Until then, he needed to maintain the safety of others. It was unnerving, really, that he was allowing her to stay. Had allowed the net to reach forth and tug him too, entwining him in his own plot.

Which turned his thoughts to the occupants upstairs. He had hoped the boys would trip over themselves to give any information, no matter how superfluous. They usually did, especially when he leveled that stare on them. But . . . tonight, though they had revealed the answers to his direct questions, they had been more reserved, as if they needed to watch what they said. She had infected them too. The large boy and scarred boy held that tight-laced zeal when speaking of her—like they would jump in front of a bayonet should one be pointed her way.

Stupid biscuits laced with warm poison.

He tapped his pen, then tossed it across the room. Shit.

He had no presumptions that any of the others would be less immune. He would search, though, and see anyway.

The bigger problem was that his mind kept saying that if he did find someone less than enamored of her, he should get rid of that person instead. The thought did not endear itself to him.

Andreas could hear Donald walking down the hall—identifying him by the sound of his long and even strides. Donald almost stood eye to eye with him.

"Enter," he said before the stride fully stopped.

Donald slipped in, long hair sweeping across his forehead. He casually flung his head to remove the sweep, and it worked for a second, then slid back down. The hair had never changed, not since Andreas and Roman had met him when they were, what, seventeen? Yes. It had been just after the main street revolt. Seven years on the streets, and Roman and Andreas had been making headway toward taking them over.

He took the chair in front of Andreas and waited, his eyes steadily watching. Steadiness was why Donald was in charge of this particular hell. Their other hells had overseers as well, with Milton acting as a sort of overall manager and enforcer across the establishments. But this one, where Andreas lived and worked, had required someone who could deal with him on a day-to-day basis.

He was well aware of what an ass he was. Only Roman could tolerate him, really. Stupid, charming bastard.

"I am giving the order for a security lock. Medium now, full in a week."

Donald just inclined his head, waiting.

"Have you observed our guests?" He couldn't help his somewhat surly tone, not that he was trying to help it.

"Yes." The normally stoic man surprised him by continuing. "They haven't asked many questions. Yet."

That questions *would* be asked eventually hung between them. Andreas didn't shift though his leg pinched. Scratching. He'd have to visit Mathias soon.

"The girl is persistent though," Donald added.

"I want to know who she is particularly close to among the staff here." Who is *besotted* with her.

Hell, they probably all were. Except Donald, who rarely broke his stoic façade. And Andreas. "And what questions she asks."

Donald inclined his head, hair slipping a fraction more. "It will be done." He watched Andreas for a moment. "And she and her family will be safe here," he said, gaze steady, eyes just an extra bit bright.

Andreas nodded sharply back, dismissed him quickly, all while trying to hold back the curses layering his tongue at the words that were both said and unsaid. Donald was infected too.

Goddamn biscuits.

Chapter 10

Golden brown hair, lit by the light streaming in from the windows behind her, made him stare in shock for a moment. When he had encountered all three locks to his office door disengaged and free of scratches and gouges, he had envisaged a great many possibilities. Except this one.

Phoebe Pace sat in his chair, head bent over a ledger, a stack of invoices beside her, intense concentration on her features.

He hadn't forgotten that she was living here for the unforeseeable future. How could he when he recalled every few seconds that she was sleeping just down the hall from him? But he had thought maybe he could *avoid* her.

Better that than to think of what deals had and could be made.

"What are you doing?" He had meant to bark it or hiss it or emit it the way some feral animal might. Instead, the question emerged strangled.

"Oh!" She looked up at him brightly. "Good morning, Mr. Merrick. I thought you might be abed a few more hours. You aren't much of an early riser."

He felt like snapping out something such as how he had gone to sleep three hours before and part of that was because he kept seeing *her* in his mind's eye. He reined it in with difficulty.

"What are you doing?" he repeated darkly.

"I have been painstakingly working on these figures. Numbers are not my strength, unfortunately, but working diligently—long and hard—I believe I can meet even your exacting standards, Mr. Merrick."

He didn't know how to respond to that. So he strode toward the windows and yanked the drapes closed, plunging the room into darkness, only slivers of light seeping through the edges.

"Too bright for a creature of the night?" she asked lightly.

He didn't answer, lighting the lamps on his desk instead, as she smartly slipped into the seat on the visiting side.

"It is as if you are expecting an attack through a second-story window," she mused. "As if someone might shoot you from a broken pane across the alley."

"What are you doing in here?" His seat was still warm in the little space that had held her rear. He shifted.

She nodded at her pages. "Math. Or I was. It is hard to do anything with such little light. You are going to go blind, Mr. Merrick," she said cheerfully.

"Why are you in my room?"

He didn't ask how she had entered. Three sets of locks on the door open and unscratched. Either someone had let her in, or Roman had left a set of cranking master keys in his bedroom.

"I had thought your room was upstairs?" she said.

"My *office*," he responded, in a more surly manner.

It looked like she tried to keep the smile from her face but then decided to let it bloom anyway. "I needed somewhere to work, and I wished to speak with you. Your office suited both desires."

He could throw it in her face that the exchange had included her promise to leave him alone in order to stay in his brother's rooms. But something about that smile prevented the words from emerging.

And that irritated him.

"Well, speak, then leave." He started writing on a piece of free paper on his desk, tasks for the day, anything to keep him from looking at her.

"I would like to use some of your staff if you would allow it."

"No." She could probably cause the lot of them to revolt.

"Just for a few small tasks. Like taking Mr. Wiggles out for walks and relief, which I have commissioned help with already," she said lightly.

He continued scrawling on the page. "You want them to look for your brother."

She said nothing for a full minute, damned by the silence, even if he hadn't been sure of her motive before. "Yes."

"Do you think to find your brother in London? Not even a mudlark would help you now."

The silence after that statement grew heavy and weighted. He rubbed his chest. Damned guilt. He had survived splendidly without it for thirty-odd years. "Fine. You can choose three of them to help you."

God, he was going to regret this. It was like loading a pistol, then handing it to the enemy.

"Truly?"

Her voice was warm and happy, and the feeling in his chest loosened. Shit, shit, shit.

"Yes." He raised his gaze, pinning her. Not so far away, really, with the way both of his arms were resting on the desk's top, his shoulders well over the edge, leaning toward her. He watched the pulse leap at her neck for a moment, unable to look away. He finally tore his gaze back up to hers. "But you can't leave this building. And if someone with loose lips inadvertently gives away your location and leads trouble here, I will kill the lot of you myself."

She smiled, bright and warm, the rays of it lighting the room as if he'd never pulled the drapes.

"Thank you, Mr. Merrick." She leaned across the desk, meeting him halfway, a stretch that lifted her rear into the air, and lightly kissed him on the cheek, a brush of warm wind and soft lips. He froze.

"And I'll have the numbers done tonight," she said, pulling back to meet his gaze. "I'll bring them to you by nine."

He was so shocked he didn't ask her *what* numbers before she disappeared, smiling, from the room, ledgers pressed to her chest.

He stared at the figures in front of him for the twentieth time. It was an easy task. Add, divide, subtract. Nothing taxing. And yet each set of numbers might as well have been recipes for apple pie written in Sanskrit.

Indecipherable and twice as useless.

The padding of steps thumped softly above.

He desired to take a look inside Roman's rooms. To see James Pace and figure out what the devil was going on there. He had listened with varying degrees of incredulity to five different men report on the arrival of the Pace family. Dressing the man as a woman had actually been brilliant. Three older servant women entering the hell had provoked not a single bit of talk outside of it. And nondescript bags containing their personal belongings had been brought in at various times throughout the day to avoid speculation that someone was moving in.

There had been a tremendous amount of forethought given to their move, especially with the nondescript baggage. The thought that she had planned the move in advance wasn't a new one. But he wondered for how long she had done so. Right from the beginning? The thought of it made him nervous. No, *she* made him nervous.

Which all spiraled back to the reason he wasn't upstairs asking questions and demanding answers from her parents—for it meant that he would have to face Phoebe Pace too.

And her lips.

So he sat holed up in his office, finding it increasingly difficult to sit still in his seat.

How the *hell* had she gained the upper hand? He could threaten anyone. He could make giants cry in their porridge with little effort. He had had her exactly where he wanted her last night. Hell, she had promised him thirty percent of her company last night. If that wasn't victory, he didn't know what was.

And yet, here he sat, feeling completely on the defensive. Had let her breeze by earlier, granting her request to investigate *them*. My God.

She knocked on the door just as the clock's hand clicked, and the first of nine chimes began. He had felt and heard her since she'd stepped off the landing. If he were honest, he had been avidly listening for her steps every time he heard the creaking of the floors upstairs.

"Enter." He didn't look up as she walked inside and closed the door. This was a business meeting. A simple transaction. "Very punctual, Miss Pace."

"You seem a punctual sort of person, Mr. Merrick. Or at the very least, one to expect punctuality."

"And here I thought you sought to defy all expectations." He looked up as he said the last, trying to inject the appropriate amount of dark sarcasm.

She gifted him with a brilliant smile. He stared at her bright lips—truly as soft as they looked he now knew. "You'll make me blush, Mr. Merrick, with such complimentary humor."

He waited a moment to make sure his voice didn't emerge strangled. "What figures do you have for me?"

"The last of the figures to straighten out the books. Or up, as you will."

He simply waited for her to continue.

"And I am settling things so that you have action on our account for our company holdings."

He stared at her for an indescribable moment. "What?"

She shrugged lightly. "Well, I did promise you a thirty percent stake last night. And combined with your other single shares, you are close to a controlling percentage already. If anything happens to us—should we go to prison or disappear more permanently—I want someone with intelligence and foresight to deal with Pace & Co. of London. It is my father's legacy," she said, the last uttered more quietly but no less resolutely.

That feeling stoked again—fire burning under his heart. Guilt.

"Why wouldn't you make this deal with your friend," he said harshly. "Edward Wilcox. With the provision that Lord Garrett, his father, cannot touch the company."

She tilted her head, a small smile upon her lips. "Why indeed. Why do you think I am dealing with you instead?"

"I don't know. I am hardly omniscient," he said tightly.

"That is not what those around you think. A god among men."

"I am something far darker, if anything." He

leaned forward as he uttered the silky words, expecting her to back away at the dark net flaring toward her. Considering their previous words, he didn't know why he expected such a thing, for she leaned forward as well. As if she wanted to be entrapped by the spell.

He pulled back instead. "Why wouldn't you offer to Wilcox? He has gained his majority and does not need to answer to his father. Garrett would be horrified."

It would actually have made things easier and more difficult for Andreas's own plans if she'd done that from the beginning.

"Edward, though he is a dear, is uninterested in financial matters. Even with his estate accounts, he is smart enough to know his limits and hire others to help. However, there is no other I would trust to pick out livestock and good, arable land." She tilted her head. "We all have our skills. But his father is still able to bully him. And Henry too. It would be a burden for them in the end, and they would not be able to save the company."

"And you think I will?"

"I know you will." She said it simply.

"You are assuming I want to."

"You are heavily invested." She tilted her head. "It is a boon to us to have you heavily invested, actually."

He didn't verbally acknowledge the thought that she might have planned this all along. But it was a distinct possibility that he would not lightly dismiss.

"Some investments turn out poorly."

"I have heard that you make very few bad investments."

"It sometimes happens." He lifted a shoulder. "I do not have control of everything."

"No?" She examined him. "I think I would like to see you out of control."

His body reacted to her words, unfortunately. Already watching him keenly, her eyes followed the sudden movement of his lower body shifting behind the desk.

He quickly leaned forward, unnerved and irritated with his own reaction. And hers. "You choose to put your company and lives in my hands? You play a dangerous game."

"I do." She watched him, head tilted up, eyes holding his. "Will you do it?"

"Yes." It was as if the word had been just sitting there, on his tongue, waiting to be said. Everything up to that point leading to it.

"Good. Do you have a copy of *The Statutes of the Realm*?"

He started to point, but then realized it was the perfect opportunity to avoid looking at her. He stood and briskly walked to the bookcases beside the door. He pulled the legal volume from the shelf and turned around, only to find that she'd followed him. Trapping him.

He hadn't realized the danger he had put himself in by escaping the barrier of his desk.

"Thank you." She looked at the volume, then back to him. He hadn't felt so trapped in a very, very long time. It made him want to snarl and push away. But instead he kept himself still, muscles tight.

She took the volume from him, bare fingers drawing over his.

"Why aren't you wearing gloves?" he said harshly.

She contemplated the book for a moment before tilting her head up so that she could meet his eyes. He wasn't sure anyone other than Roman and Nana had ever met his eyes so often.

"I wear them when necessary. But I enjoy feeling the sensations and textures when I touch things." As if she had enjoyed touching *him*. "I enjoy not wearing gloves in my own home."

"This isn't your home."

She smiled. "You are wrong. At least temporarily it is. Home is where my family is."

He had nothing to say to that. Nothing that wouldn't emerge with far more admission than he intended.

"Thank you for helping us, Mr. Merrick."

She rose to her tiptoes, free fingers curling around his forearm. Somehow he became even stiffer. Her lips brushed his cheek. Soft petals sliding along a rocky cliff face.

Something less impulsive than before—more deliberate this time.

She dropped back to her heels and smiled at him. "We always share kisses good night," her soft, husky voice said. "Mother and Father have done so for as long as I can recall."

He stared at her, on edge from the conflicting feelings such an action generated within him.

"I think it a fine tradition to continue." She released her fingers from his arm. The soft touch that felt like a manacle. "Now that you are family—"

"We aren't family." It was a tight, telling response.

Family meant things both wonderful and horrid. Family that he had picked for himself were his everything. Those he had been born to weren't worth a positive thought.

The woman before him, with her tight-knit, born-to clan would never understand such a thing. How important it was to him when he called someone family. And how rare such a thing was.

Her smile stayed firm. "Floormates then. And partners. Now that we are floormates and partners."

But before he could hold on to the sharp satisfaction of such a thought, wedged between them, her lips were warm against his cheek again.

"Good evening, Mr. Merrick," she murmured as she pulled away.

Then she was gone. Along with his increasingly tattered semblance of control.

Chapter 11

I kissed Andreas Merrick.

"Thank you, Tommy," Phoebe said, handing the dog to the boy and trying to keep her thoughts away from what had just happened fifteen minutes previously.

Tommy nodded at her, eyes wary and shadowed as always. "The building is going to be locked up tight soon. No more gambling here. The order has gone into place."

They were all strange, these odd boy-men who inhabited the halls. Oh, there were plenty of adults—wicked-looking men with slightly maniacal grins. Or those wearing no expressions at all.

I kissed Andreas Merrick.

But they all nodded politely to her when they saw her. And they all ate the treats she baked. So she continued to make more, as she enjoyed doing so. And the recipients seemed to enjoy receiving them, and so she continued to be unafraid in a situation where a normal, nonaddled person would have been terrified.

I kissed Andreas Merrick.

"Thank you for letting me know and for walking Mr. Wiggles, Tommy. Please let me know if you stop enjoying the task."

He looked at her, eyes penetrating. "You have more of that pudding you made this morning?"

"Yes."

The boy nodded and took the leash from her too, transaction obviously made.

"You may have the pudding without walking Mr. Wiggles."

Another penetrating look. "No."

She didn't protest, she just nodded in return. She had realized quickly that no one here liked being beholden in any way. "I will have a bowl for you when you return."

Here things worked as an exchange. Exchanging or trading one object or service for another. The concept of the Collateral Exchange that the Merrick brothers ran brilliantly was simply another stitch in the surrounding fabric.

She had a feeling the sentiment concerning paying one's debts sprang directly from the man at the top. Ingrained into each of those beneath him. That, and living on the streets made one obviously more wary of good intentions.

Tit-for-tat transactions were likelier far safer in every way.

I kissed Andreas Merrick.

Tommy nodded sharply, then hooked the dog up, set him on the floor, and gently tugged the leash. Mr. Wiggles obediently followed.

Mr. Wiggles was quite an ordinary-looking dog,

fortunately. Mutt born, shaggy, and brown. He looked enough like the dogs skulking in the gutters here to be beneath notice. Though he was a bit plumper than the other dogs she had seen.

But plenty small enough for the boys to handle.

Tommy stopped at the door, standing there for a moment without looking at her. "Peter said he'd come speak to you in the next hour."

Relief washed through her. "Thank you, Tommy."

He gave a sharp nod, still without meeting her eyes again, and disappeared through the portal.

She leaned back against the door. Taking a moment alone—and in blessed quiet—before she would have to return to her parents.

I kissed Andreas Merrick.

She needed to stop thinking of such things: the firm, rough texture of his skin, just a hint of coarse grain against her soft cheek.

I kissed Andreas Merrick. I kissed Andreas Merrick. I kissed Andreas Merrick.

The litany of it needed to be dealt with. She had kissed him on the cheek. Hardly something worth much note. She was a tactile person. And her family had always been so inclined. Her female friends exchanged cheek kisses with her all the time.

Andreas Merrick, however, was not a person who accepted tactile advances well. The first time she had kissed him that afternoon had been an impulse. Leaning over to happily thank him, as she would to Christian or even Edward.

But while leaning across the desk . . . after her lips had touched his cheek . . . freezing him in place

. . . the thought had wended and weaved. The impulse turning into desire, then resolve, to do it again. To bring him within her fold. To show him the pleasure of sharing simple affection.

There was nothing simple in her thoughts of it now, though, without the determination there to distract her. What was she hoping to achieve, really? She wouldn't lie to herself.

That tiny shiver that had cleaved his body when she had touched her lips to his cheek . . . she *wanted that* again. It called to her. Even though she didn't understand exactly what that calling meant.

And so she had trapped him in the corner and made him shiver again.

She had *kissed* him.

Her body gave a quiver that she didn't understand. She only knew it wasn't negative.

"Phoebe?" She could hear the frown in her mother's voice, calling her from the bedroom.

She called up a bright smile and walked the long expanse of floor to the other room.

Mathilda Pace was sewing an intricate needlepoint, tilting the piece toward the candlelight. It was a good sign, as she hadn't been able to relax most of the day. Her eyes still strayed every few seconds though to watch her husband hunched over a backgammon board, rubbing his chin, the scraggly dog missing from his feet.

It had been a . . . *mixed* day here. They typically had a small cordial of port at the end of a challenging day. She knew even the servants sometimes indulged in the kitchen after such days. Sally had once confessed it while helping her dress.

"Tommy just took Mr. Wiggles for a walk," Phoebe said softly.

She stepped farther into the room and wondered for the tenth time what it had looked like before Roman Merrick had moved his personal things. There were still rich accents that pointed to someone with expensive tastes and varied interests.

"Good." Her mother surveyed her. "Now are you going to tell me your plans?" There was a threat of demand in her tired voice.

"There is little further to tell," she said lightly.

"I know you, Phoebe Jane Pace. You are scheming."

"No more than usual. As I said, Mr. Merrick agreed that we can stay."

"I am still not pleased by any of your actions these last few weeks. And you ran off last night with the barest of explanations, Phoebe. I nearly had a conniption."

"I know," she soothed, watching her mother's hands clutch the piece. "But you were and are needed here with Father, and I will need to continue to work with Mr. Merrick. He was . . . unnerved by seeing me, and I needed to sort matters right away. I am completely safe with him. There was, and is, nothing to fear."

"Fear? That my daughter has been running off on strange jaunts, dressed in strange clothing, dealing with strange men? That we are now living in an area of London ruled by thieves and scoundrels? Waiting for bribed members of the Watch to arrest us? No, there is nothing to fear. How silly of me."

The only positive thing that had resulted from

her father's episode last night had been that her mother had been unable to trail her after Phoebe had encountered Andreas Merrick on the other side of their door. With no servants to help, her mother's every activity was wrapped around watching her husband now. Not that that hadn't been the case before, but her mother had had free moments to be concerned about Phoebe.

"And there is no reason to feel guilty, Mama." She could read her mother's expression and promptly walked toward her and laid a hand on her arm, skin to skin. "This is how we need to divide and tackle. If you are to feel guilty, then so am I for not spelling you equally throughout the day."

"You spell me too frequently already, Phoebe. You take no rest. You work too hard. You should be enjoying lavish balls and being doted on by suitors." Her mother looked away, pained. "I worry, Phoebe. And I am proficient in the art."

"You are exceptional at it, Mother. Do not underestimate your talents," she said, lightening her voice again. "If I had not returned in a timely manner last eve, you would have convinced even Father to venture out to search for a strange girl named Phoebe. Mr. Merrick and I came to terms, though, no worries to be had. I returned quickly, did I not?"

Her father had still been slowly recovering from his episode when she had returned. It had taken an hour more to settle him fully, and by that time, her mother had been too exhausted to quiz her, which had been to Phoebe's benefit.

She stared at a vase in the corner. It was enameled in striking shades of red and gold. She wondered what Andreas Merrick's rooms looked like. Would they be similar to these, his brother's? The two men were so dissimilar in some ways that the question tugged relentlessly when she was surrounded by a hint of half the answer.

"The quickness of your visits does not lessen my anxiety. Having you gone at all . . . I am more than within sense to be worried. This just isn't done, Phoebe. Any of it." Her mother's expression smoothed out—Phoebe had tried to emulate that maneuver forever. "But I know there is little more discussion to be had on the matter. Did you show him the figures?"

"Yes."

That wasn't the only thing she had shown him.

"What happened?" Her mother's eyes were sharp, obviously picking up on something in her expression.

"We had a pleasant conversation. Just as we did earlier."

Pleasant—full of fire and interest and paradox. And two kisses. And many more questions. She would need to be very, very careful. In her next steps and with him. But . . .

"I think I make Mr. Merrick more nervous than I make you, truth be told."

Before her mother could question her further and wrench any details from her, Phoebe walked to her father's side. "I say, Mr. Pace, you are playing quite fiercely. I haven't seen such impressive moves in years." She squeezed his shoulder. He looked up at her, no personal recognition in his eyes, only simple satisfaction at the compliment, then looked back to the board. Phoebe squeezed his shoulder again without comment, then returned to sit in the comfortable chair next to her mother.

Her mother peered at her above her thin glasses, not distracted in the least.

"What can I add that you do not already know? I gave him partial control of the company. Our fate is now tied to his."

Her mother's lips tightened, and she looked at her husband. "I hope you know what you are doing, Phoebe."

"As do I."

"The rumors about him—"

"Are, many of them, true. But I have a good feeling about Mr. Andreas Merrick."

Her mother watched her for a long moment, expression unreadable.

Phoebe waved a hand at her father. "Did you help him set the board this time? I think he is going for the Pace gambit. It was only two years ago that he created that move." She drummed her fingers on the arm of the chair. "I think Mr. Wiggles is helping, Mama. Now, if we can just get him to stop wetting on—"

"I worry that one of these days your *feelings* will fail." Her mother had dropped her needlepoint flush to her lap and was frowning at it. Her mother did not easily fall to her tricks. "I thought you had said—"

"Mr. Merrick is a shrewd businessman," Phoebe interrupted. "He seeks the best terms for himself and maintains continuous reservations on most everything." She kept a calm expression on her face.

"Yes, of course. Your father was always the same. Kind, but stern and savvy with business matters."

It would do her cause no good to tell her mother that Andreas Merrick would rather be hanged than considered *kind*, so she took the opportunity to set her mother's mind at ease. She tried to do so as often as she could. If it only made her own inner turmoil worse, she could handle the strain. Dealing with Andreas Merrick actually did wonders for loosening stress. She wondered if kissing him more frequently would help even more.

Her mother continued to frown, though. "Roman Merrick seemed such a nice man when we met him. And he too is chased by a dark reputation. Is it the same?"

Phoebe wondered if she'd be able to keep her mother away from Andreas Merrick for the duration of their stay. The things that appealed to Phoebe about the man would definitely not appeal to her mother's sensibilities. Roman Merrick had been charming enough to pull the wool over even her mother's discerning eyes.

No one would call Andreas Merrick charming.

"They are obviously not blood kin. Though they share similar . . . traits." Danger traveling constantly over the whorls in their very skin. "Physically he reminds me of someone, though I cannot put my finger on whom."

She wished she could, for it had caused her to feel at ease with him immediately, and even though she was usually a trusting sort, wanting to believe the best about people, even she had known that blindly trusting Andreas Merrick was not smart. Yet there had been something from the very beginning urging her to put her trust in the man and their safety in his hands.

Phoebe decided to steer the conversation in another direction, if possible. "Do you mind if I have a spot of tea, Mother?" She motioned toward the service on the table.

"Of course, dear. That nice boy Johnny sent up a pot without my asking." Her mother made a stitch, a wonderful sign, which caused Phoebe's shoulders to relax a fraction. "Such a nice boy, though I admit I miss Sally's crushed-mint tea."

Phoebe did as well. But having their three servants here would have unduly complicated matters. Keeping six people hidden was far harder than three. So she had gained their servants temporary employment with a friend in the country. A friend who could be counted upon to make them permanent retainers if the worst were to occur.

"I believe that if you are going to continue this present course, Phoebe, that we would be wise to involve Johnny further. I think he would be willing to help and keep quiet. He kept mumbling about your biscuits."

Phoebe smiled faintly. "They are nice folks here."

"You've never minded a little rough talk either." Her mother pinned her gaze on her without missing a stitch. "I told your father nothing good would come of taking you to the warehouses and docks on business."

"Christian was always permitted to go, I hardly thought it fair."

"Your brother is a man."

Phoebe ignored the strain on the "is." As each day drew to a close, it became harder and harder. "He was a boy at the time. And that hardly mattered to me. Mary Wollstonecraft states definitively—"

"You know I cannot argue with you about such things."

"A decided advantage for me," Phoebe said lightly. "On the other hand, I never fare well in arguments with you concerning manners or fashion."

Though they agreed on one thing concerning those topics. No mourning wear. Not yet. Phoebe couldn't bear the thought of it, and she knew neither could her mother.

"When Christian returns, I will have him argue that point with you," Mathilda Pace said. Christian was simply still at Cambridge, not yet home for break. Neither of them had ever spoken of it aloud, yet both of them clung to the illusion, the mental deception.

For Christian was not at Cambridge.

"And though you befuddle and prevaricate, I want to know of this Merrick. I should meet him tomorrow."

Phoebe hummed without answering and thought of three different ways to prevent such an occurrence.

"The only things I have firmly wrenched from you is that he doesn't have the beady eyes and crooked nose you amused yourself with anticipating."

Phoebe pictured the man's sharp, straight features.

Her mother moved her embroidery to the side table. "And that he is not hulking and terrible."

"No, lean and tight."

And easy to kiss.

Her mother's eyes narrowed for a second. "And that you are far too interested in him."

"He is very interesting."

That shiver . . . the way he looked at her sometimes. . .

"Hmmm . . ." Her mother gave a quick look to her father, who was frowning over his next move, then looked back to Phoebe, scooting forward in her seat so that they were physically closer.

Phoebe pushed aside strange thoughts on what she wanted from Andreas Merrick and let part of her tenseness loosen, leaning into her mother as well. Safety. Security. Love. Even with the fractures that always threatened lately, she still had her family. If only Christian were here as well.

Her mother touched her hand. "We have chosen our roles and paths. I have allowed this to occur. And I know you, Phoebe. I can see that you are setting your sights. As much as you wish it, I do not forget when you attempt to misdirect me." No, it was a blessing and a curse in this specific instance that her mother was not the forgetful one of the Paces.

"It would be silly for me to set my sights on anything here, Mother." She attempted a light tone. "But we can stay for as long as we need, I believe." She had read it there for that split second. In the deep well that was Andreas Merrick, there was something there that spoke of interest. Reticence, vulnerability, and strength. Secrets and plans. "And he can find Christian—or determine what happened to him. He has the resources. All I need to do is give him the proper incentive."

Unfortunately, if she promised never again to show her face near him, he would probably leap on the opportunity. Though she forgave herself the thought that . . . maybe he wouldn't. Maybe it would be the opposite. Given time. Maybe.

"Though I wish I could rein you in as I used to be able to before your father . . . became ill . . ." Her mother swallowed. "I must console myself with the knowledge that you have always had good instincts about people."

Phoebe didn't speak for a moment, but as the constant worry in her mother's eyes shifted to something far more focused on her, she found her tongue. "Andreas Merrick is an intense man, but ruthlessly fair." It was what everyone said of him, but she often wondered if ruthless and fair might mean different things to him than they did to her. "Quick-witted and decisive. A good decision maker."

Her father mumbled suddenly, moving a back-gammon chip.

After a quick visual check to make sure her husband was fine, and that his mutter didn't signal something dire, her mother pressed closer to her, fatigue showing in the cast of the candlelight. "Though I understand your reasons for being here and doing all of this . . . Heavens, sweetie, I understand your reasons . . . I can't lose you too." Fierce desperation was in the depths of her eyes. "If we lose everything, so be it. I can't lose you too."

"You won't," she said softly, touching her mother's hand again, refusing to entertain the possibility that it might be a lie. To reveal to her mother that she was in far deeper than she had planned. "We will be safe here."

She didn't care what Andreas Merrick verbally professed. He wouldn't allow anything harmful through those doors while they were here. She had read it there in his intense gaze.

"Christian . . ." Phoebe stared at their touched hands instead of gazing at the worried face, so similar to hers. "And our craftsmen. And just to know . . ."

"I know. I *know*." Her mother turned her hand under hers, gripping upward, a tiny bit of the misery hidden beneath the depth of her mother's outer strength showing through.

They stayed that way for long moments. The clink of the chips, as James Pace played backgammon against himself, was the only sound in the room.

"The new salts for Father—"

"Will still be there. We can wait a few weeks. We will stick together."

Phoebe bit her lip. "We won't be able to keep Father's condition a secret from Mr. Merrick for long. We were lucky father was lucid when we moved in here. You aren't prepared for—"

"Neither are you."

Phoebe paused, accepting the truth of the statement. "No."

Her mother gave her hand a squeeze. "Without Christian as a barrier, we won't be able to keep your father's condition a secret in Bath this year either."

She nodded. "And Mr. Merrick will discover it immediately if he presses to see him." Phoebe looked away, unable to put the request into words. She hadn't had to worry about it before the building was secured—as they had *had* to stay out of the eye of any patrons below. Phoebe had been using the gray wig even when she ventured down the back stairs to the kitchens.

"We will stay in the rooms. Your father is a sly beast," her mother said with no small amount of exasperation laced with fondness. And sadness. "He would probably cause a revolt if we let him out." She gave Phoebe a penetrating glance. "And you wish me to avoid meeting Mr. Merrick."

"Yes."

Her mother nodded. They had banded together in equal roles when James Pace had begun his steady decline. But it was still tenuous at times, the conflicting desires to be a daughter, a mother, a partner, or a friend.

"If he meets you, it would seem strange for him not to meet Father too. There is a better chance of keeping him from both of you through joint excuses."

"Are you sure this is a good idea, Phoebe, truly?"

"Yes."

"And not just your fascination with him?"

"No, though there *is* something captivating about him," Phoebe admitted. "A hook and a draw."

A shiver under such a stark, unbending façade. The hand around hers tightened more. "He is not a broken chair you can fix, Phoebe. Nor a lamb without a mother that needs you. He is said to be a very dangerous man."

"I know that," she scoffed, but it emerged a trifle weak. "And I don't intend to 'fix' anyone. But Christian trusted him enough to formulate plans surrounding him. Christian wouldn't be duped."

They had discussed a partial plan at one point before Christian had disappeared. It had concerned gifting part of the company to Andreas Merrick in order to secure his help. Christian had planned to speak with him. Her intuition said that choice had been correct.

Her mother's entire body issued a sigh.

Phoebe was secure in her mother's love, but she had no illusions that her mother would ever think she had a greater head for decision-making than Christian, her elder child by a mere ten minutes of birth time. "Christian would not. And Charlotte Chatsworth did just marry into the family, so the Merricks mustn't be as bad as the gossip once said."

Phoebe refrained from commenting, relieved beyond measure that her mother *had* never seen nor met Andreas Merrick yet—some of his physical similarities to the high-ranking members of the *ton* aside, the aura he carried was far more deadly and powerful. When her mother finally did see him, Phoebe would have a fight on her hands to continue to meet with him.

Though Phoebe was confident she'd be able to bring her around. Necessity dictated it if nothing else.

"At least with all of us here together, your life will not be completely ruined if someone finds out where we are staying."

"Or I could always marry him," Phoebe answered lightly.

Her mother stared at her for long moments. "I misheard you, dear."

Phoebe hadn't gotten this far without investigating every avenue. "It would take a lot of convincing, but I believe I could put forth some sound arguments."

It wasn't so much confidence as pure determination that drove her in life. When things were hard, she exerted whatever effort was required to succeed.

"I, you . . . you can't marry him."

Phoebe thought for a moment. "I believe that a parson would hear us."

"That is not what I meant," her mother said, furiously, strangely, out of sorts.

A sound from her father, bless him, took both of their attention. "Could tell. Recognized the look," he mumbled.

Phoebe welcomed the distraction and hurried over to him. "Father?"

"Ack, woman, you are ruining my concentration." He waved her hand away. Phoebe was used to the absent gesture, but the pang never grew less.

"I will never forgive myself if this brings you to ruin, Phoebe," her mother whispered from where she still sat. That she was worried about things far more dire than her daughter's ruination went without being said.

"There will be nothing to forgive, Mama," she said as brightly as she could manage, moving a corresponding piece on the board across from her father when he didn't object. "Andreas Merrick is not remotely interested in me as anything other than a novelty or business contact. Besides, it is not as if I'm risking the match of next season."

Or risking pain of death. She had promised to stay in the confines of the building, and she would do so. She didn't back out of promises, and her mother knew that.

"Phoebe, you know that if you—"

"I know. I am merely being amusing, Mother."

Though they both knew she wasn't. Every season had proven lovely and comfortable up until her father's decline. But she was the type of girl that people flocked to for support and good humor and eccentricity, not the type who made hearts flutter with desire. And no man of the *ton* had made *her* heart flutter yet. Or else she would have done something about it.

Besides, she had had other things to worry about during the seasons. Before her family had . . . accepted . . . that James Pace was not quite the same as he'd once been, he had been taken in by an increasing number of fraudulent schemes and invested in a number of shady and defunct investments. They had accepted his excuses, blaming too much stress and work. It had still taken two long years before people had begun to doubt his legendary business acumen. Christian and she had concealed the situation as much as they could.

Hiding Father away broke her heart every day.

But with Christian gone, there was nothing they could do otherwise. No one listened to two women over a respected man. They were ripe pickings for someone with Parliament's ear. They would be "compensated," then shuffled out of the company James Pace had built.

She could marry. It was always the first solution on every lip. But she was not without eyes and sense to see what could and *did* happen. If she chose incorrectly, her husband could easily have her father committed. Could take everything from their family, simply and easily.

It could not be risked. Not yet.

And she'd never been particularly flush with offers. Edward had once commented that she'd find plenty of chaps ready to settle down with a "good, respectable sort" once they'd grown up a bit. The problem was she always found better matches for any of the men who looked at her with interest. There was always a girl each man had overlooked who fit him better. It seemed to be her fatal flaw, letting the "good sorts" pass her by—actively helping them find their true mates.

Her mother's eyes were disapproving at her choice of words. Worried. Worry underlining all other emotion.

"Phoebe, you can—"

"I know. But . . . but it will all work out, Mama, I won't let it be otherwise." Christian fondly liked to say that she'd change the world for the better if every man would just throw his hands up and let her rule it. She clasped tightly to the thought of her brother.

Too many things were in flux. Too many possibilities swirling.

She wondered what marriage to Andreas Merrick *would* be like. In the abstract, of course. Warmth heated her cheeks. She was just thinking out the thought to its logical conclusion, that was all.

Would people stare at her wide-eyed and terrified?

Charlotte Merrick, née Chatsworth, had invoked such reactions. Even marrying a man who could claim not a single notable ancestor, she had barely suffered a blip on the social stage. *Something* had happened after the first waves of gossip concerning their engagement. What that something was was cause for great speculation, but the male population of the *ton* had influenced their wives to the point that not even the starchiest matron dared to curl her lip in disdain.

It was the most secretive and most talked-about news of the *ton*. Everyone exchanged coded words and glances about it. She wondered if she could pry it out of Andreas Merrick. Find out the details of what his brother had done.

In any event, thinking about marriage to Andreas Merrick was quite silly. Shivers and kisses aside.

"Blasted game is taking an age." Her father seemed to be waiting for her to move a piece.

She did so, then touched his bare hand with hers. "I love you, Father," she said softly, trying not to cringe in anticipation.

Her father patted her hand, looking up at her, recognition there for a second. "I love you too,

Phoebe-bear." She held on to the feeling, chest tight, before it slipped away from his eyes.

She leaned forward to give him a tight hug, even knowing her time had run out, swallowing around the lump in her throat.

"Ack, woman. You will ruin my waistcoat." He smoothed down his undershirt—the only thing he had covering his chest. "Dratted maids trying to unman a man when he is dressed in his best."

"I'm sorry, Fa-, Mr. Pace," she said, for calling him Father sometimes sent him into a fit if he thought himself still unmarried without children at that moment.

He waved her off. "Going to meet with Prinny, Brummel, and Avanley. Need to look smart."

She nodded and smoothed his cuff. She hoped her father didn't remember the end of that memory. Brummel had said the investment was ridiculous, and her father had been embarrassed in front of the future king. Then again, her father, still fully in control of his faculties then, had had the last laugh on that one. The investment had made everyone who'd gotten involved rich.

Brummel could have used those funds. Stupid man, doubting her father in his heyday.

"Need to make a stop at the office, ensure the company is thriving. Just a few more years, and I'll make everyone's head turn."

"Yes, sir." And he would, in the future of the memory. Unfortunately, it had taken far less time to destroy the empire he had built. If only they had known when his heyday had run out.

Someone knocked politely on the outer door.

She squared her shoulders and blinked repeatedly to absorb the gathered moisture back. That would be Peter, one of the boys who had a unique place in the middle of the younger boys and grown men. She had a chance here, if she was smart, to cultivate a better position on the game board. She couldn't destroy her chance.

Her mother's head was buried in her needle-point once more, but as Phoebe passed, her hand shot out and gripped hers before releasing it. A gesture of love and support. One that they had long shared among the three of them before Christian had disappeared.

Phoebe smiled, the wallpaper blurring again.

She walked from the bedroom with her course plotted. She would save her father's legacy and prevent his incarceration—for he would not survive prison. And she would get her brother back or she would gain them resolution.

There were far too many things in their life that held no clarity, she would not let anything else be otherwise.

And with the resolve of Job, she would determine exactly what that *shiver* meant. And how Andreas Merrick's cheek felt pressed against hers for more than a single moment.

She might be a "good sort," but when it came down to sticks and needles, she was always the one who finished the game. The last man standing, determined.

Andreas Merrick wouldn't know what had hit him.

Chapter 12

He was in hell. That was all there was to it. He had entered hell approximately four weeks ago, when she'd cheerfully skipped into his life, and now he was trapped in the arms of the devil without a way to return.

He wasn't sure he had ever felt such awful certainty that he was truly damned as *everything* in him stiffened as her hand touched his arm, once more. Her soft, happy lips touching his skin.

Knowing what was to come.

"Good evening, Mr. Merrick." Soft breath upon his cheek. The smell of honey on her skin.

Cheerful and overly helpful during the day, skipping through the fully secured building, baking and charming and plotting. Bringing him food, helping him with accounts—both her family's and the day-to-day tasks that she freed him from. Taking on tasks within the building with the boys and men who were always in and out. Who all too frequently came from their other establishments in town in order to crowd into this one during lunchtime.

Tightening him with the thought that any moment one small slip from young lips could invert everything. And the knot was drawing tighter, pressing coarsely against his neck with the threat of that change.

And each night, soft lips pressed against his cheek, drawing the noose tighter still with a breathy, "Good evening, Mr. Merrick."

Her lips grew closer to his each time. He couldn't be imagining it. He couldn't be tilting closer himself.

She translated her brother's notes about Garrett's machinations. Not realizing what she held in her hand, the key to the ruination of more than one person.

Honey drifted over the downward curve of his cheek.

She ran the carriage company. Corresponding with the craftsmen and the accountants and the investors. Seamlessly fending away concerns for James Pace to meet with them and soothing fears about the allegations against him. The goodwill the Paces held with their contacts had held them in good stead and continued on for longer than another company would expect.

Honey plied the valley to the east of his lips.

Garrett was moving. Trying to subvert this tactic and take over the company "in the interest of the public while Pace was located and brought to justice." Garrett was close to success too. They had approximately two weeks more of their current tactics.

Andreas had implemented a sequence of couriers who each carried notes a minor distance before handing off to the next in line, keeping the origin of Phoebe's notes—and her location—safe. Cornelius's forces had been strangely silent, but the Merrick men were ready.

Honey whispered at the very edge of his mouth.

She put in suggestions about how to reveal the fund's performance, due out at the end of the week.

Soft air moving just over his lips.

She took on as many projects around the building as she could. Always cheerful.

He had found himself staring at her more than once, wondering what in the hell she was. Nothing human obviously.

One day to the next. Working across from him, plying him with food, flashing that eternally optimistic smile at him on lips that always beckoned. To the next day after that.

To the here and now, his body leaned toward hers automatically these days. "I believe that is it for the night, Mr. Merrick." Her fingers drifted down the fabric of his sleeve.

It was a friendly gesture on her part. One made of shared circumstance by a person who extended her friendship to all. He didn't need friends. And he definitely didn't need *her*.

His hand twitched toward her waist anyway.

Her lips pulled over his cheek. Undeniably soft. And warm. The edge of them just trailing the hard dips and planes of his cheek, touching for the briefest moment the edge of his mouth. There were spots of color in her cheeks as she pulled back—only a breath away. "Good evening, Mr. Merrick," she whispered, so unbearably close.

All it would take was an inch. To pull her toward him and claim those lips fully beneath his. To *make* her his.

He violently pulled away. "Good evening, Miss Pace," he said coolly.

She tilted her head at him, questioning, but the soft smile remained as she gathered her ledgers and the pile of work she had been doing and exited the room with a cheerful wave.

Hell.

Hell.

Hell.

Chapter 13

She folded her hands, determined to state her case successfully. She was very pleased with the progress she had made thus far—both with her business and personal maneuvers—but this particular concern was going to require an extra measure of persuasion.

"We have been working on the Garrett situation. You have also been working with me extensively on the Pace accounts," she said. "And I have kept my promise to remain inside the building, but regrettably I need to go to Dover to complete this task."

He said nothing, his silence very, very loud as he pretended to ignore her.

"You are aware of this matter, Mr. Merrick. And I realize that I am not supposed to leave the premises under any circumstance, but it's imperative that I do so now. Therefore, I would like to hire one or two of your men to accompany me. We can leave this evening under cover of darkness or tomorrow night."

"No."

"I need to in order to get the papers signed."

"Dover is half a day's travel by normal means, and you want to take one or two of my men?"

"Yes."

"No."

"It will not be a problem if we leave at night. I will put up the money for three to stay the night a few hours outside London. I'm sure the driver will have a good suggestion since the coaching road is well traveled. I was thinking that nice man, Lefty, would—"

"No."

She tilted her head, trying to figure out the main reason for his refusal so that she could maneuver around it. "Mr. Merrick, the matter concerning this signature is in your interest as well."

"I will send someone with the papers to get them signed." He indicated his desk. "Leave them here."

"Though I do not have to—and will not—give advanced warning to him, the man who needs to sign the papers will need to see me in person, I'm afraid."

"No he does not." There was a black look in his eyes. "Give them to me. I will make sure they are signed." A dark promise.

Since it wasn't aimed at her, she brushed it off. It was how she treated most things with this man. Darkness was a part of him. And she would be lying if she didn't admit to finding it a bit attractive. Because the focus on her, though intent and dangerous, never felt malicious. He was simply an intense man in all matters.

But on this topic . . . there was malice for someone. She tucked it away for further examination.

"I am going to Dover, Mr. Merrick. We are at the end of our time in this, and the signature will guarantee more. You can stop me, of course. I could do nothing to stop *you*. But I would like to have your compliance in this request. I have a sound plan. I won't be gone but three days at most, and it will be a completely impromptu visit. And I assure you that though you might try and browbeat Edward, he won't sign unless I speak to him first, and he can see that I am not being coerced."

She almost tacked on that he was a loyal friend, but instinct stopped her from doing so.

"What's more, you know that this will facilitate the transfer. This will push Garrett out. Make him forfeit his shares completely if he denies the transfer of leadership to you. And he must attend a quarterly meeting tomorrow here in London. There is no way he can be in Dover. The timing is perfect."

Andreas Merrick watched her, dark gaze clamped on her as it always was. Plumbing her secrets, reading her soul through her eyes. She kept his gaze for long moments, calmly allowing him to read her intent.

"Fine. I will arrange a carriage and escort. Be ready at nine as darkness falls."

"Thank you."

"We'll see if you thank me upon your return."

She didn't know how to respond to that other than by nodding, so she made a quick stop in the kitchen to pack a food basket, then retreated upstairs to let her mother know of the trip and settle her own thoughts before she left.

"Who is accompanying you?" Her mother had been fretting almost nonstop since her announcement.

"I don't know. Someone capable, I am sure, Mother. Hand me the purple dress, please?" She tucked her overnight items into the small valise.

"I don't like this, Phoebe. Not at all."

"I know you don't, Mother. I am sure I would be in a similar state of panic if it were you going instead of me." She put a hand upon her mother's arm to settle her. "But I need Edward's signature. And I want to speak to him in private, in person. It is important. I know you know how much. I also know that you are worried, and your feelings are not without merit."

"We never should have sent away Sally and—"

"Mother."

"You can't travel without a chaperone. I, I—"

"You have to stay here with Father," she said calmly. "All will be well. I will likely be in a coach all by myself, any men riding up top. And I assure you that Mr. Merrick would cut off his men's ballocks were they to touch me inappropriately in any way."

"Phoebe!"

"I only state the truth." She moved around her mother and picked up the lilac dress herself, her mother seemingly unable to perform even the small tasks of helping her to leave her sight.

"Your truth is disturbing me, Phoebe." She

didn't have to look at her mother. She could hear the reflection of that statement in her voice.

She clamped her lips shut on another rejoinder. It was actually something that was quite pleasing about her interactions with Mr. Merrick and some of the others here in the building. She could say what was on her mind—and sometimes the irreverent humor was even returned. Her mother, on the other hand, frequently had a fit. But then, she wanted better things for her daughter than for her to have a rotten mouth and ill-bred reputation.

And she wasn't wrong in that desire. Their paths of humor simply diverged on occasion. And Phoebe refused to feel guilt as the simple freedom to do as she willed should always be enjoyed when presented.

"I won't be gone long. I am going to straighten our remaining financial issues. That will go a long ways toward helping with Father's judicial case, should one occur." She was also hoping Edward could shed some light there as well. "In a few weeks, we will have everything straightened out, and we can retire to Bath." She wound her fingers together as she tucked the dress in, hoping. "And we will get Father the new salt treatment."

A long silence enveloped the space as she finished packing. She was much more used to dealing with silence though. Andreas Merrick was training her well. She liked to think that she was rubbing off on him too, evening them both out.

"Very well," her mother said. "I hate this though, Phoebe."

"I know. I wish things were different."

She wished things were *better*. She couldn't be upset that circumstances had brought her into contact with Andreas Merrick, just that the circumstances themselves couldn't resolve quickly and happily so that she could pursue him with abandon.

That thought brought a smile to her lips. Poor man.

She flattened her expression as she latched the case. "I will gain the opportunity to ask around the Dover docks as well. You know I have been wanting to, as many ships from London stop there."

"I don't want you to ask around, Phoebe!" Her mother's eyes closed suddenly, fingers pressing against the lids. Pressing the tears back. "I want him back, Phoebe. But I can't lose both my children."

"Shhh . . ." She hugged her mother to her. "You won't. I promise."

"You can't promise such things, Phoebe."

"I won't do anything to put myself in jeopardy."

"We are already in jeopardy."

"In more jeopardy, then. Come." She pulled her to the chair next to her father, who was playing some odd hybrid of squares for which only he knew the rules. "Drink this." She poured the warm tea and placed the cup into her mother's hands. "Knit me something warm for autumn? Something for my feet beneath the cool covers? We will be in Bath before you know it, and it is cold there in the night air."

"Phoebe . . ."

It took another fifteen minutes of reassurance before her mother let her depart. The knock on the door had occurred five minutes previous. She hoped whoever it was had continued to wait.

Peter and Tommy stood on the other side. They were maybe eighteen and twelve, respectively, if she had to guess. It was hard to tell with people here sometimes. Their eyes always looked far older than their other features.

"Miss." Peter nodded, then politely motioned toward her case. She let him take it from her. She had a warm, hooded cloak on. Carriages could be freezing if they were not well sealed, and she had no idea what to expect.

"I should speak with Mr. Merrick before I leave, Peter," she said apologetically to the boy, man . . . *male*.

Peter shook his head as he started down the steps, Tommy taking the flanking position behind her. "He said ta escort you directly ta the conveyance, Miss," Peter said over his shoulder. "You c'n speak there."

But she didn't see the man at the entrance, so she continued to follow Peter. A dark, unmarked carriage was parked a few steps from the door. Not a Pace carriage—this one was far more drab and had no distinguishing marks. Likely a Flatley model. She squinted and could see the curve of the wheel set. Flatley, for sure. She wondered why Andreas Merrick had never contracted for a Pace craftsmen to build an unmarked carriage for him. She'd have to speak to him about partnerships and purchasing from friends, not competitors.

Two dark horses snorted and pawed the ground. Peter handed her case up, and the driver secured it.

She didn't see Andreas Merrick anywhere. Perhaps it was better that way. That way she didn't need to dissemble if he tried to threaten or make her promise to stick exclusively to the inns and Edward's residence.

She squinted in the darkness and recognized the boy at the carriage's door. Trusting to the safety they had kept her in so far, she nodded and stepped up and inside.

She felt the presence on the other seat before she saw him.

"You are late, Miss Pace."

And Phoebe wondered, as her heart picked up speed, and realization dawned, what might happen on this trip.

Chapter 14

"**M**r. Merrick."

He liked when her voice went breathy and uneven like that. Surprise and something else tinting the sound.

"I didn't realize who my companion was to be or else I would have endeavored better timing," she said.

She settled into the seat, not showing herself to be out of sorts any more than those first few seconds. She touched a blanket on the side of the seat, darted a quick look to his side of the carriage, then drew it over her lap.

He followed where her eyes had landed on his side only to see the second carriage blanket that rested on his seat. She hadn't covered herself before making sure that he too had one. His arms crossed, unsure why he felt odd at the notion. It was not an abnormal thought for someone to do something like that for someone else.

Just not for him.

"We will stop in Rochester for the night," he said, roughly.

"That sounds fine."

"We will not be exiting at the switches between. If you need to take a moment before we leave, you should return inside."

She shook her head. "I can make a three- or four-hour trip without difficulty, and I've prepared food."

"Fine." He rapped the trap, and they began moving.

Her eyes kept contact with his across the flickering shadows cast by the gas lights they passed on the street. The bobbing lamps on the carriage swayed, making the brief light undulate across her face in a sensual wave.

"I didn't expect you to accompany me," she said finally, breaking the growing, stifling silence.

That had been obvious. He saw no need to comment on the fact.

"But I am glad," she said. "Glad that you are with me."

"Why?" Everything in him stilled.

She smiled faintly. "Why would I not be? I seek your company often enough."

Something in him vigorously wanted to ask *why* again? But whereas she was obviously willing to share her feelings, he didn't feel the desire to reciprocate in any measure, and simply asking the question would show some need he was determined to repress.

"You shouldn't."

"No," she acknowledged. "I should seek it twice as often."

His arms tightened further across his chest.

She smiled at him. "You have doomed yourself to endless hours in a closed vehicle with me, however. Are you not worried?"

"Why would I be worried?" Worry wasn't his overwhelming emotion at the moment.

"I may uncover all your secrets." Her tone was teasing, but he stiffened all the same. "You blabbing them all to me, if for no other reason than to stop me from speaking."

"There are other ways to do that."

Even in the revolving shadows he could see the blush darken her cheeks. His arms loosened a fraction, and he felt the edge of his mouth lift in absurd pleasure.

"I told you that you might regret this trip, Miss Pace," he all but purred.

"Oh, I don't think I will regret it at all, Mr. Merrick," she said softly.

His arms became steel bands across his chest once more.

She smiled. "Though you have appalling taste in carriage makers. Flatley?" She looked around her, tsking, her tone obvious with its teasing. "Truly, Mr. Merrick? I shall endeavor to help you mend your ways. And to teach you to treat your partners better."

There were a number of items in that statement to concern him. "I don't require mending."

"But perhaps you require infinitely more teasing?" She turned thoughtful. "Not stopping until Rochester—you think we will be recognized?"

"It will be a point of interest that there was a carriage whose occupants did not show themselves, but there are plenty of respectable citizens who desire to remain undisturbed at various stops, as well as travelers asleep inside."

She tilted her head. "There are people who watch for gossip on the road. That does make sense." There was something about her voice that was elementally soothing. In such a confined space it was hard to escape from it.

"The desire for information is always flowing," he said stiffly. "There is nothing recognizable about this vehicle"—unlike a Pace carriage—"or our driver."

She smiled.

He turned from her smile. "But eventually talk will connect the events with anyone who observed the vehicle leaving the alley. However, an unmarked carriage leaves every hour from that alley, whether there is anyone inside or not."

He wondered at himself, telling her such things. One in a string of a hundred little secrets he had let slip. Perhaps he would need to keep her at the end of this endeavor. Lock her in a tower and throw away the key.

"That gives us some time," he continued. It was like a disease. A Phoebe-Pace-inspired disease, this need to speak so much—to explain himself. "Deception works best if it is part of a regular routine."

She watched him, her mind obviously working

quickly behind open, expressive eyes. Open and expressive, but hiding a far more cunning mind than most gave credit.

"It is on our return we will have to be most cautious, Miss Pace." Don't think of her as Phoebe, *ever*. "We will use another carriage on our return trip."

"People watch the alley?"

"Outside the alley, not in it. Inside is a secured area when we choose it to be."

The look in her eyes said she was thinking of the incident that first night in his office. He waited for her to question him about it again.

"I am pleased that the company I have is yours, Mr. Merrick," she said instead.

"I have business in Dover," he said quickly.

"That is most convenient."

He didn't respond. She was like some sort of horrid diviner's rod, poking inside.

"I am happy that our paths are headed in the same direction, Mr. Merrick."

There was something in that statement that caused him to sit stiffly for the rest of the trip.

Phoebe watched him across the space of the carriage. She was still uncertain what actually went through his sharp mind, under the emotionless façade that he normally displayed.

They arrived at a small inn in good time—just under three hours. Their driver was skilled and the roads had been freshly treated.

Andreas Merrick withdrew a pistol from a side

pocket near the window and checked it over, then slipped it into his coat.

"Wait here. Keep your hood up at all times." He stepped out of the carriage oddly but turned gracefully to the driver. "Five minutes or drive to the location we discussed."

She resisted the urge to look through the window to follow his progress. He had her case in his hand and a satchel around his shoulder. Five minutes? He couldn't promise to secure their rooms and return in that short a time. What location had been discussed? She wasn't leaving him.

He returned four minutes later without her bag, just as she was starting to fret, said a few low words to the driver, then held out a hand to help her down. She put her gloved hand in his, heart beating faster. She knew that he was simply helping her—it would cause comment to their masquerade if he didn't—but she was unused to his initiating any contact with her. It was always she who touched him. She took a deep breath, trying to calm her reaction.

He was wearing a large greatcoat and low-slung hat. Altogether, they looked like two chilled and weary travelers. He released her hand but remained close, shielding her as they moved.

She could see the innkeeper curiously watching them as they entered. She kept to the darkness of her hood, keeping her head lowered and her lamp well away from her face. Frankly, she trusted Andreas Merrick, and his paranoia, to keep her safe, and she wasn't afraid to admit such. It was simple good sense. The man was overly suspicious and prepared enough for two.

"I secured two rooms with a connecting door," he said in a very low tone of voice. She nodded to indicate her understanding. It was both a security relief and privacy challenge.

Often such double rooms were used for children or servants of higher-paying customers. The more demanding patrons paid for their own convenience instead of having servants double-bunk with the inn's staff.

He opened a door and poked the lamp inside, doing something that she couldn't see. Checking shadows? It was quickly done, then he stepped back, eyes sweeping the hall in both directions as he motioned her inside. Yes, he was paranoid—*thorough* enough—for both of them.

He followed her closely inside and shut the door, locking it. He pressed her against the wall near the door, then leaned down, ear to the floor. She stared at him blankly until she realized that he had already risen again and was strolling to the bed, having just checked, at a distance, beneath the frame. Something unsettling went through her at the thought of someone's hiding beneath.

He pulled a spindle of filament and a small weight from his satchel. He strode back to the door leading to the hall, strung the weight through the string, knotted one end of the string to the base of the handle, then strung it across, weight dangling in the middle, and attached the other end to the edge of a sconce on the other side, ripping the string free of the spindle with his teeth.

"Don't use the door."

She nodded to show she understood.

He opened the connecting door and left it open. She leaned against the jamb, watching as he repeated the actions in the other room. His movements were brisk and efficient. But then he was a brisk and efficient man. No movements wasted.

He was bent sharply at the waist to the task, all cool, straight lines. She admired the view from the rear. She wasn't in some ballroom where she needed to worry about her reputation if she were caught ogling someone.

Not that she had felt the need to ogle anyone before Andreas Merrick. But she could look freely at the object of her interest when they were alone. Privacy freeing her in a way she had never been able to be before. This was what marriage was like, being able to look one's fill. Her parents had always exchanged glances in such a way, in the seclusion of their own house.

Phoebe wanted that intimacy. The intimacy that was allowed without social repercussion.

He looked at her as he finished the wiring on the door. His face immediately shuttered. She wondered what he had seen on hers. "You should sleep. We will be leaving early. The earlier you can get in to see Edward Wilcox, the better."

She nodded slowly. He obviously wanted to return to London as quickly as possible. Probably hoping she would be unable to complete any of the other tasks she had planned.

If any of his men had accompanied her, she could have cajoled. Andreas Merrick was mostly immune to cajoling. *Mostly*. But that tiny crack was where opportunity resided.

"Edward is an early riser, and he will likely be in the fields when we arrive in the city. I will wait until noon. If it were Henry, we could go earlier. He tends to rise late, but he stays in the house."

"If Henry Wilcox is there, you will not go inside."

"Henry is a friend—"

He leaned forward into her space. "You will leave if he is there."

She watched him. "Henry is at Fairhaven, so it is an item of irrelevance. Is it not?"

If he chose to pursue the topic, she wanted to make sure he knew that she would be pursuing it as well.

The tightening of his lips said he understood perfectly.

He turned and began to rummage through his bag, his back to her. She tilted her head, something about his body position sparked a thought she couldn't quite grasp.

There were too many other thoughts running through her head, blocking it out, leaving only a warmed feeling behind. She slipped back into her room to prepare for bed. With the door opened between, she could easily hear him moving about in the other room,

She hesitated; perhaps she should speak to him about her other plans for tomorrow. Spin some tales—or just confess what she planned to do and see how he reacted. She had the notion that he was going to be monitoring her progress tomorrow anyway.

She walked back to the open doors, peeked around, and froze.

He was a tall man but not heavy. Most men of his height and lean musculature were gangly or awkward in their skin. But there was a tight strength about him that spoke of someone who knew exactly how to use his body to its fullest potential. A lethal dancer. A dark Lucifer who could bend and twist and kill.

His shirt was off, his loosened trousers barely hanging on the edges of his hips, one step away from removal. Her gaze couldn't linger on the thought of seeing a man so unclothed, especially one her heartbeat responded so readily to, as her mind was fully taken with other visual aspects. His back was a tapestry, filled by the cracked art of the streets. A tangle of scars, one overlapping another bunched beneath the nape of his neck, then dove down the tendons and sinew of his back, splitting off, snaking over his spine in lashed patterns.

There was symmetry to a number of the longer marks, indicating that they had been gifted by the same wielder, whereas others along his shoulder blades and waist were clearly single events made by a blade or bullet. There were so many lines in the longer cuts that they overlapped entirely in some parts, the only way to tell that there were two or three separate marks was to see the tails splitting at the ends. She wondered how someone could have survived being whipped that many times.

"What do you want now?"

His voice was as unpleasant as it always was when he was on guard, his posture just as tight.

She wondered if he was bothered by anyone's seeing him like this, or if it were she specifically.

Her hand was already reaching forward to smooth over the raised marks when she realized what she was doing and dropped it back to her side.

"I wanted to wish you a good sleep," she said softly, all thoughts of speaking of the next day and confirming her suspicions wiped away.

He said nothing for a long moment, hands folding his shirt, shifting things around his bag—the actions shifting the muscles beneath his skin. "And now you have." The words were no more kind, but she thought that maybe his tone lacked just a bit of its edge.

"No, not yet."

He warily looked at her over his shoulder, body stiff. Every night for a week she had kissed him on the cheek before turning in for the night. But she had always flitted away, back to her own room, a floor away from his office.

Here, there was no leaving. The beds less than a dozen paces from each other.

She almost pulled back into her room. Her first official act of cowardice. But then she moved forward with purpose.

He kept his back to her though his visible eye tracked her closely. Again the odd thought presented itself that there was something *telling* about that. He always kept people in full view.

She touched his shoulders and pulled her fingers lightly over a few braided scars at the back. It was entirely inappropriate—beyond inappropriate and entering into condemnable really—and yet she couldn't help herself. It was a form of possession that made her touch one of them with her lips.

His muscles were steel beneath her touch as he quickly looked away.

Part of her wanted nothing more than to turn him toward her. To touch, and kiss, and soothe him. To make him totally surrender to whatever lay between them. The other part of her knew he wasn't ready. And she wasn't going to push.

"Good evening, Mr. Merrick."

Yet.

His profile showed a mixture of expressions as he stared straight ahead, away from her, but he nodded sharply, the rest of his body still clenched tight.

Her hands shook as she undressed quietly back in her own room. She could not deny it—she was becoming irreparably entangled. And what he would ultimately do with the net, she did not know.

Chapter 15

He heard her all night. She wasn't a loud sleeper, but he was well used to listening for every sound in his environment, especially in an environment that was not his own. The sound of movement on bare sheets or a dream-induced sigh made him . . . uncomfortable. Made him feel the urge to toss and shift.

She had touched him. She had looked at his repulsive scars and pressed her lips to them. Soothing and steady. Unfaltering and unshakable. That was Phoebe Pace.

He needed her gone more than he ever had. And yet his fingers clutched an invisible cord, fingernails gripping his palm, as if it would hold her to him.

He wasn't feeling particularly charitable when the sky lightened. There was little on which to assuage his black mood, for she rose quickly at his knock against the open frame between them.

He didn't watch her rise, unwilling to see her sleepy-eyed and rumpled.

"We need to be gone before the light takes hold," he said, already turning to leave.

She was quick to pack her things and dress, and she stood patiently waiting, eyes looking through a crack in the drape to the courtyard beyond, when he walked through the connecting door five minutes later.

He stopped, watching her for a moment. She looked . . . wistful. Innocent.

What was he doing here? With her? There was the possibility that he would bring direct danger to her if he was spotted. Better for him to have sent someone else—or three—with her.

But he had known he was going to accompany her as soon as she voiced the request. Unavoidable. Inevitable.

Especially considering where she was going. Things were moving quickly, in another direction, away from him, and all he could hope to do was to control the casualties that would result.

He wouldn't let Phoebe Pace be a casualty. And wasn't that just a damn thing. He wondered when she would get around to asking him directly about her brother. She had to know he knew almost everything that happened in London, even with Roman absent from the city.

She had to suspect he knew exactly what had happened to her brother and what players had been involved.

He saw it sometimes. The trust in her eyes. Fragile and easily broken with just a few simple words. Warm lips pressed to his body would be exchanged for tears and betrayal.

"Ready?" she asked, drape closed again, cloak and hood drawn up as he'd been castigating himself.

He nodded, taking her case. He avoided contact with the two men lingering in the common room and strode to the waiting carriage, lifting her up and in. Their baggage was latched and secured by the driver.

They were clomping down the courtyard path a minute later. He watched through the window until they were well out of town. Not followed. It was possible someone had been posted ahead of them, though. Smarter. They wouldn't exit the carriage until they finally reached Dover. Three more changes, and they would be there.

He glanced across the space. Her eyes were closed, and she leaned against the seat. He didn't think she had meant to fall asleep. But he had heard her restless sleep as well. Perhaps he would get a room on the outskirts of the city. Let her rest for a few more hours before she sought . . . her contact.

His nails curled into his palms. He wondered if this disease she had brought upon him would be cured at the end of this endeavor. He hoped so.

In the meantime, he had to weigh the risks. He had been provided with the perfect opportunity to shore up any talk on the docks. But it meant he would have to leave her unguarded. He should have brought one of the others with them. Made the other man ride on top with the driver regardless of the gossip that would result within the ranks.

He had already tipped part of his hand to the other occupants of his building though. What difference did a further show make? Only his stubborn resistance said otherwise.

Phoebe jolted as the carriage pulled to a stop. She had been thinking of marked skin and warm lips and her utter inability to choose the correct words to keep the skin under her fingertips.

She stretched her cramped limbs. Oh no. Dreaming. "How long was I asleep?"

"You made it through two stops without waking."

"This is our last then?" She pushed fully upright, clearing the lingering sleep from her mind and trying to read the expression on his face, the tone in his voice. She wondered—a bit mortified— if she had been snoring or sleeping with her mouth agape.

"Yes."

She picked at the blanket over her—had she placed it there?—and ground her jaw back and forth as inconspicuously as she could to see if it felt as if it had been open for two hours. She held on to her embarrassment. Easier than dealing with the unease that had developed between them. "When is your brother due back?"

The question was out of the blue, and she knew she had taken him by surprise though he covered it well. For a moment she wasn't sure he'd answer.

"Soon."

"That is quite vague. Soon might be tomorrow or a month from now. How do you define soon?"

"I define it as a period of time in the near future."

She smiled. "How do you define difficult?"

"By your presence."

She grinned fully, delighted to feel the tension dissipate. "Now you are just flattering me for no reason."

He grunted.

"On the contrary," she said, as if his grunt had been a worded response. "It was most flattering."

He stared at her.

"What? Did you think I wouldn't figure out how to interpret your grunts? It is like listening to a conversational gambit with a thousand different meanings."

He recovered quickly, as always, scowling. "Why would you think it flattery?"

"You have defined something by my presence. Which means you have noticed me quite keenly. I take that as flattering."

His eyes narrowed. But then she knew he wouldn't like that particular explanation. It left him too wide open.

"I find you difficult. Not adorable."

"I think I am quite shocked to find you using the word 'adorable' in a sentence." She waved a hand. "Next thing I know, you will be petting puppies in the street."

"You are the one with the odd canine fetish."

"They make me happy with their silly doggy grins."

His stare was flat.

She simply smiled more. "Mr. Wiggles seems taken with you."

"It tried to urinate on me the other day. I prefer not to be 'taken' by something like that."

Phoebe pressed a hand to her mouth, unable to help herself. But the image was too much. Her laughter spilled around her fingers.

She counted it as a victory that his shoulders didn't tighten. Indeed, he almost looked . . . relaxed.

Perhaps he was loosening toward her? Perhaps the kiss last night had not been a mistake? Hopefully. And if so, she planned to exploit such a development.

A small voice in her head persistently reminded her that one of these nights she might prod him too far. She didn't know what would happen to her carefully laid plans then.

Visiting Edward's house on her own had been easier than she had anticipated. Andreas had ridden in the carriage with her, but when they had arrived, he stayed inside, saying that the vehicle would be waiting up the street when she was done with her appointment.

She wondered what he was going to do in the interim.

The game tightened around her.

Under the cover of her hood, Phoebe handed the butler a folded card with a handwritten note inside. "I realize this is unusual, but Edward Wilcox will see me should you give him this." She kept her voice low.

The butler, a man she did not know, looked at the folded slip of paper, then back to her covering cloak. Probably trying to deduce if she was a woman "in the way" seeking compensation from his employer. Or some street cat. She kept her posture stiff and sure. A moment later, the butler acquiesced, shutting the door and leaving her on the porch. She wasn't affronted. He couldn't trust that while he was speaking to his employer, she might not make off with the silver, after all.

Only half a minute passed before the door opened again. "Mr. Wilcox will see you."

He led her through the halls to a study, a long sweep of arm motioning her inside. The door closed behind her.

But it wasn't Edward Wilcox standing there. It was Henry.

The Honorable Henry Wilcox, heir to Viscount Garrett, was already standing and striding over to her. She kept herself from stiffening only with effort. She had the sudden thought that Andreas Merrick was going to be very displeased with her.

"Miss Pace," Henry said softly. "What are you doing here?" He tried to peer into her hood.

There was nothing she could do except to work out a new strategy as she went.

She motioned to the drapes, and he walked over and drew them. She pushed back her hood as the room darkened, and he was forced to light a lamp. She looked around the room, noting that although there was a lot of furniture, there was thankfully no good place for another person to hide.

She seemed to be adopting more of Andreas Merrick's quirks. But they were useful tools in this odd and dangerous game she now played.

"Mr. Wilcox. I had thought Edward was in residence."

"He is out, surveying the fields at the edge of town." He gripped a paperweight on his desk without looking at her. "I heard about what is planned for your father. Why didn't you come to me immediately?"

She watched the tense set of his shoulders and the constriction of his lips. She had, at times, been slightly leery of Henry. He was usually friendly, but there was a darkness to him too, buried beneath a fine veneer of civility. There had been whispers that his mother had gone mad after giving birth to Edward. That she had alternated between rage and desolation for over a year. Some people even whispered that she had killed the eldest child in that time.

The Paces hadn't known the family then, not until the viscountess was over her disturbance. But Phoebe wondered what that time had been like for nine-year-old Henry, especially with a father like Lord Garrett.

She moved toward him. "This is silly. I haven't even greeted you properly." She gave him a firm hug, which he returned.

"How are you?" he asked, pushing her back and examining her for a moment.

"I am well. Better than expected. Hopeful. As to why I didn't come to you immediately, you know why I did not."

His lips tightened. "I do. Forgive me."

"There is nothing to forgive. The whims of our fathers forever cast shadows on our actions. Therefore, we must look to the light."

"For you, there is light. Your father made mistakes that weren't even of his rational choice. For me, there is unending darkness."

She squeezed his arm.

He shook himself from his daze and pointed at the small set of armchairs around the fireplace. "Please sit."

She did. The room seemed smaller and more intimate with all of the furniture overloading it.

"I thought you were at Fairhaven," she said. She would have made alternate plans otherwise.

"I was. I arrived here last night. I had planned to be there two weeks more." His voice held a bit of wistfulness. He leaned forward, his arms crossed over his knees. "Not that I am unhappy to see you, but why are you here? The timing is . . . concerning. You risk much."

"Yes." She withdrew a folder. "I couldn't risk getting in touch with either of you using other methods. And I knew neither of you would sign these papers without seeing me."

He looked at the papers in her hands. "What are you plotting, Miss Pace?"

She shook her head and handed him the papers.

He flipped through them, checking the standard clauses and phrases, nodding as he went. He stopped at the last page and stared at the name over the third signature line for a long moment. "I believe we need to have a chat, Miss Pace," he said at last.

"We are overdue on a great many topics of conversation."

He continued to stare at the paper, eyes not seeking her out. "Do you know who you are signing your company, and our investments, over to?"

"Yes."

He finally looked at her, eyes serious and dark. "What game are you playing, Phoebe?"

"I am playing no game, Henry."

He watched her, searching her face for something. "Are you truly guileless in this, or is trickery involved?"

"It is no trick, no deception."

"No? What do you know?"

"I have mere suppositions." Such as the shape of a nose, the set of a chin. Though the number of features that were dissimilar were too many to count. It could be that her imagination had finally run wild, but she had a feeling—to the good or bad—that the evidence wasn't just in her mind's eye.

"Is he here?" He cast his eyes around the room, looking into the shadows cast by the furniture. Henry suddenly looked much older than his thirty years. "Have you set me up for death, Phoebe? And Edward? Edward is innocent."

She blinked. "No. Of course not. I would never hurt either one of you."

He ran a hand through his hair. "Mother wasn't in her right mind after Edward was born. There was . . . just something wrong with her for months on end. Father exploited it."

"Henry, of what are you speaking?" she asked cautiously.

He waved a hand, lips tight. "Nothing. Father is ever pushing me to marry you."

"Of course." She went along with the subject change, caution overriding all else. "You, Christian, Edward, and I knew that would occur months ago."

"I, I can. I will marry you, you know that. I can keep you safe."

"Don't be silly. You will marry Cecily."

Cecily Spinner was the one who banished Henry's shadows. And Phoebe had thrown them together frequently after the first mutually wistful exchange she had witnessed.

The skin stretched at his neck, tight and uncomfortable. "Mr. Spinner wants a viscount for his daughter."

"And you are the heir to one. Stop being silly."

His laugh had more bite this time, and his eyes pinned her. Yes, that stare was similar too, though Henry had nothing on Andreas Merrick's hard gaze. "I have not taken you for a fool since I was twenty. Don't play with me, Phoebe."

"I will let nothing happen to harm you, Henry." Her voice was sure and strong. Henry was her friend, and she would keep her promise.

"You cannot make such a promise. What have you gotten into?" He flung a hand toward the paper. "I do not want to know what this means. And yet I must."

"It means that I have found a solution for our concerns."

He laughed humorlessly. "There isn't anything that is more of a concern than . . ." He flashed a hand again, seemingly unable to say his name. "Don't have any more contact with him, Phoebe."

"How much contact would I have?" she demurred without outright lying. "Mother, Father, and I are closeted away, hiding, trying to keep Father safe. Our hope resides with someone powerful enough in London to wield on our behalf."

"He sought you out and wheedled or threatened you. He is *lying* to you."

"No. I sought him out."

That caused Henry to pause. "Why would you do that?"

"Instinct."

He laughed without humor. "Of course. Are you sure it wasn't some bird chattering in your ear, whispering?"

She tried not to let the hesitation show on her face, but the narrowing of Henry's eyes confirmed that it hadn't worked. "There *was*. Dammit, Phoebe. Rip these up. Hide further. Farther. Forever."

"I can't." She was in too far, in all ways.

Henry leaned forward, his movements aggressive. "He is the reason we are in this position. He . . ." He gripped the arm of the chair. "Listen, I can't tell you more without saying things that might put me in jeopardy should someone overhear. I'm sorry, Phoebe. Just believe me. He is out to do you harm."

"No." She tilted her head. "He won't do me harm. I am sure of that."

"He will destroy the company and fund. He will flush us all with it."

She gazed back steadily, mind working to assimilate all of the information she had gleaned. "He returned our debts."

"He *what*?"

She nodded. "We are clear. Well, there are still

a few outstanding debts, small ones, as he hadn't collected all of them, but a place no longer awaits any of us in debtor's prison at least."

"Why would he . . ." Henry looked stunned.

She regarded him. "Do you *know* him?"

Henry's lips clamped together. "No. Not really."

She held his gaze for a long moment. "There was a bird, you are right about that. But I am certain of my present course. I need you to trust me." She nodded at the papers. "And to help me. Your signature—or Edward's—will do as well as your father's by the words of the original agreement."

"Your father would never have—"

"He didn't." She met Henry's questioning gaze. "I inserted that language in the final contracts. Your father glossed it over, thinking he was taking advantage of my father by signing quickly. He actually laughed as he signed the agreement."

"You sly vixen," he murmured. "Christian was forever warning me, but you have always managed to surprise me, even now."

"It is because you expect women to be as you see us at social functions, with our masks in place. We are far more complicated."

"I should know. Mother was nothing if not complicated." His mouth twisted. "I try to pretend that she was extraordinary."

"Complicated does not have to mean negative."

"I know." His hand went to the top of his head, and he pulled it forward, bringing his hair an inch farther down his forehead, trying to hide behind a veil of hair far too short. "You are asking me for a leap of faith that may bring about my destruction."

"You want to take control of your own future," she said firmly. "And at the same time this will remove you from your father's path and place that burden elsewhere. This will be your decision. I trust you to make the right choices for all of us."

A grim little smile took his lips. "You are a manipulative cat, Phoebe. You say what I want to hear."

"No, I say what I mean. That you want to hear it only means that we are in agreement."

He stared at the names on the document for a long minute more. Finally, he nodded shortly, a bitter twist of lips. "And I am tired of the lies. I will sign. I will attempt to make up, if even a small part, for my past."

He signed the paper.

Andreas was livid.

He strode forward and took her arm as soon as she walked by his hiding place, steering her into a little lane down the street.

"Don't ever do that again," he hissed.

He gathered himself physically as her eyes went wider than he had seen them before.

"Whatever is the matter, Mr. Merrick?"

"You drew the shades. So that you were alone with him," he snapped, unwillingly.

Her expression didn't change. "So you were there?" She nodded, obviously not needing the answer. "It was not you who I was trying to block, Mr. Merrick, but if you were unable to pierce our conversation, that means others were equally unable."

"You were supposed to meet with the youngest one."

"Yes. I planned to speak to Edward. I didn't realize that Henry would read a note meant for him and answer me himself."

"You promised to leave—" He stopped abruptly, hand tightening. "You never said you would leave if Henry were there, did you? You changed the subject." He cursed fluently. "You will not visit him again."

She nodded and patted his hand soothingly. "No, I won't. There is no need to." She looked at him. "Do you fear that we were physically intimate, Mr. Merrick? I assure you, we were not. Nor that we will ever be. Both Edward and Henry are my friends. Good friends and business associates, and nothing more."

"Why are you telling me that? I don't care about your intimacies." He felt himself shifting without conscious thought.

"No?"

"No," he said a little more forcefully.

"I do not believe you." She smiled at him. Why was she always smiling at him? It made him tense. "I will tell you of our conversation, though, should you desire it."

He desired it greatly.

She nodded, as if he had asked the question. "Henry signed the papers."

Andreas paused. Edward, yes. Henry? That was . . . unexpected. "Why?"

"He said he wishes to make amends for the past."

"I don't believe you," he said before he realized what he was admitting. "What do you know?" he asked harshly, forcing himself to move backward, a pace away from her. He'd never forgive himself if he accidentally gripped her arm too hard because he was thinking other thoughts.

"As I said to Henry, I only have conjecture. Both of your responses lead me to believe at least some of that speculation to be accurate."

His lips twisted. "You cannot know everything." He was a little frightened, though, that she might. She was a dangerous woman.

"Of course not. If myth tells us nothing else, it is that no one listens to people who know everything." She poked him, then turned and started back toward the high street. "And since you might be forced to listen to me forevermore, I must on occasion make a misstep."

"What—" He ran after her, catching up with long strides. "What the devil are you talking about?"

But she just laughed. "Are you going to do whatever task you planned to undertake while we were here? I will rest at the innyard if so. I had hoped to speak with Edward and do some other questioning but . . ." He couldn't read her eyes, as she had the hood of the cloak up, and she bounced entirely too much as she walked. " . . . that is perhaps not wise at this juncture."

He did want to do his task, tasks now—as a *chat* with Henry Wilcox was sorely needed, but he had the sure notion that leaving her on her own was a very bad idea.

"No." He stopped her, making everyone veer around them. "Let's just leave."

Stopped, he could see her expression. See her wistful glance toward the docks. Maybe he should just let her investigate. Go question people about her brother. Find the answers. See what she could uncover, then what she would do with the knowledge.

She peeked up at him from under the hood of her cloak. "Very well, Mr. Merrick. That is undoubtedly the wisest course of action. Let's go home."

He stiffened involuntarily at the words but led her back to the carriage.

It was not a long trek, but then he was quite wishing they were somewhere else already.

He knew something was wrong before the fresh carriage horses pulled into a full gait at the fourth stop. He should have been alerted by his second involuntary visual check to make sure the weapons in the carriage were where he had last placed them. But his mind was on so many other things—mostly centered around her—that the alert slipped past him.

Gunshots rang out in the encroaching twilight.

The carriage tilted precariously. Andreas had known better, and still he had accompanied her and pushed forward. He hadn't waited to exchange the carriage that would have arrived in Dover that evening. He'd just wanted to get her away from Dover, Henry, the docks, and the dangers her curiosity threatened. And she'd said *home*, and he hadn't wanted her to be able to retract it. He would need to deal with those thoughts later.

His mind focused down to the immediate situation, letting the inner dark stillness weave up and over him.

The driver, chosen precisely for his skill in dangerous situations, turned with the movement, and they slid for a long moment on two wheels, the spindles creaking in protest. The vehicle righted itself, and he could hear the reins snapping and the horses blowing as they galloped on, the driver not wasting movement.

Phoebe Pace's eyes were wide, but she said nothing, bracing herself on the seat. She had obviously been trained to react in the event that a stage was set upon, she was the heir to a carriage empire, and, frankly, she was intelligent.

He grabbed three pistols, checking them, and unlocked the padded box secured under the seat as carefully as he could amidst the motion. He'd blow them all to hell if he accidentally dropped what was inside.

Shots rang again, closer, attempting to surround them. Prepared. Cornelius, on neutral territory, was a threat.

Something hit one of the back wheels, and the carriage tilted up for a moment and Phoebe flailed, losing her purchase.

He caught her and pulled her against him, bracing with his right leg. The driver pulled back on the reins, and the belly of the carriage lunged forward, then shifted to the side as the coachman turned sharply in front of the men tailing them, the carriage skidding to the side in the middle of the road.

Andreas clenched his teeth as he felt the bone pop

in his leg as the vehicle jerked to a stop. He didn't waste any time, though, and kicked out the door with his other leg, pistol up and firing. The assailants were obviously taken by surprise, not expecting such a thing to occur, the driver stopping dead and opening the entire side to their fire. Andreas shot two of them before they could even think on it. Three more reared back, horses spooked. He could hear the driver discharging above as well.

A bullet whizzed past, and Andreas pinned Phoebe Pace more firmly behind him.

He flung the large ball from the overly padded box toward the remaining assailants. He pointed his weapon, drew a steadying breath, then shot it as it hit the ground.

The blast rocked the coach, and he braced himself over her as he prepared for them to overturn. They tipped up for one suspended moment, then righted with another jerk that buckled his leg more. He could feel the heat of the explosion, could hear the driver snap the reins and jerk the carriage back westward, then the wind through the open door was battering his face as they flew. No one followed behind.

He closed his eyes. He'd make the driver rich once they got back to London.

A questioning stomp came from above.

He set his pistol down and pulled Phoebe from behind him. He looked her over, quickly running hands over her limbs. She stared back, blankly, in obvious stupefaction. Assuredly she would have bruises, but she wasn't in physical peril.

Andreas gave two thumps to the roof, and the

vehicle continued its breakneck pace, the scenery whirling by the open door, the sounds unmuffled.

"Are you hurt anywhere?"

She blinked a few times, then awareness started to return. She sat up and ran a shaky hand through her hair, looking through the open cavity of the doorway. "No. I don't think so."

He nodded tightly. He couldn't think of anything outside of the present. Other things, like the bloodcurdling revenge he would wreak after this, were unimportant right now. "The driver will take us somewhere safe." Or the horses would give out, but he kept that information to himself.

Suddenly her hands were upon his cheeks. "Are you hurt?" She pulled the edge of a blanket across his forehead. He realized he had broken into a sweat.

He swatted the blanket away. "I'm fine. Give me space for a moment."

Why he felt the need to tack on the last words, which were almost courteous, was immediately rejected from his mind. She moved back.

He gritted his teeth and thrust his palm against his right leg, snapping the bone and its shell back into place. Fire licked straight up his throat. She stared at him, mouth hanging open.

"Oh my God." She moved toward him. "You need—"

"I need nothing," he said hoarsely. He looked away from her eyes. They were far too concerned for him to hold. He extended his leg, then pressed it against the floor. It hurt like hell. Mathias would tsk for sure. Damn tinkers.

"Here, put it here." She switched back to sitting next to him and motioned to the bench across from them. Feelings warred within him—he wasn't sure which he preferred, her sitting far away or close enough to reassuringly touch.

"No. Leave it alone." He let comforting pain block out the insanity of such thoughts.

The horses slowed, their huffing audible through the open door. Andreas hoped it was because the danger was well behind them and not that the animals were foaming and ready to keel over. They continued along at a slow pace. He'd make sure the horses and their owner received their due as well. A debt to be repaid.

Phoebe didn't say anything, but her shoulder pressed to his, and she didn't return to her seat.

The carriage pulled to a stop, and the driver hopped down, the movement shaking the vehicle. Since there was no longer a door, he appeared directly in view, looking much worse than he had previously—but all body parts seemed to be in place.

"Sir. There is a small farm ahead."

He gave a sharp nod to the man and helped Phoebe dismount. His leg ached. He ignored it as best as he could.

Dogs were barking loudly, and a man hurried out of the house, a rifle across his arms, as they climbed the path.

It didn't take more than one look at Phoebe Pace though for them to be admitted and fussed over. The man's wife was a mothering type, who hurried Phoebe upstairs. The driver was tending the horses and carriage, leaving Andreas with the farmer and the story they had concocted.

"We were set upon by highwaymen. My wife and I will leave in the morning, after the horses rest and we make repairs. You will be well compensated," he said stiffly.

The man whacked him on the shoulder. "No worries, my good man. No need to worry about a sneak attack. The dogs will alert us if anyone sets foot on the property. Gets lonely out here. The wife delights in a bit of company, and it sounds as if you have an interesting tale to tell."

Indeed, Phoebe seemed well able to entertain everyone with stories that evening, holding the man, his wife, and the driver in rapt attention. Andreas watched her work whatever magic she effortlessly possessed. It was a good thing too, as she would touch him every so often during the conversation, as if they were a real pair. He had difficulty keeping track of anything but the warmth of her hands.

Sooner than later, though, they found themselves in a bedroom, alone. Their driver, Charlie, as Phoebe had called him during dinner, was bunking down with the horses, determined to baby the "fine beasts" until the next switch. It had started raining at some point during dinner, but the man had firmly maintained his desire to stay the night outside, saying the barn was dry and well made.

"Perhaps we might purchase those horses for Charlie," Phoebe Pace said casually, as she reached into her case—both articles had somehow remained undamaged and had held their strapping during the fray. "I think he would like that."

Andreas pushed back the drape, watching the drops splat upon the glass, some splotches hanging, dripping slowly bit by bit, while others joined together to streak down.

He hated the rain. Even now.

"It will be done," he said. It was a good suggestion.

"Thank you." Her voice was warm.

He didn't know why he felt so . . . strange. Raw.

He watched the slippery drops. As a young child, rain had been a cleansing beast. Sneaking out into the night, feeling the drops on his face. Washing away blood and tears. Burrowing under his covers afterward, dry and cleansed. But as a growing boy, rain had come to signify something far more fearsome. Such weather never meant well when you lived on the streets. Rain meant shivering through the night in wet clothing. Rain meant sickness and death. He'd seen people drown in the gutters. Lying down to sleep, never to wake.

Rain signified something he had lost. That cleansing innocence. No, not lost. He had never really had it.

A hand touched his shoulder. "Are you well?"

He let the drape drop. "I am."

"I think you would say that even if you were laid upon Death's arms," she said, lightly touching his elbow as her hand descended.

He turned, and her hand drew along his forearm. "I am fine." He twisted his arm under so that he had hers clasped in his hand instead. "Death would welcome me."

"And you? Would you welcome her embrace?"

It would be so easy to pull her to him, leaning as she was. Tug her, taste her, tumble her to the bed.

"Perhaps."

He stepped forward, into her, but as always she didn't cede ground, and his leg pressed between hers.

She winced, and that dark thread, ever present, slivered through. Narrowing his eyes, he grabbed both of her forearms and pressed her to the bed. The edges of her half-loosened hair spread out on the counterpane, the majority still bound beneath her trapped figure. Her eyes went wide, and she immediately scrambled so that her hands propped behind her to keep her half-upright on the creaking surface. He knelt swiftly between her legs. It was hard with his leg still dully throbbing, but he didn't waste time concentrating on his own pain. He lifted the hem of her dress, then pushed the layers up.

She gave a little gasp as if disbelieving what he was doing.

He pulled the lamp nearer and found what he sought. He narrowed his eyes at her.

"It is nothing," she said, trying to push her skirts back down. "Honestly, Mr. Merrick. You thrust your leg back together as if you did so every day. A few scrapes are nothing."

He didn't respond. He touched the edges of her stockings where long, angry gashes cut straight through. Slashed on something in the carriage fray obviously. "Foolish woman."

Cornelius had just gained himself three additional broken bones. Andreas added it to the tally he would inflict before he killed the man. It was one thing to try to kill Andreas—that was the way of their world—and he usually treated such attempts with apathy. It was another thing entirely to try and kill *her,* someone under his direct protection.

He reached for his bag and pulled it toward him. Finding the scissors and salve.

"They are simple scrapes," she said, trying to cover herself back up. "I had worse as a child."

He pushed her hands away and used the scissors to cut a large square in the already slashed netting. "They can become infected."

"Well, yes. But it is not a true worry."

He looked up at her face finally. At cheeks lit a brilliant, bright red. The urge to shout in triumph at her embarrassment was oddly muted. He might have been more inclined if he wasn't feeling so out of sorts himself. Under her skirts and touching her limbs. Feeling the echoes of her hands trying to comfort him.

"Infection is a powerful worry." He put the scissors away and wiped his hands on a cloth, then uncapped the small pot and dipped a finger into the green salve.

She leaned forward, half-unbound hair brushing his shoulder, skirts spilling around his arms. All of it encasing him in . . . her. "What is that? I've never seen an ointment that looks or smells like that." Her curiosity was a vibrant thing, always overcoming any weaker emotions.

He didn't answer—wasn't sure he was capable of it. He touched his finger to her leg and heard her intake of air.

"Does it hurt?" he asked without looking up. He didn't think he could risk it.

"No-o," she stuttered. "But you are under my skirts and touching my bare skin at the moment, Mr. Merrick. Perhaps a bit of quickened breath is called for?"

He paused the movements of his hand and narrowed his focus to the wounds on her leg instead of giving in to the urge to touch anything else.

"If you prefer, I can have the farmer's wife finish this."

She didn't say anything for a moment, and he refused to look up. "No. I don't want anyone else to do it."

He finished dressing the wounds without saying anything else. He had half a mind to investigate other shadowed areas under her stockings, but that desire did not spring from making sure she was unhurt.

He finished and pulled her skirts back down, his head bent to the task. A small hand rested on his hair for a moment, then pulled around to his cheek. He froze in place.

"Thank you," she whispered.

He didn't move for long moments, eyes on the exposed wrist connected to the hand on his cheek. The harsh pitter-patter of the rain the only sound in the otherwise still tableau.

It was awkward and terribly intimate. There was something rather soothing about being inside a room with her when the rain was pounding outside.

"May I tend to your wounds as well?"

And look at his leg?

He pulled away from her violently and threw the items back into his bag. "There is no need."

He would not—could not—indulge in such foolish thoughts. Such ridiculous desires.

He darted a quick look to see her reaction anyway. Her lower lip was pulled between her teeth as she reached for her bag, ostensibly to change. But there was no privacy to be had in the confines of the single room. And there was no explanation for separation that would satisfy the farming couple—not without pretending to be far starchier than Phoebe Pace had been at supper. She had touched him far too frequently while speaking to the others, as if such touches were normal.

"Don't change your clothing," he said. "As a precaution."

In case they needed to make a quick escape.

She nodded and looked the faintest bit relieved. He had to fight a sudden smile. He kept his lips flat—it would likely make her expire to see one on his face, and he could not delude himself into thinking he wanted her anything but alive.

She unbound her hair from the simple twist that she had created that morning and brushed it out with long strokes of her brush. Having nowhere else to go, and not feeling the urge to stare broodingly through the windowpane, he simply watched her. The whole mess of it fell halfway down her back. How had she gotten all of that into all those ringlets and curls weeks, months, ago? He supposed her maid had done it.

He far preferred the simpler styles she had worn since moving into the hell. The other more popular styles she had worn before, with all of the whirligigs and height-defying coils, just didn't look right on her.

She separated her hair into three sections, overlapping them repeatedly until they formed one long, braided rope.

Her fingers lingered on the end of it, playing, unwilling to let the actions be at an end. They sat staring at each other for long moments.

"We can share," she blurted out. "The bed. There is plenty of room."

There was barely enough room for two bodies if they were pressed up next to each other.

"No. I will sleep on the floor."

She stepped toward him. "But you are hurt. And I am tended. I should sleep on the floor."

He gave her a look and tossed a blanket and pillow on the floor.

She bit her lip. She always left little indentations behind when she did that. "Really, we can share."

He lowered himself to the floor stiffly. He could use his leg as a real excuse for the stiffness of his movements for once. "Good night, Miss Pace." He turned over as she climbed into the bed.

Not two minutes later he saw her lean over the edge.

"We didn't get a chance to speak about everything that happened."

"Go to sleep, Miss Pace." He tried to close his eyes, but hers held his too fiercely.

Her plait slipped over the edge, dangling in front of his nose like some sort of braided leash. As if anyone could leash her.

"Thank you," she said softly. "For saving us."

"The driver did most of it."

"Thank you for dressing my leg."

"You would have been fine."

"Thank you for coming with me."

"You would have been better off without me. It was because of me we were attacked."

She put her chin on her hand, propping it up. "Now, you don't know that. What if it was one of Lord Garrett's minions who found out about the documents?"

Cold rage slithered through him. He pressed it down. "Perhaps. But you were well disguised. I was not when I approached you after you saw Wilcox."

"Yes, why was that?"

Because I was too worried about you. He closed his eyes. "Go to sleep."

He felt a hand grip his blanket, and he saw her face far too close to his as she pulled the blanket up to his chin, tucking it around one shoulder. The other side was pinned by his free arm, and she couldn't quite move it. He watched her try. That long tail of hair hung down, brushing his free hand as she did so. He had the urge to wrap his hand around it.

"What are you doing?" he asked, voice and body tight.

She gave up trying to tuck in his uncovered arm. "Failing," she said, exasperated.

He lifted his arm finally. Better than to give in

to temptation to grip her by that long tail and pull her to him. She smiled happily and lifted the rest of the blanket, tucking it around his other shoulder.

She leaned down, a fraction closer, and for some reason unknown to man, he lifted his head the tiniest bit. Enough so she could brush his cheek with her lips. "Good night, Mr. Merrick."

Chapter 16

He had made sure she was safely back at the hell, and in Roman's rooms, before he barked a series of very sharp orders, packed a fresh bag, then left London again, but this time with five very specialized men at his heels.

Four days later, after neutralizing over half of Cornelius's remaining forces in the Thames Valley, stranding the man somewhere under a rock near London, and working through most of his frustration, he stopped dead in the doorway to his office. Again. It had become a frequent habit really.

His office.

He'd left for four days. Four. Not four weeks, not four months or four years.

A head of light brown hair turned, and a smile lifted her mouth. Welcoming him back without saying a word. Her eyes examined him, as if looking for an injury, then her smile grew when she didn't seem to find one.

A wide, warm curve of lips that made his legs feel like custard. Shakier than any time in the past ninety-six hours when he had risked life and limb. It had been four days since he had been touched by those lips, and the impact hadn't lessened one bit.

Her smile almost made him forget the scene around her.

"What the devil have you done?" he demanded.

"Oh!" This was said brightly, as if she was happy he had noticed. "I decided I needed my own workspace, instead of constantly infringing upon yours. So I had a few of the boys move a desk in here."

He stared at the petite, *feminine,* desk that was pushed against his. And wondered how the bloody hell she had managed to convince men who were terrified of him to move the desk inside his domain.

"Absolutely *not.*"

Two hours later, he was still scowling as she happily worked on . . . whatever the hell it was she was working on. Across from him. At *her* desk. How the hell . . .

He remembered saying no. He remembered cursing. Threatening her unborn children. Then there was a sort of hazy period of smiles and calm words. Then she had touched the back of his hand with her naked fingers.

And now, here he was with . . . her desk . . . pressed to his—surreptitiously watching her scratch her paper, the tip of her tongue poking from the side of her mouth as she worked. *Who did that?* It was decidedly uncouth.

Every once in a while, the pink tip would swipe

the top edge of her lower lip. Back and forth, back and forth, like a snake lazily charmed, before retreating. She tapped her chin, eyes brightening, then she scratched something else on the paper.

And he just kept watching her, unable to stop.

Suddenly, her eyes caught his. He froze, unable to pretend he had been doing anything other than staring.

She tucked a loose piece of hair behind her ear. "What are you thinking about, Mr. Merrick?"

You. Demon-spawned you. "Nothing."

She tried to peer over the span of their desks to see what he was doing. He pulled the papers into the space of his arms, hunching over them.

She laughed lightly. "Working on secret documents? Ones that threaten the very fabric of George's standard?"

"No."

She put her chin on her palm, examining him with an absurd overabundance of humor, eyes bright, an almost lazy fondness in their depths. "Are you working on secret designs for new lady's undergarments?"

"*No.*"

"I'm sure they would be very thorough and well thought out."

"What? *No.*"

She leaned farther over, her backside rising as she leaned forward.

"Stop that. Get back." *Go away.*

God, what was wrong with him? Even in his internal thoughts he sounded like a threatened child.

She stayed leaning over, her chin still resting

in her palm, closer to him than she'd been before. "Would you like to see what I'm working on?"

"No."

"I don't mind showing you."

"No."

"They aren't anything as exciting as a lady's undergarments." Her eyes lit in sudden thought. "Or a gentleman's."

"Is there something wrong with you?" he demanded.

"I find it amazing you are such a prude, Mr. Merrick. I've seen people outside my window do the most lascivious things since I've been here." She lowered her voice, as if confiding in him. "I can't credit that you've been too busy to notice the activities that go on in this part of town, and in full view of everyone. Quite educational, if I do say so."

"You are ruining yourself," he hissed.

She looked concerned for a moment. "Do you think I might be getting a bit tainted by it all? Would you like to keep me pure?"

"I—what? No!"

"How then am I ruining myself?" The suspicious glimmer of humor in her eyes increased.

When had he lost control? He wanted to identify the moment, then go back in time and squish it from existence. People didn't *tease* him. And certainly the feelings that pushed up, the stuttering, odd feelings in his stomach whenever she said something to him, looking directly in his eyes with a smile about her lips, were certainly unwelcome.

"Stop looking out the window. Or leave here. Go somewhere else. Somewhere safer."

Anywhere else. God, please. Or he was likely to do something horribly awful, like surrender his sanity and kiss *her*.

"I feel most safe right here. I trust my family's safety here. And that is all-important to me, Mr. Merrick." At the comment about her family, her expression lost its mischievousness and turned serious.

"I know," he said stiffly, that feeling in his chest, *guilt*, tightening.

She smiled, a warm smile that held no trace of aberrant humor.

It bothered him on a level he couldn't comprehend. He experienced an overwhelming urge to grab that smile and hide it solely for himself to gaze upon. A Da Vinci masterpiece he intended to jealously guard.

He tightened his grip on his pen, willing himself to think of other things.

"Besides, you needn't worry about my virtue. I am unattached outside of this building."

"Why?" He asked it stiffly. It was something he had long wondered about. She could have married and had someone take over the family concerns months ago.

Also, the phrasing of that last comment was odd.

"I trust both easily and with difficulty."

"That makes no sense."

"No?" She examined him. "You trust your brother Roman completely, do you not?"

"We aren't speaking of me."

"But you trust few others. I, on the other hand, trust most people on a basic level unless they do something to destroy that trust. And I seek to trust people on a deeper level but have had to hold myself back these last months."

He should have spoken to her parents by now and damned the consequences. Reports said that the father still had rarely been seen—holed up in Roman's bedroom. They were long overdue for a chat.

"Why have you lost your easy trust?"

She shrugged lightly. "What matters is that I wish to trust. I want to place my trust." *In you*, was apparent, but left unsaid. He shifted. She tilted her head again. "I think that is the difference between us. I wish to trust but must exercise caution. You object to the notion of trust."

The entire conversation was making him uncomfortable. The need to rub his chest pressing. "That doesn't answer the question of why you have remained unattached."

She laughed lightly, but there was something off about it, covering uncertainty. "I don't conform to the ideal unfortunately. I'm a little too firm in some ways, a little too soft in others."

"You have plenty of friends." The woman was a veritable collector of wounded birds and one-legged creatures, of the animal and human variety. He only had to look in his halls to see the evidence of it.

"Friends do not necessarily make suitors."

"I can't credit that if you set your mind to nabbing a husband, you wouldn't succeed."

"That is very kind of you." She beamed and leaned in conspiratorially. "I *can* tend toward the mercenary, when I choose."

She seemed quite pleased at labeling herself by that less-than-endearing trait.

"But temptation matters." She sounded a bit wistful again. He wondered if there had once been someone special who had slipped away. It made him feel violent. "And my friends have a tendency to find each other."

"You meddle," he said flatly, certain of the statement. "You sabotage your own chances."

"Not always on purpose." There was that look again. As if there were someone special. Of course there was someone. How would anyone not want her? She was like the sun blazing on a cool day, wiping away the chill. Sometimes he felt the need to shade his eyes around her. Reports said that she did *not* have men falling over themselves, but he couldn't reconcile that with the reality of the woman in front of him.

"You could have your pick of suitors should you choose," he said stiffly. "So I must assume you are afraid of choosing someone."

She looked startled for a moment, then her gaze sharpened, eyes swiftly taking in every aspect of his face. A brilliant smile bloomed, lighting the entire space, and he instinctively freed his hands to defend himself.

Everything about her pulled at him. Treating her as a pawn would be far easier. And yet, these conversations always felt like a queen inching around the king.

"Perhaps all this time I have been waiting for the right person," she said lightly.

He looked away from her gaze, which all of a

sudden felt too focused. He looked at her papers. "What are you working on if not undergarments?"

"I have a ten-step plan to defeat the proposed legislation to be leveled against you. Since it is still in the initial phases and not yet signed for discussion, we have an advantage. I have been working on it since returning from Dover."

He should be accustomed to her wild statements, but his stomach jerked at her words. "What?"

"I've read the papers thoroughly, and I can still hardly believe my eyes. They have blamed their own sins on you. And embroidered the truth surrounding the Collateral Exchange. It isn't right," she said heatedly.

Darkness rose from within him. "It is exceedingly *right*."

"Absolutely not." She jabbed a finger at the top page of her stack. "There are hints of retroactive provisions. One exploitation of those provisions, and they would be able to throw you in jail for past offenses—offenses that were not legally binding when they occurred."

"Those in charge make the laws." It was a true statement—he had used his power to his own advantage plenty of times in the past. That the allegations might be true didn't mean he would allow a bill to pass. He wouldn't allow anyone to control his fate. He had a few tricks up his sleeve in case the bill was introduced and someone truly pushed for one of those provisions.

But he wasn't going to let her think these absurd thoughts about his being a victim of the system. Of deserving leniency. "Don't paint a sterling pic-

ture of my character. We have done much of what
we've been accused of there. Worse even."

"I don't care. Those provisions lack honor in
every way."

"I doubt they are concerned with our honor."

"They should be," she said somewhat viciously.
He stared at her. She looked like a mother bear
ready to lash out at hunters who had drawn too
near to her family. "You are too honorable to deal
with people like this. You are one of the most honorable people I've had the fortune to do business
with. Which is why it makes my skin itch to read
these things."

His shirt felt too tight. Like it was restricting
his breathing. The urge to reach across to grab
the hand she was waving around increased to an
almost painful point.

"Beyond the more hidden possibilities, the para-
graphs clearly dictate that you will be required to
make a number of concessions that would inhibit
your ability to work at your highest capability. You
do not deserve that."

The way she was speaking—as if his worth was
a foregone conclusion . . . Dark desire swirled,
along with the need to drive her far from him.

"I have done everything to deserve it. To deserve
prison and even death." He allowed the smile to
grow, slashing into his cheeks. Perhaps it would
scare her enough to save both of them from the
horrible path they seemed to be treading. "But
then, I've never been pleased to do as others desire
me to."

She blinked, and the passionate defense crinkling her face faded to confusion. "That is rather morbid. Perhaps we should discuss why you feel it fair? Then I can modify my steps."

"No."

"They require modification, though, in that case."

"That is not what I said no to, and what's more, you know this, Miss Pace."

He caught the quick smile before she projected puzzlement once more. He almost sighed from the inevitability of their mutual destruction as it pulled nearer, inescapable.

"You have caught me out, Mr. Merrick. How—"

"—intelligent of me."

"—intelligent of you . . ." She blinked again, and for once *she* looked disgruntled. "Well. Yes."

He flipped his page. "What are you really working on, Miss Pace?"

"I am really working on the legislation. I have been since we returned, and you disappeared without a word."

If he didn't know better, he would have sworn there was a touch of censure there.

"I don't need to share my schedule with you," he said stiffly.

"No, but it would be nice not to worry about you lying in a ditch somewhere."

She busied herself with her papers, and his eyes narrowed. She was using his tactic. He refused to examine what it meant for him in light of her words.

Finally, she looked back up. "Did you catch the men behind the attack on our carriage?"

"All but one."

Head tilt. "What did you do to them?"

He gave her a pointed look without answering.

"Were you hurt?"

"No."

"That is good. I worried."

He didn't know how to respond to that, so he didn't.

She leaned over suddenly and thumped a pile of messily arranged papers on his orderly and previously pristine desk. "It is quite a weighty thing. The legislation." As if the second part was a true qualifier, but not exactly the core of the statement. That the *worrying* had been a weighty thing.

"Yes, and a bit outside of your usual concerns, no?"

"Justice is one of my concerns."

Only fools felt guilt. The twinge in his stomach must be from the lack of an afternoon meal. Something about the plate at the inn hadn't looked right. For the last two weeks, he had only been eating things he had made himself or which had come from her hands.

Except for that meal with the farming family. She had touched him so often during the meal that he hadn't realized he'd eaten half a chicken until after the plates had been cleared.

"Justice would be served by our sentencing," he said, keeping the conversation where it should be. "Unfortunately, I care little about others' perceptions of justice."

Head tilt. "Just your own?"

He didn't respond.

"I find you to be quite likable."

There was that tightening in his chest again. Like steel bands constricting. He had watched a man clutch his chest once, suddenly, before falling over dead on the street. The expression on that man's face—the fingers digging into his sternum to stop the pain—this must be how that man had felt.

"You are quite an amusing man usually. Always yelling things"—she raised her elbows up as far as her dress allowed with her fingers spread and her limbs vibrating—"like '*Leave*' and '*I want you gone.*'" Her voice had taken on a theatrical, low timbre.

She put her elbow back on the table, her chin resting back on her hand. "It's charming as long as one doesn't take you seriously."

"Sane people take me seriously."

"I'm sane, and I do not."

"You are the least sane person I've had the misfortune to meet."

The corners of her eyes pinched a little, just for the barest second, then cleared. "Well, there are plenty more people for you to meet, Mr. Merrick, so do not give up hope yet." But the tone of her voice was far too cheerful.

He watched her for a moment. Watched as her face cleared of anything remotely hurt or upset. "Do you object to being called insane or my saying that I had the misfortune of meeting you?"

"Neither, of course."

He drummed his finger on the desk, irritated and, God, how did people live feeling *guilty* about things?

"You are just fine as you are," he said gruffly.

Her expression froze for a moment, then bloomed into a smile that would slay demons.

He quickly shut down all reaction to it. She was a chess piece, and once a piece outlived its usefulness, it was discarded. That was how the game was played.

But it had always been that smile. Not her position as Henry Wilcox's possible wife nor the possibility that he could take his enemies down by manipulating her family. Those hadn't been the things that had driven him when it came to his feelings for her.

It had been that smile. Through the shadows of the theater that first night. When their eyes had met. She had smiled. Simply. Warmly. Looking directly at him, unaware that she should be afraid.

She was still unaware she should be afraid.

He was still affected every time she smiled.

"You are a true gentleman, Mr. Merrick."

"I'm not a gentleman. I don't know why you think such absurd things," he said tightly.

"Mmmm." She cocked her head at him. "If you insist." She turned back to her remaining papers.

She confused the hell out of him.

She looked up and smiled at whatever she saw on his face. "You scare the boots off everyone, yet no one sees you for the guardian you are. Like a gargoyle—a stone-faced, snarling guard over those under your watch." She covered her mouth for a moment, and he was absurdly sure she was muffling a chuckle. "A guardian of virtue."

"What are you babbling about?" he demanded.

She regarded him, one edge of her mouth turned up, and there was something behind her eyes for a moment before they were innocent once more. "My mother's worry for my virtue increases every day we are here. Wailing on about what might happen. Not realizing that my virtue is perfectly secure with you near. It would only take a moment around you to convince her that you are like one of those medieval . . ." She waved her hands around the area between her thighs and waist. He did his best not to follow the movements. "Those devices that keep a lady's virtue intact."

"A chastity belt?" he said tightly.

"Yes, exactly. What a horrible idea. I can't imagine a draft would be pleasant combined with all of that metal." She paused. "Not that *you* are horrible. I find your primness quite charming actually. It allows me untold freedom."

The entire conversation was horrifying. "How do you even know what a chastity belt is?"

"I am well-read."

"And in what book did you learn about them?"

She waved a hand. "I've read so many it is hard to remember titles."

He would bet his entire fortune that she knew the name of the book. He knew exactly where she might have found such a book. He was going to kill Roman.

"Don't touch those shelves," he hissed.

"I don't know of what you speak. Do you know of a place where I might find a good selection of libidinous texts?" She put her chin on her hand, tilting her cheek into it.

"Miss Pace?"

"Yes?"

He didn't respond because he didn't know *what* to say, really.

She reached far across their desks and patted his hand. "You are a lovely man, Mr. Merrick. No need for worry. As I said, your prudishness makes it easy for me to be free." There was something wistful to her expression again. "And it has been a long while since I was allowed the unrestrained opportunity to act as I wished. Even if I am silly."

He turned his hand so that hers was caught in his, palm to palm, his thumb pressing the back of her hand and holding it in place. She couldn't mask her sudden intake of breath.

"Does this feel silly, Miss Pace?"

"No."

His thumb rubbed the back of her hand, the smooth skin there, as he leaned toward her a measure. "What about now?"

"No," she whispered. "Not silly."

The whisper sent a fierce, almost painful, rush down his body and straight to his groin. "Does it feel safe and secure?" he whispered back.

"How—what do you mean?"

"Your virtue?" He pulled his forefinger along her exposed wrist. "Does it feel in danger now?"

"N-no." But it came out as more of a question.

"Do you not know the tale of the wolf, Miss Pace?"

"No." Her voice was breathy, her fingers clinging to his, not trying to break free.

"And the lamb who poked and poked and poked?"

He drew her hand toward him, pulling so she was half-lying across the desks, only her elbows keeping her upright. "I don't believe I have," she answered. The brown of her eyes was slowly being swallowed by black, the center point spreading outward.

"The wolf ate the lamb." He leaned forward so his lips were close to hers, hot. "Because the lamb forgot that *she* was the prey."

She didn't answer for a moment, cheeks flushed, glassy eyes on his lips. Then her eyes rose to his, meeting them, unafraid as always, with a look that made his hand tighten around hers—innocence mixed with desire. "Or perhaps the lamb didn't forget at all, Mr. Merrick."

He *wanted* her. More than he'd ever wanted anything else.

It would be so easy. Closing the distance. Confusing and conflicting all of the very real and necessary barriers that stood between them. That she had tried her damnedest to break down. He wasn't a fool. And part of him—most of him—wanted to give into it. To surrender everything to her.

But there were barriers that she didn't realize existed. And that was where the true danger resided.

Her fingers were warm and soft in his. So easy to tug her forward more. So he did. Her cheek was warm against his, her breathing heavy and audible so near his ear. He let his lips taste her skin the way she had tasted him so many evenings, let himself

have this moment. He grazed her cheek, until their
lips met, so briefly, skimming across, her breath
catching and pulling at his. But with great effort,
he kept his lips going, grazing her other cheek,
touching her other ear.

So easy to pull her onto his desk. Spread her and
taste her fully and do all manner of nonvirtuous
things to her. Consume her until she was screaming and pleading.

Damned.

He was damned. In flesh, in spirit, and through
the consequences of past actions. He couldn't have
her. Couldn't let her break down those last walls
and discover the secrets and horrors beneath.

He could, however, turn the tables on her. For
all of the madness she'd been driving him to.

"Good evening, Miss Pace." He whispered the
echo of her words to him each night and felt her
start in response.

And now he should let her go. *Right* now. Not
pull his hand up her arm, slowly, assuring himself
that she was real. Listening to the hitch in her breath
become ragged gasping. Not pulling that hand up
across the skin of her neck and into the nape of her
hair. Not tilting her head back so that he could see
her eyes, wide and dilated and *wanting.*

Just a taste.

He could have a taste. He could have anything
he wanted. Those eyes said he could. Those parted
lips invited him in.

Just a taste.

Surely a taste would not spell his doom?

"Are you going to devour me?" she asked,

breathless, spread forward over the desk, arching up to him.

"Do you want me to?"

Just a taste.

"Yes."

One small taste. He willed his fingers to let go of her, but his hands hooked under her elbows and pulled her up and all the way across the desks, papers scattering everywhere, irreparably mixing together, confused.

He pulled her so that she was kneeling in front of him, rocking back on her heels, dress spreading around her. And attached his lips to her neck. Slowly pulling at her beating pulse, trying to lengthen every exquisite taste. Needing something in this woman as he'd never needed in another.

Damned.

Phoebe arched back as his mouth moved over her skin. Yes, this is what she had wanted. Ever since the farmhouse. Ever since the night at the inn. Ever since she had first kissed him on the cheek. Ever since she had met him and he had looked at her with such fire. Ever since . . . forever.

She couldn't seem to recall a past that didn't include the want of him.

Want that increased with the motions of his right hand. Fingers so slowly traveling over her skin. Hooking into the fabric at the back of her neck, unbuttoning her dress. Pulling it away.

Desire that stretched through the motions of his mouth. Lips traveling over her neck, down her throat. Over her chemise and breasts.

Need that multiplied under the motions of his left hand. Fingers drifting along her knee, under her dress, over her thigh, up, up, up. Curling into her in a way that she hadn't even dreamed of.

She could barely breathe over the sensations—so new and so old—as if her body had been preparing for such a thing for weeks, yearning for exactly what he was doing to her.

And it was as if he was savoring every touch. Not rushing each delicious brush or lingering kiss. Tasting her and savoring the feel of her around his fingertips.

She could do nothing but hold on. Her chin brushing his hair as he did the most delicious things to her breasts with his mouth and the most scandalous things below with his hand.

"You taste just as I imagined."

She was sure it was her imagination that had conjured his voice. But she responded anyway. "You are everything I conceived."

Suddenly his lips found hers and she could barely take time to register the awe at the taste of *him*—all heat and danger, hardness and hunger—before he arched her back again and sucked hard at the tip of a breast. His thumb brushed against her, his fingers thrust within her and she gasped as shudders rocked her. Lovely, glorious waves. She felt his fingers, so deadly and hard, as they softly drew over her skin, lips whispering words she couldn't hear in her hair. But words that sounded like an apology, of begging her forgiveness.

She tried to calm her own harsh breathing enough to be able to hear him. Her body leaned automatically anywhere his fingers touched her. Buttoning her back up, smoothing her out. His lips pulled along her neck as if in a last taste.

And even later, curled up in her covers, she re-lived the memory of it. Thought on how he had denied his own pleasure, the release of his control and surrender.

She didn't think it possible to feel *more* deter-mined, but the determination coiled to claim him completely for herself.

Chapter 17

The sun was shining brightly. Birds squawked merrily. And Andreas gripped the pen tightly as he scratched his signature on the line, the name blurring.

"I now pronounce you man and wife."

Phoebe Pace, now Phoebe Merrick, stood at his side, smiling brightly. She put her hand to his cheek. "This is the happiest day of my life," she murmured. A knife appeared in her hand, dripping red, jabbing downward toward his already shriveled heart. "And I want you to know just how much I hate you, *Duncan*."

Andreas shot up in bed, knife in his left fist, breathing hard.

He pressed his chest, right fingers feeling the puckering of scars, old and new. But no gaping holes dripping blood.

He gave a harsh laugh and hurled the dagger to his left, embedding it in the wall. Just as quickly he picked up another and held it against the sheets of the bed, habits ingrained. The light told him it was just before noon. He had gone to bed at dawn. Another wonderful night of *sleep*.

Dreaming of her, of the taste of her, the sounds she had made, the feel of her in his arms. The *want*. His desire. His damnation. The nightmares of his twisted web winding around him and making him wake nearly screaming.

He pushed the covers aside and shoved his right leg off the bed. He needed to see Mathias today— he had been putting off visiting the man's strange mechanical castle for far too long.

He walked to the secret panel, hesitating for a moment before he triggered the mechanism, then spun the lock. He pulled the papers free. Parish records and dated entries. He gripped them tightly in his fist, a sudden wish to burn them to ash colliding with his need for the ultimate revenge against the man whose name was listed as father on the line above the other faded name—the name of a boy long dead.

Insidious thoughts whispered of things more important than revenge. But he had lived with the burning need for retribution for so long, building his life around the demand, that he didn't know how to rid himself of the desire for it.

And now there was Phoebe.

He had wanted to take her. Completely. He wanted to do so *right* now. Take what she so innocently and knowingly offered.

The insurgent thought that he didn't even know what game he was playing anymore was not a comforting one. He was dancing to *her* tune, certainly.

He needed to change that. *He needed to change that.*

He couldn't watch her smile dim when she realized the truth. Couldn't watch the light leave her eyes.

He gripped the page. It didn't matter. *It didn't matter.*

He should just tie her in ropes and ship her off to the country. What he should have done weeks ago. So much weakness. He shoved the papers back into the safe.

A door slammed, and someone shouted. He was halfway across the room when a body slammed into the hallway door, and someone pounded on the panel.

Horrific images filled his thoughts, as he sprinted to the door. Phoebe Pace lying on Roman's bed, throat slit. *Fear.* He yanked the door open and a man fell inside, hitting the floor, hands outstretched, a brown blur soaring over his back.

The man scrambled to his knees and threw himself at the door, collapsing against it. The handle jerked from Andreas's grip as the door slammed shut. Andreas had a hand and a steel blade pressed against the man's neck in the same instant. The man choked around his fingers.

"Where is she?" Andreas snarled. "Who hired you?" He could smell smoke. Footsteps were pounding heavily on the stairs.

He was just about to kill the man and run to find her himself when the trespasser looked up. Andreas's fingers automatically released.

James Pace stared at him, eyes wide, no recognition or even minimal awareness in his expression. Then something lit. "Your Highness! You must hide me. Quickly."

Andreas withdrew the blade slowly. James Pace, not realizing how close he had come to certain death, rose to his knees and examined the bottom of the door. "They'll be here soon. Slimy buggers can fit under the cracks."

All manner of realizations slid into place, and the confusing matter surrounding Phoebe Pace's actions finally snapped together. "Mr. Pace," he said stiffly, flicking his blade back in place up his sleeve. "I believe you are expected across the hall."

"Gads, man. Of course they are expecting me. The beasts want to murder me."

The man looked as physically healthy as someone cooped inside for long periods of time could be. Andreas, like much of London, had speculated incorrectly that James Pace was on his deathbed.

To many people, this fate was worse.

The shouts increased as footsteps hit the hall from both directions.

"Showed them though." The man's face looked viciously satisfied. "They'll be putting out the flames for hours."

"Flames?" Andreas stiffened again.

And as if by divine intervention, he heard her voice, from the direction of the steps. "Mother, are you hurt?"

There was a hysterical answer from the other side of the hall. But that didn't matter. All he cared about was that the first voice was surrounded by the shouts of his men and on the path to a cleared exit.

"Dodgy little crusts tried to attack from the drapes again," James Pace muttered. He suddenly focused on something behind Andreas, eyes widening. He lunged, and Andreas stiffly watched as the man stretched out in the air and tackled the wide-eyed dog to the ground, the furred bastard yipped twice as they rolled.

"I've got you, Deer Meat." He pinched something invisible from the top of the dog's fur and after squashing it together, staring between his fingers as he did so, he flicked it to the side. "Here, got the ratty bastard off."

If a dog could look exasperated, this one did, its chin on the carpet.

"This one here is Deer Meat," James Pace said, presumably to Andreas, while petting the dog. "Took a nice-sized chunk out of my ankle the other day. Thought I was a reindeer. Likes the taste, Your Highness."

Andreas forewent the mention of the dog's name being Mr. Wiggles. Frankly, Deer Meat was preferable.

"*Where's Father?*"

He wasn't paying attention to anyone else in the hall, but he could hear everything *she* said. His ear specially tuned to her voice.

"*No, Mr. Donald. I can't go. I must find my father.*"

The entire floor could be burning down and collapsing, and she would still try to find her father. Of that, Andreas was sure.

He walked forward and reached down, gripped James Pace by the upper arm, and dragged the squawking man—who was still holding the dog— to the door.

He opened the door. Boys ran down the hall in both directions with buckets, empty and full. Andreas thrust the man and dog into the chaos and closed the door. He leaned against it for a moment.

"Father!"

He could hear her father ask her who she was, and to unhand him, but the voices grew fainter, the steps on the stairs depressed with their weight. The smell of smoke was dissipating, and voices were calling out that the fire had been contained. He walked to the window to check the alley. The guards had kept to their posts there. Unless the entire building collapsed, that was as it should be. Neighborhood distractions had been used before to gain undetected entry to the building.

A tremor vibrated around his midsection. A single waking image of Death having causing it. He hadn't experienced one of those in a long, long time. They usually stayed in his nightmares. Unpleasant.

A single woman was upending his world, and he was letting her. He needed to change what he was doing.

He had always said he wouldn't change for anyone.

Another peculiar sensation registered as the tremor subsided. Andreas looked down at the puddle he was standing in. The one where the dog had been.

All in all, he sort of hoped the floor burned down after all and took him with it.

She thanked the high heavens that the building was fully locked down and her father had passed out, giving them time to do as they needed. It had taken several hours to calm him and hang new drapes. Luckily, very little had actually been damaged, and all of the things that had were replaceable.

She bit her lip trying to imagine what Andreas might say about the afternoon's events. No one had pierced their privacy since they'd moved in. Likely because of uncertainty at first, then to direct orders later. And they had been *so good* at keeping her father away from everyone—always keeping him in the bedroom when one of the hell's inhabitants visited. They had gotten sloppy for a moment. That was all it had taken.

Yes, she wondered with great trepidation as to what Andreas Merrick would say and do. No one had been able to locate him on any of the lower floors, and he hadn't answered the door to his personal rooms. When she had requested they check on him to make sure he was well, the boys, and even Donald, were quite firm that no one, but no one, opened that door but Roman or Andreas.

She would have approached him immediately, confronted him about the matter on her own terms, if she hadn't been needed to help subdue Father. And Andreas had reportedly slipped out of the building before she could separate from her parents.

So she had returned to her normal afternoon routine—the part that didn't include pestering Andreas Merrick—which instead included haunting the kitchens. Before they had secured the building, so many weeks ago, she had needed to sneak down to bake, outfitted in her gray wig, pretending to be just another cook. Then the boys had begun to move out the gaming tables and other gaming area furniture, armchairs and lounges, bit by bit and day by day. The noise of the customers and gamblers dimming until that area was finally silent.

Now she had full run of the building, and her hair had free run as well. She pushed her palms and wrists into the dough, one ear always listening.

"He didn't."

"Yes, he did. I tell you, I saw it."

"Mr. Merrick don't go to no tinker's shop."

"He did. I saw him two hours ago," Tommy said belligerently.

"What would he need there? A wind-up toy? It were someone else you saw."

"It was him, I say. He looked shifty too."

"Now I know you are cracked. Shifty? You wouldn't have seen him if he didn't want to be seen."

"*You* are cracked, old man. He is as easy to spot as one of them lions at the menagerie amidst a pack of geese."

"Only if he wants to be the lion. He let you follow him." The man shook his head, and she could almost picture the forbidding stare he wore well. "And that's odd behavior, boy. You should be terrified."

"I'm not scared of him."

"You're shattin' your trousers. And don't call me an old man. You're gonna end up with a split head, boy."

Silence greeted that. Tommy preferred to show his mutiny expressively.

"What were you doing following Mr. Merrick, anyway?"

"I wasn't."

She wished she could see what Tommy was doing, but she kept her attention on her actions, rolling the dough, keeping out of notice. This was her fault.

"Just happened to see him, is all," Tommy added.

The older man snorted. "Keep your head, boy. Don't be stupid."

"I'm not stupid," Tommy hissed.

"Then mind your business. I'll give you fair warning since you're somewhat new. Though you should know better. The Merricks take care of their own." He paused. "And *the Merricks take care of their own.*"

"I can handle myself," Tommy's irritated voice said.

"You aren't a total dunder, and you've been settling in with the boys and Boss Roman mighty fine, but you go poking around Mr. Merrick . . ."

Phoebe would have to have a talk with Tommy as soon as possible. This was entirely her fault. She had been poking into Andreas Merrick's affairs for months—entranced by the rumors, his correspondence, and the way he handled his business affairs.

Nothing could compare to her interest in the man himself, though, once she had met him.

The memory of a conversation with a man on the street, a few nights after she had met Andreas Merrick, tickled.

The trinket seller had checked both ways before he had motioned her farther into his stall. "He's not human, ma'am," he had whispered. She had been in full disguise, having learned to be cautious.

"Is he a dog?" She had joked—for a less likely image wasn't to be had. Dogs had masters and subservient natures. Happy, barking expressions and joyful exteriors. Andreas was less a dog than anyone she had yet met. Unless he was of some wolfish breed, solitary and territorial, snapping and mateless.

"He's something *unnatural*."

"Unnatural?" Her humor had gotten the better of her again. "Like a demon? Spun of darkness and fire?"

The man had solemnly nodded, and she hadn't been able to contain the grip on the edges of her mouth.

"You should not laugh so, Ma'am." He had shaken his head. "He'll come for you in the night if you aren't careful."

He had leaned forward, crooked brown teeth chewing his tongue as he had looked in both directions. "It is said the devil himself tried to kill him in his mum's womb, and has sent minions to complete his failed task each day since. And that Merrick has destroyed all those who try. Biding his time, working through all of the dark creatures until no one will threaten him but Satan himself. Then he will overthrow him and take the devil's throne."

Her smile had abruptly slipped, finding nothing funny in what such statements implied. Especially after he had saved her life, whatever he denied.

"And you find fault with this? His dispatching of those who try to kill him?"

"Nay. Just in how it happens. There's a tale that tells of knives in the dark, plunged into his flesh, and he, demon that he is, laughing, pulling the steel free, decapitating his enemies instead. Rising and walking away with nary a limp."

The thing that had intrigued her most about the tale, then and now, was the idea of Andreas *laughing*.

It was something she longed to see, actually, real laughter from him. He had laughed a few times, but each of those had emerged attached to darker intent, a tie to darker emotions behind.

But she prided herself on her ability to see the bigger picture, the end of the game. He had been genuinely amused a time or two since she had met him. She just needed to nurture such seeds.

Seeds like those that had sprouted last night. She shuddered, her body heating again for the thousandth time that day.

She turned her attention back to her surroundings. It was with twofold purpose that she spent most of her time that wasn't spent with either Andreas or her parents in this domain. Everyone in the building eventually gathered in the kitchen areas, spending time by the heated ovens and plucking foods from the tables. The central meeting place and the one most revered. Heat and sustenance. There could be no room that screamed survival more.

And though she too loved both the warmth and food, her current needs—to find information about her brother, to save her family's company, to know about the Merricks—centered on the chatter that was freely given in such a place. Secure from outside elements, they talked of everything that was happening around them.

If Andreas Merrick knew what his employees talked about under his nose, he would be extremely displeased.

Then again, maybe he did know. It was hard to picture him as anything other than omniscient and omnipotent. And though stories were freely exchanged here, these same chattering boys and men were absolutely silent outside the walls. She had tried to talk to a few of them, before she'd approached Andreas Merrick directly that first night. She'd been coldly rebuffed, no matter what outrageous amount she had offered. Blank faces had been almost eerie in their absolute lack of expression.

She had spent the rest of the night *after* meeting Andreas—and being given their debts back—figuring out how to infiltrate his men and domain.

She had guessed correctly that Andreas would want nothing to do with her directly, so she had brightly and confidently told his men the next morning that she was there in order to repay her family's debts with Mr. Merrick's permission. She was decently sure that he hadn't allowed any of the messengers to verify if the statement were true.

And the man didn't think he allowed his emotions to make decisions for him . . .

There had been something about Milton Fox's expression that morning, though. As if he knew what she was doing and knew something she didn't. He had gone along with her statements—not denying them, but not helping either. Letting her actions that first morning determine his course. She must have passed whatever test he had created, for he had been supportive of her efforts from the next day forth.

Now that she was simply part of the building, anointed by their demon boss and staying under his obvious protection, no matter that she had engineered much of it, they parted with information freely. Though should Andreas Merrick kick her out, those little faces would go blank once more, she had no doubt.

She had been very careful about which questions she had asked in order to preserve goodwill. By working, mostly unnoticed, in the kitchens, they shared more than they would if she was in their direct view.

Andreas Merrick would be *very* displeased if he realized what allowing her to stay here truly meant.

"Won't necessarily be the actual Merricks who get to you first either, if you catch me," the older man said, pulling her back to the eavesdropped conversation. "We're all Merricks here. Peter should have told you."

"He told me," came Tommy's grumpy reply.

"You were settling in, boy. What's got in your craw?"

"I don't like him. He's a bastard."

"Boy," the man said warningly, "Merrick has a lot of responsibility. He's bound to be a mite grumpy."

"Right. Doesn't mean he has to be a shit to Miss Pace."

There was silence for a long moment. "You don't know what you are speaking about, boy. Not at all."

"He should—"

"*Shut your trap.*" It was said in a tone that was full of warning, brooking no argument.

There was a long and oppressive silence before Tommy broke it. "Fine. Can I go?"

"Yeh, just you watch yourself, hear?"

She definitely needed to speak to Tommy. It was entirely her fault that he had followed Andreas. But she had been hoping to remove a suspicion she'd had since the beginning, and it had seemed a good idea at the time she'd broached it to Tommy.

She had no idea why Tommy thought Andreas was mean to her, though. He was veritably *protective*. And someone mean wouldn't have . . . She blushed and kneaded harder.

All in all, her inquiries were going in circles. Which meant that the truth *was* here. Her plans required some rethinking however. For as much as the thought of staying here, hiding here, forever, held seductive appeal, it wasn't a reasonable solution.

And her mother . . . she could still remember

the tone of her voice when they had arrived back from Dover—the clipped words from her mother's mouth. "I inquired about speaking with Mr. Merrick while you were gone. Imagine my surprise when I discovered that *he* was with *you*."

That hadn't gone well. Chastity belt comments aside.

No. Eventually they would need to leave. After making sure Father wouldn't be incarcerated, and that the company would thrive in their absence, they could retire to the country and figure out how to cure him.

Voices drifted out to be replaced with others.

"Going on the raids tonight?"

"Petey switched me." The voice sounded a little hesitant. "My shoulder's still a little sore."

"Yeah? You should get the Bones to look at it."

"Mayhap." Shuffled feet. "You think I'll catch hell for switching?"

"What? Nah. We do it all the time. And if you don't want to participate in raids, you don't hafta. Most of us take pride in it, but there are some who'd rather stay out of such things. As long as you tell Donald or Milton or Peter, they will find you other tasks to do. They don't want people participating that don't want to. Blood spills badly otherwise."

"What about the Merricks?"

"Well, orders come from them, don't they? You ever seen the demon bastard take people with him that he hasn't handpicked? Nah. He doesn't take notice of most of us. Usually he does stuff himself. It's Mr. Roman who forms teams. And he's a keen one with people, he is."

Shuffling movement. Perhaps a hand set on a shoulder. "You stay out of the demon bastard's way, and you'll be fine. He don't seek people out. Ever."

"Thanks."

The boys walked off, leaving the kitchen empty once more. It was like waves on the shore, people coming in, chattering, then breaking and leaving. The silence was smooth and untouched once more, waiting for the next wave to crash.

She lifted her eyes and froze at the sight of a man—*the* man—across from her leaning against the opposing counter, arms crossed, almost languidly watching her work. The one who it was just said never sought people out.

"Listening to gossip, Miss Pace?"

Her heart raced at the soft, sly accusation. The easy remembrance of the events of the night before, and the sleepless night after, made her rub her suddenly dry lips together.

"I . . . I'm sure they didn't mean anything negative."

He raised a brow. "Do you think I care what the little bastards say about me?"

"I suppose not."

He looked amused for a moment, before covering it, face going unreadable once more. She stared, wishing she could freeze the amusement about his mouth and eyes. It made him devastatingly beautiful, really, and she wanted to stare at such a thing, chin on hand, all day if she could. Art that was far finer and more intriguing than any at a museum.

Seeing expressions move across his face was riveting. When he was even remotely feeling a positive emotion, he was breathtaking to observe.

"My question remains, are you enjoying the gossip?"

"I don't know what you mean. I am simply kneading dough."

No need to admit that she had kneaded the dough so hard by that point that it would be a brick when it emerged from the oven.

He examined her for a moment before gracefully rounding the barrier between them. He was moving more easily, and there seemed to be less physical tension to him today.

But the thought of it flitted away as he drew closer and the expression on his face made her heart beat a little faster. Dark sarcasm could be fended off with easy charm. Beastliness could be undermined by happiness. But that intense, stripping gaze was harder to contend or resist.

He lifted her hand, and she almost felt as if she were someone else watching the action. So seldom did he initiate contact with her . . . though the previous night . . . when he had gripped her hand . . . when he had pulled her close . . . touched her . . . made her fly. . .

"Abusing the dough, Miss Pace?"

His eyes were on the pummeled brown ball, but his fingers continued to hold her wrist, palm up, her fingers half-curled into the air.

"All air needed to be removed."

Sort of like her lungs at the moment.

"I would say that you have accomplished that task."

"I didn't think you came to the kitchens, Mr. Merrick," she said, *breathed* it really, trying to get her thoughts in order. She needed to be on her game with him, or she'd be quickly destroyed.

"Where else would I find food?" His fingers slid from her wrist. It was a moment before she could move.

She hastily pushed her fingers back in the belly of the firm dough. "I assumed you had it sent to you every meal."

"I'd starve if I did that."

She blinked. "They won't bring you food?" It seemed such an odd concept based on everything else she knew about the occupants of the building.

"They bring plenty." He pointed to the ginger cake on the platter next to her. "Did you bake that?"

"Yes." She was a bit mystified, and she knew it showed. "It just came out of the oven a half hour or so ago."

He cut a slice and bit into it.

She blinked at him, then unobtrusively checked everything about him from his height to his eyes, his posture to his visible scars. No, even if he had an identical twin hidden away, the other couldn't possibly have the same scars on his neck and hands.

His fingers turned over her hand again, and something was suddenly placed into her palm. She looked down to see a slice of cake nestled there.

He had touched her again.

"You look as if you could use something to eat. Do you feel unwell?"

"No." She felt *out of sorts*, not unwell.

"Miss Pace?"

"Yes?" She looked up at him, her mind a little hazy.

"I asked if you were enjoying the gossip?" He leaned back next to her against the counter, almost lazily. But she wasn't fooled. Every movement he made had purpose. He didn't waste anything.

"You plan to keep asking that until I give you an answer."

"Of course. It is the only way to pin you down." There was something in his eyes that spoke to other things, that made it feel as if the ovens were blazing behind her. "Or else you will just evade and twirl and do something to make me try to forget what question I asked."

Well, that was a discomfiting response. "I cannot help but hear some of what you deem gossip, yes." Far easier to answer the question than to let him think on her methods further.

"Putting yourself in the kitchens helps to facilitate such situations."

"To facilitate the completion of my baking? Yes."

"Your word games won't work."

"But you seem to enjoy them. I don't want to disappoint."

That faint smile tugged his lips again. She couldn't help but lean closer. The skin around his eyes tightened, the deep blue color of them darkened, but not with anger.

There was something almost *loose* about him. It both excited her and made all the hair on her neck stand on end in warning.

"I'm not sure 'disappoint' is a word I'd use for you, Miss Pace. Perhaps anger, annoy, rile . . . please. But not disappoint."

Yes, the ovens had to have been lit.

"Oh. That is rather . . . pleasing to hear."

He watched her for a second, and she could have sworn there was a moment of hesitation, that he was going to reach for her and pull her to him, but he crossed his arms. "Are you going to tell me about the morning's events?"

She put the slice of cake down on the counter and squared it with her fingers. "What would you like to know?" She looked up through her lashes. "What do you already know?"

She was sure she wasn't the only one who knew how to listen for gossip without drawing notice.

"Why don't you start where you feel it best."

"That is a disconcerting request, Mr. Merrick. What if I tell you something that I might not have needed to otherwise?"

"That is the point." His voice was almost gentle. She looked up fully, examining his face for the expression that would match that tone, but it was already gone, replaced, if not by the cold façade he usually sported, then something equally as expressionless.

"We experienced a small fire in your brother's bedroom. Everything is fine now. The drapes had to be replaced, and we will pay for that, of course. We cleaned the walls too, as there were a few scorch marks. The boys used a few buckets full of water to extinguish the flames completely, so there may be a bit of light water damage. But the woods and linens are almost completely dried now. We will reimburse any lingering damage that has not yet been accounted for."

She wiped her palms together, discarding crumbs, and smiled reassuringly at him, hoping that explanation would do.

His face remained stoic. "Your father is not of sound mind."

She couldn't fully contain her wince. "No." There was relief that he finally knew, along with the tiny knot of fear that she might have misjudged him. "You saw him, didn't you? He was in your room when he was missing during the fray."

"Yes."

She bit her lip. "There are times when he is fine. When he remembers. This morning was not one of those."

"I am sorry."

She stared at him for a long moment, then nodded. Thankfully, only her relief remained. "Thank you."

His arms remained crossed. "You aren't going to exclaim over my suddenly sympathetic nature?"

"I have never thought you an automaton, Mr. Merrick. Or unfeeling. I think you as human as I am. And I appreciate your concern. Very much," she added softly.

She wondered with supreme intensity what was going through his mind at that moment, for his face gave nothing away.

"How long ago?"

"That we fully noticed about Father?" She could have dodged the subject a moment more—turned it back to him, with humor about how long she had noticed his nonmachinelike state. But not after that exchange. She shook her head. "It has been building for a while. We pretended . . ." She clamped her lips together. It was always hard to admit it without tears. She shook her head and strove for a light tone. "We wanted him to be well."

"You have hidden it well. Remarkably well."

She wished she could read the expression on his face. "Yes. Under the impression that he became an inept recluse rather than not altogether there." Her smile strained. "A rather poor exchange."

"So far you have kept both the business from failing and your father free of prison or an institution. A fair exchange by any standard."

"But not for long. The scale waits to tip one way or the other. If Christian were here . . . but he's not. I have sought your help, and you have given it. If our plans don't work, I will let the business fail or be consumed by Lord Garrett before Father goes to prison, of course." She picked up the dead dough again, needing something to do. "But Lord Garrett is behind many of our troubles. I don't *want* him to be rewarded."

"Yet you are friends with Garrett's sons."

"Edward Wilcox is nothing like his father. Neither is Henry—not for a long time now, though I've heard that he tried his hardest to emulate him when he was younger."

"The seed usually runs true."

She sighed. "That is like saying that each dog in a litter is a replica of the sire. It is possible to deviate from a course, even one set down from birth."

His eyes were shadowed. "A nice sentiment."

"I think it simple truth. Though it is hard to deviate from the path others expect from you even if you grow into something more. Mother still thinks I'm daft occasionally. The lighthearted, quirky relief for our family."

"And you aren't?"

"Sometimes, yes. It is in my nature to be blithe. And other times it is just easier to pretend that ease and play the role."

He leaned over and cut another slice of cake. "I think I like it when you are smiling, from within, no matter how that occurs."

She stared at him as he ate and watched her. It was as if the world had turned upside down but hadn't swept her with it. Standing on the ceiling now, stomach suddenly in her throat, waiting to fall to the floor in a tangle of limbs.

"I . . . really?"

"Is it so hard to accept?" He seemed so relaxed. It was alarming. Yet there was that watchfulness still in the back of his gaze, as if awaiting her rejection.

"I . . . well, it is not your usual comment."

"Perhaps you have forced me to employ a new strategy."

"Oh?"

"I dare not want to be the keeper of cold, metallic belts. Not if you find them uncomfortable against your skin."

Was he . . . flirting with her?

"Your skin is always warm against mine," she whispered.

His eyes were stripping her again. But this time she could feel the remembrance of his mouth and hands on her skin as he did so. "Yes."

His lips against her cheeks, the feel of his fingers caressing hers.

Breathless and wanting all of it again, she watched him. All points of her body leaning toward his. Watched the various emotions pass over his dark blue eyes, his sharp cheeks, and oddly full lips—lips that were usually thinned by displeasure. She thought it beautiful—that openness on his face as for once he didn't shutter the emotions mixing and chasing across.

And it decided things for her, really.

She could plot madly when needed, but when it came down to basic traits, she was an impulsive spirit, relying on instinct and emotion. And instinct and emotion said to follow the end of the thread that had been between them since the first time she had seen him catch his breath in a darkened theater.

She shifted forward slowly, just that extra bit, since he had complied so well in bringing them so close together.

Shifted straight forward. Not cocked to the side, so cheeks would brush together. She half expected him to pull back, but then again . . . he was a still and steady man. Rock hard. She pressed her lips slowly to his. His mouth was firm. That was unsurprising. But his lips were soft as well. Above the steel. The opposite of the man, really, who had such a dark and forbidding shell but was surprisingly gentle underneath.

He'd deny it. And perhaps the truth of it was that he was gentle only to those he cared for—and that the people in that category numbered few—but he had given her a glimpse of it. That gentleness focused on her. And it quickened her breath, thinking of it, made her press more steadily against him, uncertain and confident at the same time.

She had never initiated a real kiss before. Only those on the cheek. Warm lips to scratchy skin. Or the brush of his lips against hers. The taste of him on her tongue as she'd moistened her lips afterward. But her parents had always been affectionate souls. And she had gotten more than one eyeful of the ladies of the night on the streets outside. Observed them from her window, pressing against men, eager, or at least pretending to be so.

But there was something cheap in thinking such thoughts. For those women did it for coin. And she blamed them not at all for the choices they made, but she wanted something far different from the man whose lips were motionless beneath hers.

And suddenly they were anything but still.

Heat, overwhelming heat. It was like nothing she had ever experienced before last night. Like being burned alive and feeling no pain. Only the scorch and the flame. And his hands were wrapping around the back of her neck, tipping her up, bringing her closer, claiming and branding.

My God. She wanted to wrap herself around him, to pin herself to him, the heat melting them together, never able to separate.

His lips consumed hers. As if he had been waiting years, decades, to unleash such passion. Waiting there, leashed and growling, behind a cold and steely façade.

And she couldn't think of a single regret as he stole the breath from her.

She had never been so right. That this was a man to whom one sold one's soul. For he was assuredly pulling it right out of her. With every breath that passed from her lips to his. Piece by piece, never to be regained. Held for judgment or set free.

"Miss Pace?" An outside voice called. "Are you in here?"

Her lips were suddenly released, the hands in her nape slipping through the strands there, and he was gone.

She gaped at the empty space in front of her, breathing hard, a hand pressed to her chest.

"Miss Pace?"

She turned to see a large boy appear in the doorway. Robbie, who had the largest frame she had ever seen on a boy of fifteen. He was looking at her strangely, concern beneath his shyness.

"Yes, Robbie?"

"Are you well?"

"Oh, oh, yes. I, I almost pitched myself into the oven when I tripped."

As if she had tripped against Andreas Merrick's lips.

The boy looked from her to the oven, and moved closer, placing himself between her and the oven, in harm's way. "Are you hurt?"

"No, no, of course not." She dredged up a reassuring smile for the kind boy. Tucking her thoughts on what had just occurred into a nice, warm corner of her mind, to examine later. For it was a certainty that Andreas Merrick was gone and not returning for the moment.

"Oh, good." Robbie shuffled his feet. "You said you were going to prepare cottage pie and treacle pudding tonight? May I help you?"

She smiled and put a hand on his sleeve, calming her racing heart further. Calm. Calm. Calm. "Of course, Robbie. Let's get started."

He gave her as close to a beaming smile as she'd ever seen on him. It had taken a bit for the boy to warm up, and she suspected deep abuse in his past despite his size, or perhaps because of it, but he had become a fast friend in the kitchens once he had determined she meant him no harm.

She ran a still shaky hand down her skirt. Calm. Calm. And instead thought of what she had gathered from her contacts here as she chatted with Robbie. That someone in the Merrick's employ had observed what had happened to her brother was becoming more and more apparent. That she still felt completely safe here, even with the secret of it swirling, was strange.

She looked at Robbie from the corner of her eye as they worked. It could be someone like Robbie, too frightened to come forward. Or . . . or something else.

She was going to beard Andreas Merrick in his den tonight, over supper, and pry it out of him, however she had to do it. It was time—past time.

But she hoped he would force her to kiss him senseless first.

Chapter 18

However, by the time she had finished her part of the supper preparations, she couldn't find him. She worked in his office, tense and hopeful. Alone. Uncertain and eager. But he hadn't shown.

She had finally asked, casually, in the kitchens when she'd gone to get a tray for her parents, and been told that raids were commencing and that Andreas was leading them. Something about revenge for the attack on the carriage and the last day that slimy bastard Cornelius would see of the sun.

That had gained the boy uttering it a prompt elbow to the gut from one of the others—everyone nervously exchanging glances.

The only things she knew of Cornelius were what she had learned by listening unobserved. Few people would part with information concerning him directly. She had a feeling that was due in no small part to Andreas's tampering.

The boys had fallen over themselves to assure her that everything would be fine. The demon bastard never lost. Not even to another underworld lord. For some reason, that last bit of news hadn't made her feel better.

It had made her nervous and tense in an entirely different way. But the building had been quiet, to the opposite of her turmoil inside. Her parents retired early, as usual, leaving her in the growing silence, stretched out on Roman Merrick's plush sofa.

That changed a few minutes before midnight. Stomping and yelling could be heard up and down the stairs. A few victorious shouts. Phoebe scrambled up and pressed her ear to the door, waiting until she heard the footsteps on the stairs.

She peeked out and the lone person in the hall stuttered to a stop at the end. They stared at each other for long moments, then he walked stiffly toward his door, the limping very obvious.

Giving it not one extra thought, she closed the door behind her and ran toward him. He opened his door quickly. She half pushed, half slipped inside with him before he could bar her entrance.

She flitted into the middle of the room and turned, hands out in submission as he stared darkly at her. In another person she would have said she saw fear there for a moment.

But his face contorted suddenly and his hands went to either side of his left thigh, blood soaking through the fabric.

She heard the intake of her own breath, felt it vibrate from her chest. "Oh my God." She started toward him, but his suddenly outstretched bloody hand stopped her.

"Stop. Leave." There was a wealth of emotions strangled in those two words.

"Absolutely not. You are hurt. Have you sent for a doctor?" She listened for footsteps, but the hall was silent.

"No. I don't need one." He drew himself back upright. "Go back to your room, Miss Pace."

"There isn't a chance of that happening." She inched forward, as if approaching a wild animal. "Let me see your leg. Please."

"I don't want you to see my leg. And I am not in good humor." Everything about his voice and expression indicated it, but there was vulnerability underneath. One that everything in her latched on to. "So kindly get out. I will speak with you in the morning."

That hint of exposure just made her more determined to erase the remaining barriers between them. She watched him, quickly trying to figure out the best course of action.

"I am fine," he said tightly, his voice deeper and harsher than usual. The tightness of his body, his expression, and his voice only strengthened her resolve. "Now please leave."

"No." She took a deep breath. Andreas Merrick was hers. "If you aren't going to send for a doctor—"

"I don't need one."

But blood had finally seeped to the floor, alarming her further.

"You most certainly and obviously do." She took a step toward him, only stopping when he turned his blackest glare on her. "Is this when I ask you if *you* are taken by madness, Andreas?" she asked in a low voice.

Something shifted on his face for a moment,

perhaps at her use of his name, but then it grew hard once more. Implacable and dark. "I do not want you here, Miss Pace. I don't know what right you think you have to enter my rooms, then remain after I've asked you to leave."

"Indeed, I follow direction poorly. And sometimes you are a rude, brutish man." She moved forward, in direct opposition to the expression on his face, which was growing darker with each of her steps. The shadows drawing in with the creases of his narrowed eyes, the tightened line of his mouth. She gave a determined smile. "But I like you. And I'm going to help you."

"Well, how about I don't like *you*." His voice was tight and stressed, that vulnerability harshly buried beneath. "Now will you leave?"

"No," she said, tone going gentle. "I like you well enough for the both of us."

His face tightened again, but it was obviously a reaction to pain this time, as he all but collapsed on a very elegant chair.

She dropped into the chair across from him and reached for his bloody leg.

He pushed her hand away. "No. *No*." But there was a fine line underscoring the words, threatening a break, echoing the sheen of sweat on his forehead and above his lip.

"Let me see your leg."

"Get out!" he roared.

She took a deep breath, but she held firm. "I have every thought that you will treat this yourself and not seek help elsewhere. But you need help, and I am going to help you."

"I want you gone. That will be the most helpful action you can undertake." The last word was said with a low, hissing quality. The echo of it prickled across her skin. "Stop helping me, stop kissing me, stop invading my territory."

And there was that vulnerability again. A desperation.

"It is a sad fact that things we want are often not the things we receive," she said lightly, reaching for him once more.

He caught her hand in his, holding it between them. "That must mean you *want* to be helpful."

"You are a mean-spirited man. You realize this, yes?"

His lips twisted, but it was more of a grimace. "Keenly."

"But, as I said, I like you. And I am going to help you."

He just watched her for a long penetrating moment, before abruptly pulling the unmarked right leg of his trouser up sharply, over his knee. "Are you going to match them together?" The words were bitter.

She looked at the exposed limb for a moment in shock, then reached forward to feel the steel encasing it. It was almost like a clockwork, how everything seemed to move and shift together. "How . . ." She touched the skin of his leg between the flat bands and bolts. He shifted, and she lifted her hand. "How long have you had this?"

It was genius. She had never noticed anything amiss in the shape of his right leg through his clothes.

"Years." His voice was dark and deadly. If he had been another man, and she another woman, she would have stiffened, waiting for the blade to pierce her exposed neck.

But she wasn't, and neither was he.

She examined what she could see of the scar beneath. And the brace on top. Something very bad had happened to his right leg at some point.

She remembered him snapping it back into place in the carriage. A weakened joint that popped out frequently? The metal surrounding would brace it. Most men would just use a cane. There was little surprise as to why he didn't, though, when she thought about it. But the secret of it . . .

He had just trusted her with the secret of it. Most likely in an illogical attempt to drive her away, as he was on the thin edge of eruption. He would destroy their relationship without thinking twice and probably think it for the best.

But he had trusted her with an obviously *very* closely kept secret. There was something relieved and resigned in his tenseness. Angry and unguarded.

She stared him hard in the eyes. "It is fine. Let's look at your left leg." She wasn't going anywhere.

Andreas Merrick was nothing if not a dominant man. And every facet of his facial expression threatened dire consequences. But if she were ever going to have given into his threatening gazes, it would have been well before now. Well before she had an actual vested care for his well-being.

"I am not going anywhere," she reiterated aloud.

His nicely shaped lips disappeared in a thin, hard line. He opened his mouth, and she had the very sure notion that he was about to say something completely unforgivable.

She clamped her other hand onto the one holding hers. "It doesn't matter what you say, I will not leave tonight. Your words will only matter for how things go between us after this. Tomorrow." She kept her eyes fixed to his. "I hold you in high stead. I have a care for your well-being. If you have any sort of care for me at all, you will say none of the black thoughts echoing in your head right now—though hopefully not in your heart—and simply accept my help."

It was a little like looking into the face of a deadly animal backed into an alleyway.

"I will not begrudge you ungracious words," she continued calmly. "Just nothing unforgivable."

His gaze held hers for long moments, and she thought for a second that he was going to do it anyway. But his gaze shuttered, and he gave a sharp nod.

She squeezed his hand, relief draining her. "Good. Fine. Yes." She took a breath. "Where are your medicinal supplies?"

He pointed to a shelf. There were a number of bags, vials, and cordials. Needles, tinder, and tape.

She quickly walked over and gathered everything she could, trying not to knock over the very expensive statues guarding the area.

A quick, fleeting glance at her surroundings said that all of his furnishings were elegant and hard. Like him.

No one would ever guess from looking at the exterior of the building that such expensive spaces were to be found in the Merricks' private chambers. Everything that existed in Andreas's realm was secret.

She poured capped water into a bowl. She didn't have to ask if the water had been previously boiled. That shelf stated in all manners that all of the supplies were for this very purpose.

She wouldn't be surprised if someone as prepared as Andreas Merrick freshened the dressings and restocked the supplies each morning.

She quickly took a pair of scissors and went to work cutting his trousers. In any other instance, she would have been redder than red, but determination had taken over. She could suffer a lady's embarrassment later.

Parting the fabric, she pressed her lips together to refrain from gasping and reached for the water-dipped cloth to clean and determine the extent of the injury.

He lifted a bottle and held it to her. It stung her perfectly wound-free fingers as she tested it. She gave him a sharp look, but he gave her a "get on with it" signal with his hand. She dabbed a bit on the edge of the gash.

He grabbed the bottle from her and shook it over the wound before she snatched it back. She took a deep breath and liberally coated his thigh.

He made not a sound. But he had procured a bottle of liquor from a nearby cabinet and was drinking like he was preparing for a week in the desert.

As she'd never seen him drink liquor before, it was quite a sight.

She contemplated her next action. She had never stitched something as deeply gashed as the wound on his thigh, but she had some experience sewing wounds since her father frequently harmed himself—or someone else accidentally—with his sometimes bizarre actions.

Although there was still blood sluggishly emerging, the wound did not appear life-threatening. After three flights of stairs and however many streets he had traveled, he was lucky.

She picked up the needle and thread to start the stitches, contemplating the mechanics of sealing the cavernous gap. Suddenly his hands pressed the skin on either side together, thinning the gash. Like it was a paper cut that simply needed pinching.

A stream of blood trailed out.

She met his eyes, kneeling between his legs, her hand on his left knee. "Are you sure you don't want to call someone else?"

He stared at her for long moments, those intense eyes swallowing her. "I'm sure. I would do it myself if you weren't here."

She looked back at the gash. She threaded the needle.

Then she leaned up and kissed him, her free hand pressed to his cheek.

He tasted like liquor, unsurprisingly. But also of fire and brimstone. He responded immediately, lips pulling hers against his over and over.

She pulled away, focused her concentration to a pinpoint, and stabbed the needle in.

He didn't say anything for a few minutes, just let her work and gain a rhythm. She tried to pretend

she was working on a needlepoint sampler that
needed fixing.

"You are now the third female to stitch me up,"
he said finally, tipping the bottle again. His voice
sounded resigned. As if all the anger had drained
right out with the snip of his clothing. Or more
likely, the fifth tip of the bottle.

"Third?" She questioned in the light voice that
worked best with him in times of stress. "I believe
I'm a bit jealous."

"Don't be. Roman's damn wife was the second."
He grimaced and took another drink.

"You don't like her?"

"She's not completely awful."

She sat on the smile that threatened. "Were *you*
jealous? When they married?"

She figured he wasn't going to bat her away at
this point for asking such questions.

"Shit no. That woman would drive me crazy."

"No. *Of* her."

Charlotte had taken away his partner after all.
And it was obvious that Andreas Merrick didn't
believe in superficial attachments. It had to have
hit at his core having his brother separated from
him, even in a minor way.

"Ah." He looked drunkenly contemplative for a
moment. "Maybe a bit. But Roman is deliriously
happy. It's nauseating. I'm glad."

That was a patchwork of admissions. She had a
feeling he avoided alcohol for just that reason.

"What happened? To your right leg?"

"I irritated someone."

She clucked her tongue. "I would like to have words with that someone."

"You have."

She blinked. "What? Who?"

He smiled darkly, the alcoholic haze clearing for a moment. "It matters little."

She glanced at the brace, still uncovered. There were tiny steel knobs that looked as if they could pinch. "Do these hurt?"

"Sometimes. I get them modified every few months."

The tinker. Earlier he had been more at ease. It must have been hurting him previously, and he must have gotten it fixed that afternoon. "Oh, Andreas."

It was a tactical mistake. She realized it immediately and quickly pushed farther into his space, between his legs, batting his hand as he tried to move her away. "Stop it. I didn't mean it that way. I simply don't like to see you hurt."

His muscles were all tight, but his chest was moving in and out at a good clip.

She concentrated on his leg again and silence stretched.

"It's a surprise to have the other one injured. Everyone goes for the right leg usually," he said eventually, sounding even more resigned, like she had finally cut the last string he possessed. "It's like a curse."

"Or a blessing," she said, examining the numerous small scars. "How many times have you been hit in that leg?"

"Too many to count."

She thought on it for a moment as she briefly wiped her hands on a towel.

"The stories. Someone, or more than one some-one, stuck a knife into your brace at one point and lived to tell the tale, didn't they?"

"Yes."

"People are terrified you aren't human because you receive what appears to be mortal wounds, yet walk away." If it had been a tale about some name-less other soul, she might have been amused.

"Even one's worst feature is useful sometimes."

"But surely at some point, someone must have seen your brace or guessed?"

He shrugged, but his eyes were dark on hers. Telling her quite clearly that she should run and run fast—as the reason no one knew was because none of *those* had lived to tell the tale.

She smiled instead. "It is a good thing I am trustworthy then," she said lightly.

He didn't say anything for long moments, but his head dropped back against the chair, throat bared.

She paused. The action of it tugging at her . . . Her mind finally caught up, and something clogged her throat.

When he had turned his back on her in the inn. When he had allowed her the upper position at the farmhouse, sleeping next to the bed instead of across the room from it—she could have dropped anything on him. Exposing his neck now, and his obviously closest guarded secret.

She coughed to clear her throat and focused on finishing the last stitches.

"I assume your brother knows." She somehow managed to say it without her voice breaking.

"Of course. But few others." He was looking at her through half-slitted eyes as she worked.

She had absolutely no idea how he had kept it a secret, unless it were true that he had killed anyone who had seen his leg. "I won't tell a soul. Ever. Even without the threat of death." She tied the thread and reached for the salve to layer on top.

"I know," he whispered.

She just barely kept from jerking at the admission. She smoothed the jellied substance on the wound instead of saying anything else.

She cleaned up all the supplies, moved a lamp to the bedroom, then reached down and helped him stand, putting his arm over her shoulder. She was actually the perfect height to do so, to lift his weight just enough. And she was stronger than she looked. She had wrestled too many times with her father—trying to wrest flame from his fist—that she could do this small bit of moving Andreas, even with his superior weight.

She got him to the bed and pulled back the covers. He was asleep as soon as his head hit the pillow. She tucked him in, then contemplated her next action. She could go back to her sofa and worry about him all night . . . or . . .

The bed was surprisingly big. Large enough for her to lie down on and not disturb him. She crawled under the covers on the other side. She lay there for a moment, hand tucked under her cheek, looking at his dark hair splayed over the pillow. Then she leaned over, pressed a kiss to his hair, and reached back to extinguish the lamp on the side table.

"Good night, Andreas."

He woke up to a body splayed under the covers next to him, taking up more than half the space, arms and legs outstretched. Light brown hair scattered in every direction as well.

Not some strange dream then.

And he suddenly realized he hadn't had any nightmares that night. Liquor always made them worse, so he never partook unless he had to.

No, the only thing that had been different had been sleeping next to her.

Dangerous thoughts.

Not even the pain in his legs could diminish them from spiraling.

Andreas gripped his fingers together. Usually he could keep such thoughts at bay in his office. Keep writing, keep adding, keep working. But it wasn't working here, especially with her sleeping next to him.

There was a forked path in front of him. The path he had always planned to take grew narrower. The second path, a mere suggestion of a trail, was now paved and wide. Enticing.

He touched a lock of shiny brown hair that had migrated to his pillow. He had thought it bred out of him long ago—that simple hope for freedom.

And the entire game was almost at an end on all fronts.

What would he do after he gained his final revenge? Roman had long asked him that question.

To which he had always sniped out an automatic response. But now, with an end in sight, he had to question his choices and their consequences. What might they bring him after?

After.

It was odd to entertain such thoughts. He trusted few people. But that was his least concern when dealing with Phoebe Pace. She was a trustworthy person. Odd, in the end, that it wasn't trust that was the problem.

He trusted her. And that said a lot. No, that would say a lot for most people. That said . . . far more than a lot for him.

No, it wasn't trust in her that he lacked. It was trust in himself. To do the right thing.

He laughed without humor. He had been born to people who *took* as their divine right, later raised on the streets to take what he could, while he could. He couldn't rid himself of the fear. That he would invest in something and have it snatched away. Inbred for long enough that he couldn't shake the dread.

Trust had nothing to do with it. If she discovered . . .

One eye peeked open, and she stretched. He withdrew his hand from her hair.

"Good morning," she said sleepily, a smile curving her lips. One of those smiles he wanted for his own, with a desire that would destroy him.

"Good morning," he said hoarsely. Liking the way that she looked on the pillow next to his as the sun rose.

If she discovered . . .

She sat up, cheeks pink, hands pressed against them. Rose was a good color on her. And so unusual. And yet, that smile on her lips was not one of embarrassment. It was one of happiness.

Happiness. His gut clenched. Fortune truly hated him.

For if Phoebe Pace discovered it had been he who had shot her brother, what would happen then?

Chapter 19

It was noon. Andreas should be back from the tinker's shop by now. In his office.

He had refused to stay in bed—as if there were nothing wrong with him. She didn't understand such things. It was as if he were immune to pain.

He had tested his weight on first one leg, then the other, walking forward in a variety of motions, shifting, before he figured out how to make his walk look the same as it always did—with one leg bound in steel and the other stitched up only six hours previous.

Astonishing really.

She had thousands of questions, and few answers. But he had said nothing, and she had simply watched him—and even more startling, he had allowed her to watch him—until he'd tightly said he was going to get the brace adjusted.

She wondered if his grumpiness was a result of constant pain and pretending there was nothing wrong.

She carefully arranged food and utensils on her

tray, taking a moment to rearrange things until they were suited just so. Her heart began to beat harder.

She had made the trek to his office many, many times before. But never had she felt such a wild anticipation mixed with abject panic.

She knocked and received a brusque, "*Enter.*"

She poked her head around the door and gave him a sunny smile. "Pardon me for interrupting, Mr. Merrick." He looked up at her with a raised brow that clearly expressed his thoughts on her actions' apology.

"Am I interrupting?"

His eyes narrowed. He was obviously contemplating something deep and interesting. He just wasn't the type to think about mundane subjects for long stretches of time, not like she could, examining for an hour how water dripped down a pane during a storm. His pen tapped against the desk. She always wondered how he didn't flick ink everywhere. How did his desk stay so clean? It was as if the ink itself was afraid to cause a stain.

"Miss Pace?"

"Yes?" She focused back on his face. "I can return later if you need me to." Coward, coward, coward. She was so nervous that she could barely make her lips work.

"I said to enter, did I not?"

He turned back to his papers, and she slipped inside and closed the door softly, balancing the tray in her free hand, standing right in front of the door. He finished something with a flourish, then set his pen down in its holder and leaned back in his chair.

"Well? Did you burn down the kitchens?"

"What?" She blinked. His face was a strange mixture of expressions—resignation, anticipation, tension.

"Something dire has obviously happened if you are pussyfooting around me."

"I wasn't—am not—pussyfooting."

"You usually charge right in and plop down in front of me, at a desk *you* added to this room, lips bleating away."

"I don't bleat," she said, disgruntled, more so that he had correctly identified her tactics than that he had compared her to a woolly animal.

"Well?"

She inclined her head, watching him, a smile pulling at her lips the more she watched him. "Do you need to beat back the silence now too, Mr. Merrick? You don't usually prompt answers verbally."

His eyes narrowed, his expression closing. "What do you want, Miss Pace?"

She was glad to see he wasn't becoming complacent with her. It pushed her into motion. She saw the way he stiffened as she walked toward him, and it made her relax a measure more, as he picked up his pen, pretending to ignore her again. She took a deep breath and softly let it out between her lips.

Perhaps the unabated tension between them was not so one-sided. Their shared intimacy, discovering such a closely kept secret when she stitched him up, then waking up next to him, had simultaneously broken everything open between them, which in some odd fashion had thrown up an awkward barrier that even she did not know fully how to breach. Like two people who suddenly knew each other faster than regular pacing dictated and had to figure out how to acknowledge that fact.

She did not know how to proceed after yesterday's events. She was willing to wait, but when Andreas Merrick's defenses were at their weakest spot, they were still difficult to scale. And any lag *she* allowed would just allow *him* to fortify his defenses more.

"Let me begin again. Good afternoon, Mr. Merrick," she said cheerfully, and twisted her palm in a circle, placing the tray on his desk with a flourish. "I've brought lunch."

He was working hard on something. He always was, really. She had been beyond surprised to realize that he really did control all financial and operational aspects of their empire. No wonder he rarely left this room.

Sometimes he disappeared into another room on the second floor. She had been told by a few boys that when Roman Merrick was in residence, the two sparred frequently in the large room, and that it held all manners of weapons. But she hadn't been witness to such activity. Apparently only Roman was privy to whatever happened inside. Andreas always entered alone and always locked the door behind him.

She had heard him though. It sometimes sounded like he was determined to destroy the building from the inside.

She saw him peek through the hair hanging in front of his eyes as he kept his head bent to his tasks. "You cooked it?"

"Yes. I assure you, though, that I didn't use anything rotten."

She waited for him to joke back, but he nodded, reached for one of the biscuits, and brought it to his mouth.

She took that as an invitation to sit. She had brought enough for two on purpose.

They ate in silence for a few minutes. It was usually nice simply to sit with him—the silence pleasant and full. But after what had happened yesterday, she couldn't sit still and silent for very long.

"You seem determined to ignore me now, Mr. Merrick," she said in between bites. "Are you embarrassed that we kissed in the kitchen?"

She could have raised a different subject but she had a positive feeling about this less threatening line of questioning. She licked her lips in anticipation.

He paused for only a moment in his litany of work, work, work, *bite,* work, work, work. "No."
Bite.

From previous experience she knew if she let it, he would allow the conversation to drop until it was well within his own best interest to raise it again—to disconcert her. "Well, good. For I am not embarrassed," she said. "I quite enjoyed myself. It was a singularly gratifying experience that I hope to remove from the singular."

A splotch of ink splattered the page. He cursed and reached for the blotter.

She leaned forward. "I think that is the first time I have seen you make a mess. Does that mean you are unnerved by me saying I enjoyed kissing you and wish to do so again? Even with my inexperience in such matters, I would say that you seemed to be enjoying yourself as well."

"Miss Pace."

"Yes?"

"Do you have no decency?" It was said almost in resignation.

"No. Not if it interferes with good sense."

His hand dropped, and he looked at her. "You believe decency and good sense unrelated?"

She gave a firm nod. "In this case, yes."

He sighed and threw his pen down on the desk. A tiny trickle stuttered out. It was a week for amazement apparently. He rubbed a hand over his eyes and sighed again. "Yes, I enjoyed myself."

She beamed at him. A slew of normal, human gestures *and* an admittance of happiness. Or, at least pleasure. Her smile grew larger as he peered at her through his long fingers.

"I am going to regret admitting that to you."

"Come now, Mr. Merrick. You do not regret. You have said so yourself."

"You'd be surprised," he muttered.

She leaned forward, entreatingly. "Would it make you feel better to curse or threaten me with something horrendous?"

He shut his eyes and leaned back in his chair. He looked tired, resigned. "No. I would simply be wasting my breath." He opened his eyes and looked at her. "What do you want, Miss Pace?"

She leaned as far forward as she could, leaning on her elbows. "May I kiss you again?"

He stared at something in the corner over her shoulder. "Just when I think I can fall no deeper into hell, the hole just keeps going."

She blinked. "Oh." That smarted a bit, even through the armor she had constructed before entering.

He looked back at her, and his face was unreadable for a moment, but there was something almost vulnerable about him. "Fine."

"Fine what? Fine, as in, yes, I can kiss you?"

"Yes."

It was not the most exciting response she had imagined. "Er, well, before I leave then, I suppose, yes? Allow you to get back to work then?"

"I suppose."

Had that been amusement in his eyes? She decided to count it in her tally to the positive.

She was ever an optimist.

From there, the conversation turned beautifully awkward. She swallowed her own embarrassment as best as she could and concentrated on exploiting his.

"So, how did the return visit to your tinker go?"

He tapped his finger on the arm of his chair. "It was satisfactory. Mathias was beyond happy."

She blinked. "Truly?"

"The man would like nothing more than if he could turn everyone into full-scale automatons."

"And what about Cornelius?"

His body went still, deadly still. "You shouldn't even know that name."

She tilted her head. "Is it a danger that I do?"

"I don't want you involved in any of it."

"Well, that is too bad, really. Are you going to tell me if I need to worry about you reappearing with a bloody arm next?"

"No."

She chose to deliberately misinterpret his answer. "Good. I have a care for your safety."

He didn't respond.

"Is he dead?"

She didn't think he was going to respond to that either, but a low-voiced reply emerged. "Yes." He picked up his pen, not looking at her. "He signed his death certificate on our return from Dover."

"You hadn't been planning to kill him before?"

His fingers pressed against the edge of the pen, then released, pressed, then released. "It is complicated. This world is complicated."

"Very well." The question pressed though. "Do you plan to stay in this world indefinitely?"

He didn't answer, and that gave her hope. The Andreas from weeks ago would have responded with an unequivocal yes.

She nodded as if he had answered. "Did you speak to our men in the financial district?"

"Yes. They sealed the fund documents and accounts. Garrett's reported response was . . . satisfying. I am finishing the pages that will hasten his removal from these shores permanently."

"Good." It was good. Everyone would be free once Garrett was gone. She didn't want anyone else to die. She had a feeling the man across from her understood that. She was surprised he had admitted to Cornelius's death. She wasn't going to reward his honesty by being a hysterical nag. She *didn't* understand this world. And she wasn't going to criticize what she didn't understand.

That didn't mean she wanted to *stay* in it, though.

Andreas's pen made a sudden flourish on the paper, almost as if he had just sealed Viscount Garrett's fate by doing so. "Garrett's only salvation was in Cornelius's winning—and in rebuilding his reputation through your company. I have been steadily ruining him for too long for him to have other opportunities available now."

"You've been corralling him into this spot for a long time."

He looked at her through his lashes. "It was a different spot a few months ago, but yes."

She almost asked if he would have ruined them along with Garrett had they not met, but she knew the answer already. She could choose to move forward with him, or argue over decisions that had not occurred in the end.

What was important was that she sensed a change in him. Or the *verge* of a change. A change that only he could choose to make. To go forward with life—but in a different way and with different goals.

Not that he would ever stop being Andreas Merrick however he chose to continue. Which was well, for she liked him—all of him—grumpiness and darkness included.

"Henry and Edward have both said their father would never agree to banishment."

And there was the darkness, curving his lips. "If Garrett doesn't leave England voluntarily, he will be labeled a traitor and run the risk that his title and line will be abolished." He smiled, utterly satisfied. "Little matters to Garrett more than the knowledge that his own seed will continue the viscountcy."

"You truly think he will be labeled a traitor?"

"In the same way your father was marked for prison and ruin, people need to blame someone. A financial crisis looms. Mark my words. And those in power see the stirrings."

"My father—"

"Was a very convenient scapegoat. Circumstances were perfect. He will be fully exonerated within the week."

She believed him. When he said something in that tone of voice, it happened.

He continued speaking, and she wondered briefly on his apparent ease conversing these days. "You helped me trace and tie Garrett to many of the rotten aspects of the fund speculation. He will take the fall, and rightly so. Easy enough for the word 'traitor' to be applied when foreign governments are involved. England will rue its speculations in the Latin quarters."

He rolled his quill along the desk top, smiling. "And if Garrett does something stupid in the interim, we will be waiting."

Rolling his pen was an odd gesture. It meant he was likely up to something.

He looked up and his eyes, heavily lidded and intense, met hers.

"I . . ." She wet her lips. "Well, I suppose I should

retire for the afternoon. Let you work." Which had been the promise of their bargain, the current price of a kiss.

He rolled his pen for long moments more. "Very well." He rose, then walked around the desk.

She nervously watched his advance. It was strange doing this in a less-than-spur-of-the-moment manner, and she regretted a little, her stupidity in suggesting it. But at the same time . . . something said that if she could tolerate a little discomfort, she would be rewarded. The same feeling that had guided her in all her actions with him.

Chipping through the uncomfortable exterior in order to get to the treasure underneath.

He stood in front of her, and oh, he wasn't going to make this easy on her. She could see it there in his eyes and posture. But he also wouldn't be here, standing in front of her, if he were opposed to kissing her.

She licked her lips. His dark eyes were intense, holding hers.

She reached up to his chest, straightening an already straight seam. Then she reached up to his shoulders and put a little pressure on them as she lifted on her toes. His lips were warm as they touched hers. And the fire was there, underneath the contact, itching and dancing in her belly, waiting to be ignited completely.

But the kiss was oddly . . . gentle. Between her hesitancy to completely throw herself at him—she did have a little decency after all—and his actions in letting her lead, she supposed it wasn't really odd. But . . . it was nice all the same. A different kind of feeling than what had happened between them in the kitchens or two nights ago on this desk, and different also from the kiss before she had made that first stitch, but no less intriguing in its own way.

The kiss stretched, her lips not separating from his for long moments.

She pulled back a notch, only enough to see his eyes. "Do you think that you might want to initiate another kiss too? At some point?"

"Perhaps. At some point," he replied, his voice just the slightest bit uneven.

She nodded and dropped back on her heels, looking down. The slight embarrassment of the request and her forward action in kissing him were trying to overcome the feeling of rightness that she felt when near him.

"Good day . . ." She looked at him, and the impulse gripped her again. " . . . Andreas."

She turned to go, but his hand captured her wrist. He had the strangest look on his face. Usually so rock steady, but she could see the very visible fight in his eyes.

She tilted her head. "Is there something you need before I return upstairs?"

"You are the oddest creature."

She nodded again. "Yes, I have been told so before." She wouldn't let it hurt. She'd pushed the thread that connected such thoughts to her feelings away long ago. Hidden deep down. She was odd, it was true. She had been told so for so long that she accepted it as fact. Better to embrace the oddities and celebrate her strengths. Far easier and more productive. "Did you need something further, Andreas?"

His name easily slipped from her lips again, and she found she liked it there.

"I find it beyond comprehension, but yes, I do." He reached forward and one finger touched her chin. Her breath caught, heart picking up speed quickly. "You tilt your head when you are curious. Therefore, you do so often."

She swallowed. "That, and you are quite tall."

"Or you are just short."

Had he just . . . teased her? "To you most people likely are."

His eyes were intense on hers, and so near to hers. His fingers curled around her chin. "You are the oddest creature."

"Yes. And you are repeating yourself," she said, a bit disgruntled within the onslaught of tangled emotion.

"You are one of the most confident people I've ever encountered, with a core so vulnerable to hurt. Do you realize what you are even doing, showing me such vulnerabilities?"

She swallowed again. "Perhaps it is stupid of me. I cannot help but be interested in you. And"— she looked down for a moment, only his hand and the darkness of his wrist in her view—"I do little by halves."

"I as well." It was said in a low voice. He said nothing further for long moments. "When I take something, I take *everything*."

She had the feeling that he was giving her an opportunity to turn tail and run.

She tilted her head. "When I give something, I give everything."

So many expressions chased across his face that she was uncertain what to even attempt to read there. Need, victory, despair.

"I know," he whispered. His lips brushed against hers, once, twice, one taste, then another. She could barely catch her breath, then his lips were parting hers, opening them beneath, and the tinder exploded into flame. Consuming once more.

Taking everything. She offered it all freely, simply hanging on as every bit of her caught fire. Even the fingernails gripping his shirtsleeve burned.

His mouth pulled from hers suddenly, as if ripped away by will alone, and she gasped.

Strong lips pressed against her ear. "And I will find myself in hell for admitting it, but I have discovered you to be completely undeniable," he whispered, then pulled away and strode back to his desk.

She stared at him as he walked away. And she thought she probably looked quite foolish if someone were to look upon her, but the beat of her heart thumped so hard in her chest, and the breath had been stolen from her lips, and the thread hidden so deep inside gave a twang, vibrating. Turning her world on end.

He didn't look up from the papers there, but there was a hesitancy to him that she had never seen before, that her suddenly acute senses focused upon.

"Good day . . . Phoebe."

Chapter 20

Andreas got a surprising amount done. Focused and determined to do so. Wrapping up things as he went. It was stunning, when he looked at things in a new light, but there were a large number of things he could wrap up and put in the "never again" pile if he so chose.

Life . . . life could be different.

If only . . .

No, he couldn't think like that. He had carved this empire from blood and steel. And sheer stupid determination, at times. It was what he had.

But what he *might* be able to have . . .

He twitched and cursed violently as one of the steel bands bit into the junction of his left knee. Mathias had crafted a temporary brace to keep his left leg steady enough so he could walk on it without anyone the wiser until it fully healed, but the disadvantage to making it seem as if there was nothing amiss was that he had to be very careful of new movements.

He was getting rid of the left brace as soon as

he was able. He wished he could do so with its counterpart, but the right joint had been too badly damaged. The bone was too prone to popping out for him to get rid of the brace in his line of work.

His reputation had not been gained from hobbling around with a cane.

Still, a line of sweat broke on his brow as he pushed the bands on his left leg back into place. For the moment he was safe from Phoebe's prying eyes and could give in to the pain. And none of their men would dare enter.

His brother chose that moment to stroll nonchalantly into the room and his life again. "I leave for a month and come back to a bloody building full of fowl."

Andreas stared at him, but Roman merely blinked at the double desks, then negligently dropped into the chair on the other side of Phoebe's, looking happy and relaxed and completely *pissed* underneath it all—a tightly held thread with Andreas's name on it.

"Real fowl," Roman stressed. "There are at least fifty birds in the building down the street. Did you suddenly develop an affinity for the taste of chicken?"

"No." Andreas gritted his teeth and struck the last band back into its slot.

Roman's eyebrows shot up, but none of the mingled emotions in his eyes changed. "I would say it is good to see you, but you look like shit."

He wasn't foolish enough to believe that Roman hadn't received the shortened version of most of the events that had occurred in his absence. Probably on his way up, the boys tripping over themselves to secure his favor once more by supplying every detail.

He took a moment to look the blond man over, at the healthy and relaxed glow that emanated above the irritation. Good. He could deal with the underlying displeasure. That, otherwise, Roman held happiness in his palm was his main concern. "Where is your wife?"

"At the house."

Andreas grunted. "One-eye?"

"He stayed to moon over Viola some more."

One-eyed Bill's fascination with Charlotte's mother was enduring. And it served the perfect excuse for him to be near Charlotte and the Chatsworth ladies whenever Roman was absent. Andreas was sure Charlotte wasn't unaware of that aspect of the situation. There were enough rough-looking men surrounding their Grosvenor Square house, and accompanying the women when they were out and about, to dissuade the devil himself from collecting a soul inside.

And Roman was adjusting to life outside. That was . . . favorable in many ways. And Andreas was always happy to see the stupid bastard.

"How was your trip?"

"Fine." Roman smiled. "Let's talk instead about what you've been doing in my absence."

Healthy and relaxed aside, there was no doubt about it, Roman was thoroughly pissed.

None of the tactics Andreas used to distract or remove people would work with his brother. "I took care of matters that required such care."

"Mmmm . . . and I seem to remember a distinct promise that you made to me stating that you were going to wait to take care of Cornelius until after I returned."

"Well, you only missed by a day."

"Andreas."

"He almost killed Phoebe Pace."

Roman watched him closely. Andreas didn't even try to hide his expressions. Roman was a master at reading people, and he knew Andreas better than anyone.

"You were hurt killing him," Roman said.

It wasn't a question. That meant that someone had noticed. "How did you find out?"

"Some of the boys saw you limping last night and elaborated on it during their overzealous report."

Snotty bastards and their hero worship.

"How you put up with those little shits, I'll never understand."

Roman waved a hand. "Like you have to anyway. I'm sure you made Milton handle them."

Andreas said nothing, resignation overtaking him. Consequences were for underlings, dammit, not for him. Unfortunately, that type of previous thinking was what was going to cost him Phoebe Pace in the end. Consequences were reaching around and squeezing him like a constrictor on its final press.

"Where is Milton, by the way?" Roman asked far too pleasantly. "At the highway?"

Andreas pinched his lips together. Roman obviously knew.

"Andreas?"

"Shropshire."

"My God, that bit was true? You sent Milton to *Shropshire*?" Roman sat forward, looking at him as if he'd lost his mind.

"We needed someone to assess the situation there. You knew that before you left."

"You sent *Milton*?"

"Yes," he said defensively. "He is qualified."

"*Qualified?* You could have sent two newer recruits and one of the older boys to do that task. Who has been handling things for you?"

"I've managed."

"You sent away the one person who could have handled everything on my side in my absence, leaving you to your dark hole. What the devil were you thinking?"

He hadn't been thinking anything outside of keeping Milton away, that was the problem.

Roman's eyes suddenly narrowed on him. "What did Milton do? No one will say. That means they don't know."

"Nothing."

Roman's eyes narrowed more on that quick response. He examined him closely. "Milton Fox would not steal."

"No."

"He is good at handling your anger." Roman examined him as if he'd turned into an odd form of ermine in his absence. "He wouldn't step on your toes."

"I just sent him on an assignment, Roman," he said in a surly voice. "He's not six feet under."

"What did he do, show interest in Miss Pace?"

When Andreas didn't reply, Roman's eyes went wide. "Oh dear God. Andreas, you didn't?"

Andreas didn't get a chance to respond before Roman started madly laughing. "Charlotte is going to die."

Andreas had a knife in his hand, twirling it on his desk. "Not if you die first."

But Roman just continued to chuckle, of course. Andreas's threats had never worked against him. Ever.

Because he knew, for him, they were empty.

He looked at his brother, at his cheerful expression, fierce feelings running through him. He could still remember that day so long ago, lying crippled in the detritus of the alley, freezing, watching Death stalk closer. And then blond hair had popped into his vision. Talking a mile a minute, the strange boy had pulled a blanket from somewhere and offered him a chunk of stolen bread, talking crudely around a bite of crust he was munching. Never stopping for a moment, even as he'd pushed Andreas onto the blanket and dragged him into an abandoned building, tucking him away.

Overly chatty bastard even then.

"It would be worth it," Roman said lazily, his expression beyond pleased. "So, Miss Pace is living here, I hear? Couldn't wait to rent my rooms?"

"Yes. Now get out and go home." He motioned to the door with the knife.

"Nice desk you've added." Roman smirked, putting his feet on top of the feminine abomination.

"You should be terrified by its existence. I can assure you that *I* didn't bring it in here. She's corrupting all of your thugs. I heard one say he was going to become a *cobbler* because she complimented his leatherwork."

Roman tried, unsuccessfully, to hide his smile. "Well, you do always say that you don't need lackeys. Think of it as her culling the herd for you."

Andreas glared hard enough to sear strips through most people's trousers. "The situation is not amusing."

Of course, Roman would walk from the room with trousers intact and never find any of this upsetting. Roman was always of the opinion that if one wanted something, even if it meant living in poverty, one should go get it—that if a perfectly good thug wanted to be a *cobbler,* he should be encouraged to do so.

Thoughts like that were why *Andreas* was the brains behind the operation.

Thoughts like that were perhaps why Roman was deliriously happy, and Andreas was still entrenched in a world of coldness.

"It is beyond amusing, brother mine."

Roman had been on the streets a few months longer than he had and had shared all of his knowledge—sometimes in long streams of uninterrupted dialogue—seemingly content simply to survive. Andreas had wanted far more, and after he'd recovered, after he'd fashioned stray bits of wood and metal together into what he'd needed to support and hide his weak leg, he had dragged Roman along with him to ruthlessly carve their nook in the world. Then their larger piece. Then their kingdom.

Even now, Roman would be content to retire with his wife and live happily in some tiny hamlet in the country. Happy driving her wild and seducing her every chance he got. Perhaps fleecing the neighbors if he grew a little restless. Happy.

But Andreas needed the drive. Needed the empire. His revenge would be complete soon. And there would be no family for him. Roman would make him share his family anyway. Andreas grimaced. He could see that dark path stretching before him. Short little bodies, Lucifer's blond curls, snotty noses, and food-encrusted faces peering up at him, wanting to be lifted and spun. Wanting to hug him and be hugged. Ugh.

The vision of a tiny heart-shaped-faced girl with large brown eyes took form for a moment. He pushed it violently away.

"It is an interesting addition to this room, though." Roman tapped the desk with his heel. The light in Roman's eyes, and the way he had waited to bring up the subject said he knew more than he was letting on. Like always.

"It is an abomination."

Roman threw a pair of dice, sending them skittering across the wood tops, eyes never leaving Andreas's, even as Andreas reached out to stop them. "So, why is it still here?"

Why is she still here? was the real question he was asking.

"You will know when you meet her."

"Right. If you recall, I know *you*. You can get rid of anyone in five seconds flat."

"Not her," he grumbled.

Roman examined him. It was sometimes impossible to know what his brother was thinking behind his masks.

Andreas didn't know why he opened his mouth, but words emerged without permission. "Something hurts in my chest whenever she looks my way. Whenever she touches me."

Roman's stare went blank for long seconds before a grin slipped across his lips. "She makes your chest hurt?"

"Yes. As if I've been felled by a blow." He rubbed his chest absently.

"Felled by something." Roman looked amused. "Odd for someone to want to keep a person near who makes him hurt."

"The pressure decreases when she smiles." His damn lips wouldn't stop *moving*. As if he had needed a confessional and a priest had finally, *finally* appeared. "And she smiles often."

Roman raised a brow. "You are partial to someone having amusement?"

"I like it when she smiles. It makes me feel . . . something."

Roman didn't say anything for a few long seconds. "By God, you have it bad."

"She kissed me."

Under normal circumstances, Andreas would have fiercely celebrated the look of utter astonishment on his brother's face, but he just wanted to finish his confession and be done with it. Then he could button it all up and ship it off to parts unknown. Never to return.

"She knows about the brace. I slept without

nightmares next to her. She makes the best biscuits you've ever tasted."

Roman's mouth opened and closed, nothing emerging for a moment. "Biscuits? You eat her food?" His feet dropped from the desk, and he leaned on it, as if he needed the prop all of a sudden. "My God. You *love her*."

Andreas scoffed, feeling uncomfortable. "Love? Go be poetic with One-eye or thrice-damned Downing."

Roman's expression went flat, serious. "Does she know—"

"No."

His brother regarded him, his expression clearly saying that he was positively itching to say more. But he clamped his lips together and nodded, regular mask quickly back up. But Andreas could see the plotting, the whirring gears in his sharp mind. "Very well. Tell me about Cornelius. And Garrett. Everything. Then I'm going to kick the shit out of you in the sparring room."

Andreas had no doubt that he would try.

Love? A nice sentiment for nice people. And while others might lump Roman into the same category as Andreas, Andreas took all of Roman's sins as his own, leaving Roman free to love and be loved in return.

But Andreas didn't deserve such. He never had.

Chapter 21

Phoebe hugged her robe to her throat as she stood outside his door. Her parents had been sound asleep when she left.

A birdie had made a very casual comment to her in the kitchens—after making sure it had been just the two of them present—that Andreas had serial nightmares, but that he hadn't had any the previous night with her there.

Dangerously winged thoughts. Birds could be devilish creatures. Especially blond ones.

Her mother would have apoplexy if she woke to find her daughter gone, so Phoebe had left a note saying she was in the kitchens. Hopefully if it was found before she returned, it would be found at dawn. It was not unusual for her to go down to bake at first light. The idea that her mother might find the note in the middle of the night, though, was beyond terrifying. Phoebe had managed to slip back in that morning before they woke.

Following birded tweets was not without risk. But she had read sincerity beneath the words and hoped her intuition would not lead her completely astray.

She finally raised a hand to knock. The door immediately opened upon her first strike. "Oh." She let her hand fall. "Are you on your way out?"

"No." He stood in the doorway, his expression unreadable. "You've been standing outside for the last three minutes."

He didn't seem to be the type to wait politely for someone to knock. He was more likely to shoot someone hemming and hawing outside of his door.

Astoundingly, he answered her unvoiced question. "I knew it was you standing there."

She couldn't stop the smile. A balm of soothing calm slid over her skin and started to settle in. "May I come in?"

For a moment she wasn't sure he would cede, but then he held the door open and stepped to the side. It amazed her still that she couldn't tell that he had any injury at all—his movements were so fluid.

"What do you want?" he asked, but the question wasn't brusque. It was more . . . awkward.

"Company."

He looked at her for long moments, then motioned toward a set of chairs. They weren't as comfortable-looking as the ones in Roman's suite, but then again, they matched the man who owned them perfectly, lean and hard.

"Drink?"

"What do you have?"

"Wine. Weak cider. Water. Whiskey."

"A veritable plethora of 'W' drinks."

"If I ever have walrus piss, I will offer it as well."

She stared at him for a long moment, then laughed, relaxing into the stiff chair. "As adventurous as that sounds, cider would be wonderful, thank you."

She turned her head to examine the room more fully as he poured two glasses. She had been a bit busy last night, and this morning she had been gawky with lingering embarrassment.

The room was expensive. That was the only way to describe it. Everything glittered.

"I feel a bit like a child who is going to run amok and destroy everything in here."

"Your father managed not to destroy a thing. If you run amok, I can simply replace said 'mok.'"

She took the offered glass from him. She swirled it for a moment, looking at the surprisingly plush rug in front of the fireplace. Step twelve in her fifteen-step plan said it would work perfectly. "Do you have wood for the fire?" she asked innocently.

Ten minutes later, as the fire blazed in the hearth, she had managed to coax him to the floor, long legs stretched out in front of him, while she lay on her belly on the rug. He looked infinitely more comfortable. She really had to wonder if the man used pain as a focus somehow.

"How can you lie like that?" he asked.

"Without a stiff busk, anything is possible," she said confidently, then conspiratorially. "I must confess to a most unladylike nature."

He snorted. "Hardly a confession."

"Psh. You're not being a gentleman now, Andreas."

There was something in his eyes that she very much liked every time she used his name. "I did warn you. Besides you are a hoyden if ever there was one."

She winked at him, liking the relaxed state he was in. "Only between the hours of ten and two."

"More like two and ten."

She laughed. "I was in trouble frequently as a young girl. I am sure that surprises you not at all."

His look was all the answer needed.

She laughed again. "One escapade even required a prince to save me. It was a glorious adventure. I was the envy of all my friends."

"Oh?" His voice sounded tense all of a sudden.

"Yes, His Royal Highness, then Commander in Chief of his Royal Majesty's troops, Duke of York and Albany, et cetera, et cetera, ruined his best boots in order to save me from the path of a carriage. The loss of those boots was worth every penny, I feel. I would have been called Phoebe the Flat, otherwise." She tilted her head, admiring the way the flames were snapping behind the grate. "Or perhaps Phoebe of the Dented Noggin."

"You were saved by Frederick?"

"Yes. He even stopped by our home twice while I recovered from the lumps I took when I fell into the street. I was determined to marry him at eight years old. He was charming, heroic, and magnificent."

She looked at him to join her merriment. But there was a cool stiffness to him that hadn't been there before. As someone who had made many verbal blunders in the past, she knew she had said something wrong. She just didn't know what it was.

"I was eight. I got past it quickly, I assure you. I don't still hold a torch for him."

His shoulders loosened. Jealousy? But she didn't think that was it.

"I should hope not."

"What? You think it would make me a bit mad?"

"You?"

She smiled. "Everyone is a bit mad. A little madness is fine. Christian always called me an unfettered spirit." It still hurt to refer to her brother in the past tense in any manner.

"Unfettered. Is that what you have been all these months you've been holding your family together? Unchained?"

She looked at the liquid in her glass. "You make it sound like dire duty."

"You should be at parties worrying about what dress you are wearing."

"Come now, Andreas, what a waste that would be. Who would draft your legislation arguments then?"

"No one."

"Then I must say with forced frivolity that it is a good thing the world is mad."

He didn't respond for a moment. "You didn't yank the company from your father a year ago."

She looked at her glass again, concentrating as she swirled. "Sometimes Father was lucid for long periods of time, and we didn't want to let him think we . . ." She bit her lip. "I worsened matters with my dreadful emotions, I know."

"You didn't."

She examined his expression and let her fingers loosen from her glass. "That is kind of you. Thank you. But it is hard not to fault oneself when one's villain is amorphous and ever-changing, and full of emotional decisions and consequences."

"You could blame the other men who took advantage of your father. What were their names?" His tone was casual.

She wagged a finger. "Absolutely not. There is a dark slope there I do not wish to pursue."

"Yet you are having your revenge on Garrett."

She tilted her head. "Mmm . . . I can't deny that helping you draft the documents against him has been satisfying knowing what he wanted to do—and already did—to us. And that I wish Henry and Edward to be free. Perhaps I don't see it so much as revenge as legally making sure he cannot harm us further."

His nonresponse made her straighten on her elbows. "What we spoke of earlier . . . I thought it was agreed we would legally tie his hands by presenting evidence to Parliament if he balked. Do you have side plans of which I am unaware, Andreas?"

"Of course I do. Do not tell me that you expect otherwise."

She opened her mouth for a moment, then shut it. "I expected you to deny it."

"Why?" He swirled his drink. "I find myself unable to deny you much these days."

She stared at him, at the echo of his earlier words. Words that had stuck with her all day. Which she had *clasped* to her.

His eyes didn't leave hers. "You simply open

your lovely mouth and touch me with your soft hands, and I do whatever you like."

"I . . ." The fire in the hearth was less hot than her face. The flames of it springing from her belly. "That is a lovely thing to say as long as you aren't calling me manipulative."

"I was thinking adroit."

"That sounds far better."

"I thought you might like it." His finger pulled along the rim of his glass.

She inched her way over to him, using her elbows and knees, braid hanging loose over one shoulder, and leaned her head in his direction. "You do not smell of alcohol."

"Do you think I must have been drinking to say such things to you?"

"A small part of me, yes. Though I think very highly of you, you know."

"Yes. It is something that continues to startle my mind."

"You are a very confident man, Andreas, even arrogant. It startles *me* to realize that you feel such debasement sometimes."

"Are you saying that you do not have attacks of uncertainty as well? I believe we were just speaking of one of your fears."

She examined his face, and the way that he was so easily confessing to having faults and fears. Unstated or not, that a man like Andreas Merrick made such an admission *meant* something.

She pushed herself to her hands and knees, then sat on her heels directly in front of him. "You always make me feel strange."

His gaze sharpened, and she plowed ahead. "I don't mean that in the negative. But you do, and have, ever since that night I met you. I can't say I rightly felt that way before that night, though there was something about you across the theater that made me want to get you to smile at me in return. Still, it was that night we met. I had never felt such a reaction to a man before. Something tight and uncertain and exciting. Wild."

His eyes were hot on hers, and his fingers were wrapped more tightly around his glass.

"I still only feel such a reaction to you," she added softly. "And one of my enduring faults has always been to seize those things that hold my interest. It is quite unladylike of me I suppose. I have never made a very good lady."

She watched as he seemed to struggle with something. Struggling to maintain that last measure of reserve—whatever final barrier lay between them. "You make a fine person. If someone calls you unladylike, I'll kill him."

"From you," she said earnestly, "I take the threat of murder on my behalf as the highest compliment."

He almost smiled. She saw it there at the edges of his mouth, for a moment. But then he leaned toward her. "You should."

Her eyes dropped to his lips, watching the end of the last word form.

"I feel that strangeness again," she said, but suddenly it felt like her voice was coming from a great distance. She watched his lips part. Firm and seductive at the same time. "Or perhaps not so much strange as very, very alive. Do you think I might be allowed to kiss you again?" she whispered.

He was watching her lips when she asked—the echo of the question tickling his ears.

A kiss seemed a fantastic and terrifying idea. But he would have given her anything she asked for at that moment.

"Yes."

She leaned the last few inches toward him and touched her beautiful lips to his.

Could it be called a kiss, this meeting of skin where one person pulled the soul from another? Her mouth parted beneath his, and the space that opened between them just forced his soul to flow faster, a straight conduit from him to her.

He could feel her smile against his lips. An open-mouthed smile on full, soft lips, still touching his, still tugging out his soul. The temptress of the dark, binding him to her.

"It is like a rebirth when you kiss me." Her voice was shy, but sure, beneath the softness.

Too open, too honest, to be of the dark. Temptress of the light then, absolving him of sin before destroying him completely.

"I want such a thing to last forever." Her tongue darted out, licking her lower lip, the edge of her tongue touching his, being so near still. "Even should I wither from lack of food, lack of drink. I would be happy to exist solely on the feel of your lips against mine, I think."

He had never been good with words. Not for anything other than threatening someone or issuing commands. He was a man who spoke with action. So he connected their mouths again and let her drain him completely, should she choose to do so. Willingly giving her the power to destroy him.

His shirt disappeared and her dress became undone and she was arching underneath him as he set about touching each bit of skin on her body with his lips.

A long time later they lay sprawled on the rug together. Half of her hair was out of the braid, messy about her head and shoulders. The glint of firelight cast a glow on the individual strands sticking out.

She drew a pattern on his chest, matching up one scar with another, dragging her finger between them like a twisted maze game.

"What are you doing?"

"I'm playing mazes on your chest. I always loved to do them, and it gives me an excuse to touch you."

He would think up a dozen excuses to hand her for the future.

"How did you meet your brother?" she asked.

He couldn't stop himself from stiffening. She pressed more firmly on the paths across his shoulders and upper arms, kneading his muscles back down.

"Please. I want to know about you. Let me in."

For some reason, he couldn't rediscover his ability to say no.

"He dragged me out of the gutter."

He could feel her throat work against his chest. "What were you doing in the gutter?"

"Dying."

He looked down at her and saw her lip curl between her teeth, but she continued to touch him, almost stroking him now like some sort of feral beast who needed calming.

She let the silence drag out, though not uncomfortably. Not with the way she was touching him.

For once, he gave in to the urge to fill the void. "I've always done a poor job of dying unfortunately."

"Where were your parents?" she asked in a curious, non-confrontational manner. He knew she had already connected most of the dots. The apparent ones, anyway. She didn't know the actual reason he had been ordered killed.

He smiled an old, chilly smile. He pictured the back of his mother's head through the carriage window as it drove away.

It took him a moment to realize he had vocalized part of his thoughts. But the stilling of her hand proved that he had.

"Both of your parents left you to die?"

"My mother left me to die. A last act of generosity—or ennui—on her part as she stopped the driver from completing the task given to him by the man who had been listed as my father."

He could see the emotions churning from her eyes as she looked up at him. He didn't want her pity.

"It was the best thing that could have happened," he said tightly. "I hated them, and I hated living there. It became unbearable after they threw . . . my nurse . . . out. She always took care of me." Nana, poor Nana. Tending all of his wounds, holding him in the night—the only one who had cared, and she'd been almost destroyed for it.

With her hand, Phoebe made a soft, soothing motion along his chest. "I'm glad you had someone," she whispered. "And that you got out alive."

"I got Roman, the stupid bastard, as a result, so it wasn't a complete loss."

"Tell me about meeting Roman then," she said, voice deceptively light.

"He wouldn't stop talking. The man can hold a three-way conversation by himself. He dragged me away. Fixed me up."

"It is hard to imagine you lying in the gutter, dying," she said. "I dislike the very image."

He lifted her braid and played with the end.

"I thought they'd killed Nana." Damn. He hadn't meant to say that. "As soon as I recovered enough to hold a pistol, I planned my revenge. Would have quite literally died for it if it hadn't been for Roman."

And even then he had lived much of his adolescent years gloriously plotting out various outcomes in excruciatingly bloody detail. The woman next to him would be horrified.

"You were wronged. As someone who feels . . . strongly . . . for you, I want blood myself."

He stared at her.

She tilted her head to look at him fully. "The question is—you have spent so much time waiting and plotting, what do you plan to do after?"

He didn't know. It had never mattered. He had just pushed forward, doing everything he needed in order to set himself up as the most powerful, to set the stage for Garrett's utter annihilation, putting off the final act of revenge until he didn't have to worry about Roman anymore. Roman was happy now, with a good life set before him. And so Andreas could exact his revenge—he had been dodging death for it.

But things had steadily changed since Phoebe Pace had bounced in and taken over everything that belonged to him, internally and externally. He stared at the woman in front of him. What did he want? After? Did he deserve an after?

"There is nothing wrong with wanting justice. You just can't allow it to consume you." She stared directly into his eyes. "You have for a long time, but the consumption has slowed now, hasn't it?"

He had the absurd urge to look away from her, but couldn't bring himself to do it. "Yes," he said softly. "But I cannot purge the desire fully."

She nodded. "And he shall pay. But you shouldn't pay anymore."

His fingers circled her wrist. "You need to understand that I didn't start these events in order to help anyone else. I am a bad person."

"Sometimes, yes." She patted his fingers. "But sometimes you are quite a good person. And everyone has faults to work on."

She smiled softly at him. "I have many, for instance. But my abiding interest in you isn't one of them."

Her lips were so near. And then suddenly they were *under* his. And he knew it was because he had moved first. Spread her beneath him. Because he knew abruptly and irrevocably that she was *his*.

And he wasn't going to let anything interfere with that fact.

And an hour later, as she was arching and moaning under him, he was as positive of that as he had been of anything else in his life.

He likely tore half of his stitches as they moved together. And he didn't care one whit. As long as there were still a few that remained, pulling the edges together, he could resew the rest himself. He could bleed out completely as she kissed him, writhing beneath him, clutching him, her warmth surrounding him as he thrust in and out, wanting to be buried completely inside her forever—he could have bled out and died, and it still would be worth it.

The first light of dawn crept slowly, but surely, forward as he lay in bed, fingers carding through her hair. He had gotten a few hours of the best sleep he had had in years. He was so unused to such rest that he was wide-awake, his brain working too quickly for such an early hour.

He had a few options available—to what his direction would become.

Options that had moved past using the papers from the vault in his final act of revenge. Gaining the ultimate revenge and legally stripping Garrett's true sons of their title and the legacy that Garrett had been so obsessed with since he had realized the truth of Andreas's parentage so many decades ago. Andreas did not need to threaten a charge of treason in order to enact a killing blow. Garrett had been anticipating and panicking over *legacy* ever since he had seen *Andreas Merrick* six months ago. So little time really in the grand scheme of things for Garrett—never understanding for so many years as to where all of his bad fortune had sprouted. And why.

But legacy revenge wasn't part of Andreas's option set anymore. He wanted something else far more. Something that superseded vengeance. That could not exist if he did not choose a new path.

And that was where he had to rally. Quickly. To decide.

He could confess everything. Let Phoebe shoot him. Go to his grave at least free of guilt.

Or he could try and bind Phoebe to him so completely that she wouldn't be able to break free no matter what was later revealed.

He stared at her lying there, smile lovely and wide as her eyes opened upon him. The choice was obvious. He rose and dressed.

"A bit early for you to be up, isn't it?" she teased, and he had the solid notion that she was still half-asleep. She had obviously slept soundly as well. It was a strategic mistake, though—she should have been back with her parents already. Then maybe she would have had some choice in what he was about to do.

"Watching you dress in such a mechanical and focused way, Andreas, I'm feeling a little doubtful that we shared the same lovely experience a few hours ago."

He smiled at the teasing note in her voice and

pulled his shirt over his head, not bothering to set it fully to rights—and without answering her, he walked determinedly to the door.

"Andreas, wait, where are you going?" Her voice sounded uncertain now. Wary. "What time is it?"

"It is time I speak with your parents." He walked from the bedroom.

"What?" It was all but a shriek, and he could hear her throwing on her clothes.

He didn't stop to think that with the quality of sleep he had finally received combined with their actions the night before and the total upheaval of his world that he might *not* be thinking clearly.

Because in a newfound state of bliss, but backed by old, coiled fears, it all seemed a perfectly good idea at the time.

Chapter 22

Phoebe tripped in behind him and grabbed at his shirt, trying to pull him back through the doorway before her parents could see them. Her mother and father stood there already, though, likely disturbed from sleep by the loud knock and subsequent opening of the door. He had been too far ahead of her. Long, long strides ahead.

And he had keys to their rooms. *Of course,* he had.

Phoebe froze, hand fisted in the back of his shirt as she met the eyes of her mother, who had just picked up the note Phoebe had left—a note she had left *just in case,* she thought hysterically. Mathilda Pace looked bemused.

There was a chance! She pulled at Andreas's shirt with all of her strength.

He reached behind, smoothly detached her hands, and took one of her hands in his, bringing it, and her, to his side.

"I formally request your daughter's hand in marriage."

Her mother's eyes went wide. "What? Why?" She turned those wide eyes on Phoebe, taking in her state of dress fully. "Phoebe? It says the kitchens . . . Not real . . . What have you *done*?"

Phoebe cringed. It was possibly the most mortifying and horrifying moment in her life. "Nothing. Nothing! Andr—Mr. Merrick is attempting amusement. There was an accident downstairs—"

"I am not." He was looking straight at her mother. "I don't believe we've met. I'm Andreas Merrick. I formally request your daughter's hand in marriage."

Her mother was without color, gaping like a fish, with nothing clearly recognizable as English emerging from her mouth.

"Good man, Your Highness. Course you can have her," James Pace piped in from the corner.

"James!"

"Father!"

Her father's eyes narrowed on her suddenly. "Wait, who are you?"

The action never stopped hurting, no matter how many times it occurred. But she opened her mouth to softly tell her father she was a maid, when Andreas stepped in front of her. "She's your grown daughter, sir. You are unwell. I'm asking for her hand, do you grant it?"

She tried to pull him back, but he was an unmovable force. She peered around his arm to see her father's face—expressions chasing across and folding in.

"I . . . I don't feel well," her father said. Her mother turned to him immediately, but just as immediately turned back to her daughter, clearly torn between where she was needed most.

"What are you *doing*?" Phoebe tugged on Andreas's hand, hissing. "I never said *I'd* marry you. You didn't ask *me*."

He turned suddenly, dark blue eyes piercing her. "Will you marry me?"

Her mouth was moving, but nothing was emerging from *her* mouth now as his eyes pinned hers. It was as if someone had cursed their family to silence.

He tilted her chin up. "Will you, Phoebe?"

She stared at him, at the gentleness in his eyes, unable to look away.

"Will you?" he whispered, lips so close to hers.

"Yes?" she choked out.

His lips turned up in amusement, but his eyes were still intense, shadowed. "Is that a question?"

"A bit of one, yes. Where is this coming from?"

"Well, we did have s—"

She clamped her free hand over his mouth and looked to where her mother was gently touching her father's shoulder. Phoebe closed her eyes, then tugged Andreas toward the door, one hand still stretched to cover his mouth, the other connected to his. "We are obviously not going to discuss this here," she hissed at him, then called to her mother. "I'll be back with breakfast, Mother. Don't go anywhere."

Her mother's eyes promised slow death for her only daughter. But Phoebe pulled the door shut. She put a hand to her forehead and closed her eyes. "I'm still asleep. I'm still asleep."

He pulled her hand away. "Phoebe."

Firm footsteps pounded up the stairs. As soon as the blond hair crested, light blue eyes connected with dark blue. "Andreas. Uh, Miss Pace." Roman's mouth was trying not to curve into a grin as he took them both in. "You are both dressed rather strangely this morning."

"Roman."

Roman gave in to the grin, then his face turned serious. "Garrett is on the move. He left just before first light."

"Good."

"Four men are following him. The last report had him in Surrey and moving west."

"Perfect."

"Yes. There is something else though—a suspicious man was reported outside of Nana's house."

Andreas immediately stiffened.

Roman squeezed his shoulder. "We'll keep Nana until everything settles," he said. "Charlotte, Viola, and Emily will love to have her. I'll go collect her now."

As Andreas slowly nodded to Roman, she again saw everything she needed to about him. About how he felt for those few he deemed under his protection. Her intuition had been absolutely right all those months ago.

"I will go as well." Andreas looked down at her, *almost* apologetic. "We will speak later."

That cued her previous mental state. "We certainly will not speak *later*," she hissed. "After what you just did, you will speak with me *now*."

"Go inside—"

"I'm not going back into that room." She poked his chest, hissing. "Are you mad?"

"Phoebe—"

"No."

It had to be a trick of the morning light, because she swore a grin tugged the edges of his mouth. "You can hide in my rooms then."

He exchanged a look with his brother, and Phoebe experienced sudden outrage that she had no one to share a look with on her side of things. The side of the *mistreated*. She didn't know Charlotte Merrick well, but she determined right then that they would be fast friends.

She walked back across the hall with the two men, dress sliding around awkwardly on her otherwise naked frame. She needed her shift badly. Damn man and . . . whatever damn madness had possessed him this morning.

"The men guarding her house?" Andreas asked Roman as he grabbed something from a shelf.

"Still in position."

Andreas walked to another series of shelves on the other side of the room and began shoving things into a bag. She couldn't identify what they were, but she could hear the clinks as one item hit another.

"Andreas, we don't know for sure—"

"No one knew where she was three days ago. Garrett likely got lucky in his desperation."

Roman gave a tight nod. "I have twenty men assembled downstairs."

"Good. Go home. I will bring her to you."

"Like hell I'm going anywhere else. Not with you carrying that arsenal."

Andreas pinned him with a look. Phoebe watched, fascinated. "Go home to your wife, Roman. I promised I would keep you out of these things from now on."

"*What?*" Roman hissed, a sleek blond, lethal great cat. "Promised whom? Charlotte would never ask that."

"Promised myself. Now get out of my way."

"No. And you know you'll never make it past me."

There seemed to be some truth to that statement, as Andreas's eyes were stiff, but calculating. "Go home, Roman."

"Nana is mine as well, Andreas," Roman said tightly, obviously upset as a heavy street accent had started to thread the words. "She has been since you rediscovered her a decade ago. And *you* are mine too."

"And you are happy. I want you to stay happy." Andreas's voice was soft. Phoebe's breath caught.

"Stop trying to die then."

"I'm not. I think Miss Pace has to marry me first before she successfully kills me."

Phoebe was too involved in the interaction between the two men to glare properly at that.

Roman narrowed his eyes. Then he pinned a glance on Phoebe, and his smile reappeared slowly. "Well, that's settled then. Let's go."

Andreas nodded sharply and seemed to accept that was indeed that, argument over, with Roman set to accompany him. Phoebe stared at Roman as if he held a secret elixir that she could take.

They started for the door. She immediately followed.

Andreas stopped abruptly. "Stay here and lock the door."

"I'm going with you."

"Absolutely not."

Roman grinned lazily and leaned one shoulder against the door, waiting.

"You are not leaving me here," she hissed. It was obviously a cattish type of day all around. "I am not staying in this building." Her mother would find her *anywhere*.

"You aren't leaving this building."

Ten minutes later decked out in boys' clothing, complete with a low hat, her braid tucked beneath, she was ensconced in a carriage—not a Pace one, *again*—squished between Roman and the roguish Lefty.

Roman hadn't stopped chuckling since Andreas had thrust the clothes at her and tightly told her to change. "Nicely done, Miss Pace."

Lefty jumped out to help another man pack something else on the top of the rig, leaving them alone for a moment.

"By the way, Mr. Merrick, you never told Andreas that you met my family before you left on your trip. Why?"

Roman's smile dropped. "I take it the subject hasn't come up between you two?

"I tried to bring it up the first night we met, but he is rather . . . protective of you. When your name came up, he closed the conversation down." She shrugged.

Roman leaned back against the seat. "That is unfortunate. He will deal less well with the knowledge now. Tell him tonight, or if you'd prefer, I'll tell him before we spar tomorrow. Maybe that would be best actually," he mused. "He will be wroth with me." He gave her a sideways look. "With Andreas, it is best to get the aggression out immediately. Otherwise, he will clasp it coldly. Once something is in his grip, it is nearly impossible to pry it free."

She tilted her head at him. "Yes."

He chuckled again. "You will be good for him. I knew it long before I met you, when he wouldn't stop going to the blasted thea—"

He cut off abruptly as two more men piled inside. And if there was one thing she knew about the pair of brothers, they wouldn't speak of anything important in front of others.

Which strengthened her confidence since they had had the very personal, though short, conversation in Andreas's room in front of her. He would never be rid of her now.

The trip across town was mostly silent, and the men looked bored. In the past, she had seen them in the kitchens vibrating with energy before raids. She supposed escorting an older woman to a new house wasn't quite their type of excitement.

A few of the men cast curious looks her way. She had discovered that they had all known who she was under her earlier disguises. Apparently she hadn't been as anonymous as she had thought. She'd think on *that* too later.

Roman suddenly stiffened next to her and blasted his fist against the roof, then flung an arm backward across her chest and everything around her went to hell.

Andreas watched the carriage ahead of him plodding along on its slow course through town. The two most important people to him sat inside, off to escort the only other person he deemed his. He clenched his fists. The itch between his shoulder blades said he shouldn't have let Phoebe leave the hell.

But Roman had tilted his head. Signaling that he would look after her. And it had made it easier, because Andreas seemed unable to say no all of a sudden.

They had men on horseback, men in carriages, and men who had slipped into the morning shadows on the street. Twenty-two men—and one stowaway—to perform a simple escort.

He had separated into a different carriage from Roman and Phoebe, reluctantly, trusting that his brother would take care of her. He and Roman rarely traveled in the same vehicle together. Just in case. And of the two of them at present, Andreas was far more likely to be targeted if danger should arise.

He twitched as they drew closer to their destination. He would have to caution Phoebe on their way up the walk not to mention Garrett to Nana.

Sometimes his name alone provoked an episode
. . . memories still black even with time. He closed
his eyes for a short moment, feeling Garrett's neck
beneath his fingers. But no, he had given up that
course.

He kept his head against the side of the carriage,
watching at a sharp angle through the window in
order to see the carriage in front. He felt extremely
uneasy. Perhaps it was just because Phoebe was accompanying them. Or from the lingering guilt and
concerns over confessing to her.

No, if there was true danger, Roman would be
feeling it too.

The carriage ahead lurched as the driver pulled
sharply on the ribbons to some given command
from below. Roman. Shit. True.

Andreas gripped the handle of the door and
lifted his pistol. A man separated from the shadows at the side of the street and aimed directly
at the other carriage. A lieutenant or some other
man, easily disposed of usually, but on point today.
The last dregs of Cornelius's force—men trying to
find someone to carry their banner.

Garrett did possess some charisma.

Andreas's pistol discharged. His bullet knocked
the shooter from his feet but not before the man's
close-range shot was fired.

The peculiar thought that he was never letting
Phoebe Pace enter a carriage again, heir to a carriage empire or not, slammed through his mind as
the nightmare took form. The carriage containing
Roman and Phoebe crumpled as the wheel burst
into a thousand splinters. The rig detached, the

horses bolted, and the carriage skidded across the cobblestones with a terrible screech.

Andreas was out of his carriage and firing again before Phoebe and Roman's carriage finally stopped, striking another conveyance stopped at the edge of the street. The horses attached to the other vehicle spooked, surging upward.

He ran over, compensating for the cobblestones as he moved. The brace was an asset as long as he could endure the pain of the knobs bruising the flesh beneath.

He pulled the carriage door open from the top, expecting others to cover him as he did so. The shots were quickly quelled though. The attack had been a last effort.

The long-term problem resided in the fact that there could always be a last effort from someone with nothing to lose.

Phoebe emerged quickly, thank God, with Roman right behind her. She had lost her cap in the crash. And he was absolutely sure of the thought that she would never see the light of day again once he was done securing her safety—bricking her in the walls, if necessary, when they returned.

Roman lifted Phoebe out to Andreas, but his eyes were tracking their men grouping around the downed vehicle. Collecting the signals they were sending. "Four strong. All down. No one's seen Garrett," Roman said, as he vaulted from the vehicle, easily landing in a half crouch before rising to his full height.

They were only a few blocks from their destination. Andreas nodded sharply. "Cover all sides."

He motioned to Phoebe. "Let's go. We need to get inside."

He couldn't credit it, but he could have sworn he heard her grumble—"A Pace carriage wouldn't lose a wheel like that"—as she hurried ahead.

He couldn't leave her exposed in the open, and he didn't trust the situation enough to put her in another carriage without him. They would formulate a plan at Nana's.

Frankly, this type of danger was not amusing. He wasn't used to personally caring about people in dangerous situations. Roman could take care of himself, and the others were good men but not friends.

When he entered the house, he expected Nana to be baking or puttering around her garden. Not to see Henry and Edward Wilcox trying to lift her from the floor.

"Get away from her," Andreas hissed, new pistol in hand.

He and Henry stared at each other, for what felt like a lifetime. It had been a long, long time—it had *been* a lifetime—since they had seen each other, eye to eye, this close. Henry slowly raised his hands in surrender. "We are here to help, just as you are."

"Oh, boys," Nana fussed. "I always hated it when you fought."

Andreas clamped his lips together, promising death to Henry with his eyes if he spoke otherwise.

"We've made our peace, Nana," Henry said, eyes not leaving Andreas. "You'll be happy to know."

"Oh, good, dear. I'm so happy to see you boys all together where you belong."

He glanced quickly at Phoebe's face. Saw the lack of surprise. Still, having things confirmed aloud was . . . well, final. He could hear Roman asking Edward what the hell they were doing there and how they had entered.

"Roman!" Nana exclaimed, his whispers catching her attention. "Such a good boy."

He wondered how Phoebe would feel about Nana? Everything was a little foggy for some reason. He could hear Edward saying that Nana had invited them inside. That they had found some document on their father's desk saying—

"Jane!" Nana reached up to grab Phoebe's hand warmly in hers as if this were all some strange family reunion. "Look, Roman," she said. "It's Jane."

The room grew cold around him. *Jane?* Andreas pinned his darkest look on Roman—who just smiled charmingly, though there was a worried light in his eyes.

That *bastard.*

Andreas stood stiffly, wondering at a thousand things suddenly. What was real? Roman's smile dropped instantly. Always able to read exactly what Andreas was thinking. *Bastard.*

"Andreas, it isn't what you think."

"Isn't it?" he said blackly.

"Well, it is. A bit," he placated.

Phoebe—Phoebe *Jane* Pace, shit he should have figured it all out sooner—pushed into his view. "We met, the week before I first came to your office.

But I'm not going to feel guilt for anything that brought me to you." She gave him a dark glance.

For some reason that dark look made him feel better than one full of calm.

And then there was no more time to think.

"So *sweet*." That most hated voice emerged from a doorway hidden to the side. And he watched Nana gasp before her eyes rolled back and she fainted.

Phoebe whipped around to see Lord Garrett emerge. Nana's hand slipped from hers.

She knew instinctively that if she and Nana hadn't been in the room, blood would already be spilling across the floor. But Roman and Andreas just shifted their positions slowly.

"Yes. She is." Andreas sounded flatly irritated. She suddenly knew she would pay dearly for being here if they made it out alive.

She thought on it. No, at this point, still better quick death here than by her mother's slow hand.

"You can't kill us all," Roman said pleasantly, inspecting his nails, then his knuckles. She could see the barest glint of steel as the nail he had been examining pulled something from his wrist into his palm.

"I don't care," Garrett said, pistol steady on Andreas. "I have made arrangements. As long as *he* dies, that is all that matters. He should have been dead a long time ago. I should have finished it myself after I crushed him. He was broken in five places—bleeding everywhere. No one survives that much blood loss." Duncan Wilcox, Lord Garrett, spat, pistol shaking for a moment. "You won't *die*. *Why?*"

She could see Roman and Andreas sending signals back and forth. Quick flicks of their fingertips. Roman inching to the side so slowly that she only noticed because she was staring right at him.

"I didn't want to do anything that could please you." Andreas smiled coldly.

"That bitch was supposed to make sure you were *dead*." Garrett seemed to need verbal resolution before dispensing death. That could only be to their advantage, though she had no idea what she should be doing to help.

"Mother always was a contrary woman."

"Her devil spawn. His seed still running down her thigh when you were born. That *bitch*. And she said *nothing* while you were marked legitimate forevermore in the eyes of the world." Garrett smiled suddenly, madly, though. With the feral edge of a man with nothing left to lose. "But she didn't care about you, did she? It only took a few whispered words to get her to consent to your death. Satan's spawn."

"The devil always swindles his own."

Phoebe looked quickly between the four men. The features that Andreas shared with Edward and Henry were not those of Lord Garrett. Of *course*. Her hand covered her mouth, everything finally slotting into place.

"Your bitch finally figured it out," Garrett said derisively.

Andreas went still as death. "I will rip out your

tongue before you die," he said, voice flat and absolutely sincere.

She suddenly saw Roman, shifting on the balls of his feet, a diabolical look glittering in his eyes like those of the devil's right hand. How had he gotten over there? He had been moving so slowly. And what was he doing with his hands?

"I won't make the mistake of missing this time." Garrett steadied his hand, the pistol aimed straight at Andreas's chest.

"Edward, be a dear?"

She thought Roman had said it, but the thought was completely knocked from her along with her breath as she hit the ground and went rolling across the floor.

Gunshots exploded around the room. When she finally looked up, Andreas was covered in blood. Again. But he was still standing, eyes dark. Next to her lay Edward, absolutely dazed, but unharmed. *That was who had tackled her.* And Lord Garrett . . . Lord Garrett was flat on his front, stretched out. Henry Wilcox was standing above him with a pistol still outstretched, eyes vacant.

She scrambled toward Andreas to assess the damage. Shot in the arm. Grazed, thankfully. The hysterical thought that she had said something about that very injury just last night wove through her.

In her peripheral vision, she saw Henry bend on one knee over his father, pistol hanging loosely from his fingers. Edward shuffled over and put a hand on his shoulder. Andreas stared at the tableau for a long moment, then his eyes went to Roman, and something was exchanged between them. Andreas's eyes turned to meet hers again.

"I'm sorry, Andreas," she said softly. No matter what existed in the past . . . she shook her head and squeezed the hand attached to his uninjured arm.

He tilted his head to her, and she leaned up and pulled her lips across his, uncaring of the audience.

They made it to Roman's house with Nana, then back to the hell and Andreas's rooms without further incident. Phoebe barely remembered either trip.

She had somehow managed to convince her mother to grant her a stay of execution when she'd seen them return, Andreas's arm splattered with blood, as they'd walked down the hall.

Phoebe had seen the resignation underneath the outrage in her mother's eyes. It would be an interesting and awkward chat later, but she would talk her mother around in the end. Andreas was who she wanted.

Phoebe rummaged through Andreas's shelves, worrying less about the expensive statues this time while locating the supplies she needed. Andreas leaned back, head against the chair. Again.

"Am I forever doomed to bandaging you up, then?" she asked, plucking the salve.

He cracked an eye. "Maybe."

Her heart swelled. Maybe . . . maybe there was hope.

She was quiet for a long time as she worked.

"Henry could go to prison if the wrong story emerges," she said finally.

Andreas grunted. That was on the bottom of the agenda of topics he wished to discuss. He looked at the ceiling. He had hated Henry forever. Henry, who he had once blamed for turning their mother against him. Though he knew, he had *known,* it had been Garrett and a weakness in his mother that had been to blame. Having seen enough of madness by now to recognize the look, he could see it in his memories of her. Especially in the memories after Edward was born.

Still, *Henry* had silently watched the beatings, the pain inflicted on Andreas. He had smiled. Had seen his opportunity to become heir.

He could keep Henry from prison and scandal. There was one person who could ensure it. Andreas had never asked the man for anything. He had never, ever planned to, either.

The long stretch of road extended in front of him. A gleaming knocker and hall of gold. Of bent pride.

"Tell me of how you met Nana," he asked Phoebe, not wanting to think of those other things. Nana was safely ensconced in Roman's Grosvenor Square fortress. But there were a lot of decisions that needed to be made in the next few days.

"I, well, your brother—your brother Roman," she amended. "He—"

"I only have one brother," he enunciated.

She pulled the bandage a little tighter on the next wrap. "Very well. Your brother found out about my father's condition. He introduced me to Nana."

"Roman said that he couldn't bribe your staff."

"He couldn't. That didn't stop him from knocking on the door and inviting himself inside to speak with me."

Of course. Of course, Roman had done that. He had known Andreas was interested in her. And it reiterated what Roman had said earlier, away from Phoebe, little snippets of information.

—*"You never showed interest in anyone. I followed you to the theater the third time you went— watched you from the shadows while you watched her. I knew from that moment that she was yours."*

—*"The plan had only been for her to tell you she had already met me and that she had met Nana. And to secure new negotiating terms. I had no other part in her plans or actions. You. You gave her a chance to chip away at you."*

—*"I want you to be happy too."*

He had been an idiot to think Roman had given up after not being able to bribe her servants. But Andreas had thought his brother was too caught up with courting Charlotte at the time to care about much else.

"Is that why you were never afraid of me? Roman shared all my secrets?" he asked tightly.

She thwacked him in the forehead with her finger. "No. Stop that. He would say nothing of the sort. I *only* knew that you had someone in your life who was similar to someone in mine."

So she knew about Nana's episodes.

"And that you hadn't committed her. Were committed *to* her. I do admit the knowledge gave me the boost of confidence I needed a few times that first night in your office. But you . . . you were a mystery beyond that that I wanted to solve all on my own, Andreas." She touched his cheek briefly, then went back to her wrapping.

"Nana called me Andreas only in private, our special name in that dark house." He didn't know why he needed her to know such things, all of a sudden. "My middle name was Andrew . . ."

She touched the bare skin at his neck, a small caress, but one that didn't overwhelm him.

"She was my nurse. Henry's nurse. She took care of me, even with Edward newly born to care for. Whenever Garrett visited my rooms. After. But Garrett found out. He tossed her out like garbage on my tenth birthday. Did something horrible to her. There was so much blood. Garrett crowed that it was a birthday present befitting a thief."

Blood thief. Birth malefactor.

Her lips pressed together. He could tell she wanted to say something to him, comfort him. But she smoothed a hand down his arm and kept working. It was better. He sighed, letting out the bulge in his chest in one big breath.

"It took me years to find her—and even though I still looked, I thought her dead. It might be more truthful to say she found me in the end. But she . . . something had split her mind, whatever he did to her that day. I cannot tell you how much I longed for his death then, when I realized it."

Another stroke along his arm.

"Roman kept me busy, pushed me. Said that we could destroy him later. He knew it was a suicide mission otherwise. By the time I got to the point where I could easily destroy Garrett, I was too hard. Wanted everything stripped from him piece by piece. I waited and plotted. Enjoyed small victories, making his life less pleasant with each strike. Death was too easy."

His mother's infidelity had made Garrett bitter, the notion that his heir was not of his own blood had turned him crazed. But *Andreas* had pushed him into the man he had been last night.

"I never fully realized the consequences of such actions until I saw how people who I cared about were affected."

"Nana said in the carriage that your mother sent her to you before she died."

He stiffened. "Nana is not right in her thinking sometimes. She wishes it were so."

"Maybe it is so," Phoebe said softly, finishing the bandage and sitting back. "I never met Lady Garrett, but it was said she was a sad woman. Henry said she mourned and raved alternately."

He touched her hand. "I don't wish to speak of this." He kept his voice calm.

She examined him for a moment, then nodded, then gave him a quick kiss. Her hand lingered on his cheek a moment before dropping.

"Your brother gave away none of your secrets. I did my own research," she said softly, her eyes keeping contact with his. "And I trust my instincts."

"Your instincts have gotten you into trouble," he said. Trusting him was proof of that.

"And they've always gotten me back out, for the better. I do not deny that I have done some less-than-brilliant things, but always with good purpose," she said.

She tilted her head. "Like with you. Trusting you *was* a risk, but not so much of one really. Not once I met Roman and your Nana. Not once I met you. You like to make yourself out to be much worse than you are."

And here it was, what he feared each and every time he thought on it. "Once you realize it is the opposite, you will leave."

It just slipped out there, his voice harsh and damaged. Words that he could not pull back. That hung and twisted around his neck like a noose.

Her hand slipped over his and she leaned into him, head tucking against his for a moment. "Someday you will be unable to hold to that belief. And then I will have proven myself to you."

"You have nothing to prove." His voice seemed permanently stuck in its harsh cadence.

"Perhaps those were the wrong words. Perhaps it is more that you will accept me too." He opened his mouth to argue, but she continued before he could. "Accept that I will stay by your side, always."

"You can't promise that."

"Why?"

"Because you can't."

He couldn't admit why though, even now. He couldn't do it. Couldn't destroy this thing he wanted so much. Her.

He didn't know how to confess. Didn't understand how such a thing had happened. He never had to speak to anyone on the same level as he had been for years. No one except Roman, and Roman simply accepted him exactly as he was and had always done so. Had forced himself into Andreas's life when he'd been ten and still vulnerable.

But he wasn't ten anymore. He wasn't vulnerable. That wasn't what this pit in his stomach was.

"Andreas—"

He pulled her toward him, kissing her instead. He wouldn't do it, wouldn't confess anything. Wouldn't ruin this. For she would leave him. Of course she would. There wasn't a doubt in his mind.

He would bury the evidence so deeply that no one would ever find out.

Bury himself in *her* so deeply that she could never disentangle from him.

If he could marry her . . . claim her . . . bind her to him . . . then maybe . . .

And amends. Yes. He could make amends. Apologize first without uttering the words. Soften the ground. Then she would forgive him anything. That worked, right?

He couldn't stop touching her. It was as if the connection of his skin with hers settled something deep within him. Something he hadn't known had been ticking and twisting within him. Just a small touch from her was like a soft pet on raised cat fur, smoothing it down, calming. And the more she touched him, and he her, the more settled he became.

She made things brighter and warmer. For him, a man who didn't deserve the sweetness that was Phoebe Pace.

She shuddered against him, and her lips went to

his ear. "Every time you touch me, it becomes more clear that my life held so much less light before you were in it."

He didn't know what to say. How to even speak around the clench of muscles that had tightened throughout his body? How did one respond to such a thing, especially when he felt the exact opposite was the truth? She was his light. Perhaps if he had Roman's smooth way with words, he could come up with something worthy of such a statement. But he was little more than a very well educated and powerful thug, regardless of his true parentage.

"I do not know how that could be," he whispered back. "As there is nothing but light for me wherever you are."

Such an inadequate way to say that she was everything that was bright and right about his world.

But something in his pitiful words must have struck a chord within her, because her eyes softened further, widened, her lips opening. It was such an instinctive thing, the reaction that response provoked. *Claim her.* It was all but screaming inside of him. That she could be his, irrevocably, if he took the opportunity.

If he made sure that she couldn't leave him, no matter what she later discovered.

Creamy skin. Lips full and panting. Eyes swallowed by black.

It wasn't just that she was responsive. Responsive, by God, her body moved beneath his at the lightest touch. No. It was that she responded as if she were connected *to* him. That their movements were all an exotic, crazed, but still choreographed dance that only the two of them knew. He drew his fingers along her rib cage, then down over her stomach, and her hips arched—his fingers staying on the same plane, his fingers, her skin, not separating, not forcing a centimeter farther in or apart. Perfectly in tune as they moved together.

His. His, his, his.

He curled his fingers into her, and her hands wrapped around his neck, pulling his mouth to hers. Her tongue tracing his lips, his mouth catching her gasp, her body arching against his as he stroked her.

He almost lost control.

He had to stay in control. It was the only way that he would keep her. He had to be on top of everything. Make sure that he anticipated everything he needed to keep her at his side.

He took careful hold of his restraint and withdrew from her at a rate that would maximize the pleasure between them.

"I love you," she whispered.

He pushed in suddenly, madly, against his own will. The sensations were so overwhelming that it was almost painful. This want of her. To bury himself so completely inside of her.

To erase himself and let her warmth overtake and claim *him*.

Every shred of control was gone. He struggled for a moment to grab it back, but she was hot and tight and *his*. Clenching around him instinctively, trying to keep him with and inside of her. He shuddered as he pulled against the warm resistance, stroking backward. But he was a starving man, and being inside of her was the feast. He fully sheathed himself again, pushing as far as he could and savoring every last morsel.

Her eyes closed, her head tilted back as if he had pushed in so hard that he had physically moved her upward on the bed. Maybe he had. Her lips parted, and she gave a hitched breath, then tightened her legs around him and somehow he was just a hairsbreadth farther inside her and she gave a breathy little laugh, a half gasp.

Her eyes abruptly opened, and it wasn't control or restraint that stopped him for a moment. His heart had ceased to beat as glazed eyes, certain, with a well of sweeter emotions surrounding the absolute heat in the center stared back.

"I do love you, Andreas."

And then there was no more control to be had. If he had ever had it. He didn't know, for everything in him seemed to be connected right here, to this moment, these moments, to her. Sparking outward and reshaping his world.

Chapter 23

He debated whether to crawl through the window or present himself directly. The first option was far easier. He struggled with himself all the way through the second, even as he handed a card, requesting an appointment, to a stuffy butler. To his credit, the servant didn't blink at his appearance as he took the card, motioned for him to wait in the parlor, and disappeared. Andreas looked at the expensive trappings of the obvious bachelor lodgings without pausing to take in any in particular. He didn't think he would remember a single thing about this room over his own colliding thoughts.

He wondered what the butler might say to his master—whether he was the type with a warning or if he was tight-lipped to the end. Andreas expected that either way he would be reluctantly added to the schedule—a week or two in the future. Andreas would nod, then use the window approach later that evening. Though the thought of it made his stomach feel strange. The way Phoebe sometimes did. Nervous. Like he might cock up something important.

Andreas firmly pushed the feeling away, clenching his stomach and willing himself back to level.

He needed the man's help, that was all, and he had a favor to trade. A simple transaction, time of the essence. The stuffy little man returned, and Andreas had already shifted his weight to leave when the actual words penetrated.

"—will see you now, if it is convenient."

Somehow Andreas managed to nod, and he followed the expensively clad butler into the recesses of the house. He needed to get rid of the sudden pressure in his neck, and he jerked it to the side and back again, uncaring that a maid had stopped in her task to watch him pass, wide-eyed, duster drooping in her hand.

The butler showed him to a room, announcing him in bored, structured tones. The words sounded strange, as if the name he had carried for so long was wrong on the butler's lips. A click signaled that the butler had exited and pulled the doors shut behind, but Andreas didn't look away from the man sitting at the desk to confirm such.

This was a meeting that he had long thought could be his death sentence. His attention honed to a single presence. If there was someone waiting in the shadows, Andreas would send up his first prayer in twenty years as he fell to the ground that Phoebe would live a long and happy life without him.

The regal man behind the desk stared piercingly at him. "I've long wondered why Roman Merrick never came knocking on my door when he enveloped so many of my contemporaries, and even my own brothers—stuffing them in his pockets." There was an odd twang as he tapped something against his desk once. "Now I know why."

Andreas didn't respond. He had avoided this man for two decades, for exactly this reason, and now with him no more than ten paces away, it felt as if he couldn't loosen his shoulders enough to utter a single word of response.

The man continued to stare, eyes taking in everything, every aspect, every twitch of muscle that Andreas was ruthlessly trying to squash. "So. What do you want?"

"A trade."

"A trade?" The man studied him with cold dark eyes, reflections of his own. "For what, Andreas Merrick?"

"Fair procedure for Henry Wilcox. In exchange for whatever you want."

"You are reported to hate Henry Wilcox."

It did not surprise him that this man might be aware of such personal information even if he hadn't been aware of his true name. Or that he seemed to know already what had happened with Henry Wilcox and Lord Garrett. He had controlled an army. He dealt in information, just as Andreas did.

"We are not . . . friends."

"Then why would you seek to help him? You might have hated Duncan Wilcox, Lord Garrett more, but that would be no reason for a man like you to help his son."

"No."

"I can put the pieces together." The man tipped his head. "And add the numbers. I know whose son you are and what that means. She did not name you by the name you carry, though. The cold bitch would have called you something familial."

"Duncan."

The man gave a cynical laugh. "I imagine Garrett was not particularly pleased when he discovered the truth."

"He was not."

The man continued to examine him. "I always did wonder on the timing of the oldest child's birth. As I said, it is easy enough to add and subtract. But I never heard a word." He absently fiddled with a pen for a moment, still taking in all the details he could. Andreas had never felt quite so stripped to the core by anyone other than Roman, Phoebe, Nana, and his mother. He supposed what people said about family seeing straight to the heart was really true. Discomfort bled through him, just as it had when he'd first met Phoebe.

The man across from him continued. "The oldest child died."

"He did." A sliver of the old bite remained. "Twenty-some years ago."

Those eyes saw everything. Andreas held still but his barriers were being stripped away anyway. "I see." A pause of a beat. "Your mother and I were not friends . . . it was one misspent night. She was the light of a ball when she chose, or the darkness of a crypt. But I do know she fell into a deep depression after her eldest died. She must have truly believed you dead."

"I'm sure that is true." He would have been had it not been for Roman.

"When did you discover me?"

Andreas almost didn't respond. He thought of Phoebe, though, running free, yelling that holding tight to demons only dragged one farther into their pit. His shoulders tightened anyway while he spoke. "I saw you riding in Hyde when I was twelve." Good money to be had cross-sweeping and favor-taking outside the gates of Hyde. "I didn't wonder anymore after that." There hadn't been any need. He had been repeatedly beaten whenever the viscount had looked upon his unmarked face. Bruises to cover his features had almost been a rite of passage. It hadn't been too difficult later to realize why.

"You are heir to Garrett's estate, to the viscountcy. He legitimated you."

"Yes." Andreas wondered how different his life would have been if Garrett had known before his birth and not recognized him. Would this man have raised him? The man's brother had a number of well-bred bastards who moved freely in society and the world.

"You could claim the estate. It wouldn't take much. Especially with Henry Wilcox disgraced and in prison." The man's eyes were piercing. This man could easily move forth the legislation and sway everyone to his side. The circumstances would be obvious to all, and there would be direct consequences for him, but his eyes were serious, studying Andreas, weighing him, the offer real, the reasons behind it shadowed. For surely he could see the idea in Andreas's mind. In the movements he and Roman had undertaken for years.

The man across from him assuredly knew all of this the way he held himself and awaited an answer was evidence of such.

"I do not wish to claim the estate." It was the easiest and most brutal revenge. But his need for such had dwindled to a mere trickle, a puddle quickly soaked up by the green grass surrounding it. "I don't want Wilcox to pay for the actions he has taken. He . . . helped me. And my . . . friend calls him a friend."

The man tapped a finger. "I see."

Andreas usually couldn't be bothered to care about the intricacies of the worded, coded statements other people loved. He used his understanding of human nature to identify threats and eliminate them. Making personal contacts wasn't his area of expertise or desire.

And until Phoebe, he hadn't needed to bother. But the woman continually confounded him. And the desire to please her bled into the desire to understand her. Which seemed to have flowed over into other aspects of his existence. He wondered what his sire's statement truly meant in the context of their conversation. It looked as if indeed he did understand the entirety of it, but, as with Andreas himself, he wasn't easily read.

"I'd like to formally thank you for saving Phoebe Pace's life as a child."

The perusal continued, deepened. "A mischievous child, but a vibrant woman. A good person to call a friend."

Yes, it seemed as if he did understand.

"Any children of hers will surely have an easy time in society."

Andreas tried to stimulate movement in his limbs, but they seemed to be frozen. Frozen by the favor explicitly given.

Frederick waved a hand. "But for pesky matters of the Crown and legacy." He looked Andreas over fully again, slowly, and smiled. "Ah, but for the rules of succession. Would give this country a right shock."

Andreas didn't know what to say, so he said nothing.

Frederick began to tidy his papers. "I will look into the other matter. Seems I recall that Duncan Wilcox had a bit of a problem loading his own firearms back before he became viscount. I think I will have a talk with Henry Wilcox, or rather, the new Lord Garrett, about the matter."

Andreas nodded sharply and rose. "Let me know what you require in return."

Frederick nodded, and Andreas turned to walk to the door, business concluded. He'd never know if the man would have turned him aside had he shown up on his doorstep so long ago. At twelve, seeing the prince ride through Hyde, he had been sure that would have been the result. He had had way too much pride and street sense by then to give it even partial consideration. Being abandoned twice . . . well . . . and he couldn't trust a man, a stranger, of Garrett's world not to let it slip to Garrett that he was alive.

"By the way, I would never have thrown out

a son so fine," the man said softly, as Andreas reached the door.

Andreas paused with his hand on the handle, the comforting coldness of the metal gone, replaced by a layer of thin moisture, odd and uncomfortable, thoughts of Phoebe in the mix. Untamed emotion and swirling awkwardness/mischief over rock-hard certainty and loyalty.

"Good day, Your Royal Highness." And before he could recall them, he let the words emerge. "And thank you."

Chapter 24

Phoebe was concerned. Andreas was acting peculiarly. Always watching her for something. Asking small, leading questions about things she had always wanted and inquiring after things she received. Making small notes in his margins.

With anyone else, she might have thought he was trying to find her a present. But Andreas?

The whole week had had an odd feel to it as they tied up loose ends and danced around the subject of moving, and the twitch of it was approaching a head.

One of the men had approached her earlier thanking her profusely for encouraging him to become a cobbler. An anonymous benefactor had left him enough money to do so, and he was setting up a shop immediately.

Phoebe had just stared at him for a moment before shaking herself out of her surprise long enough to congratulate him warmly.

Then her mother had bemusedly shown her a document gifting Mathilda Pace with a fine prop-

erty in Bath. One that would be passed down th
matriarchal line, with a solicitor set up to tak
commands from the women of the family alone
Some sort of inheritance from an aunt neither o
them had ever heard of. Giving them complete in
dependence from the men in their lives.

Then Phoebe had found a beautiful piece o
poetry on her desk that listed one dozen stanza
as to why she was more than a "good sort." Sh
had stared at it for at least an hour, not knowing
how to respond. Was Edward having a joke? It ha
to be from him. He was the one who called her
"good sort." Made it out to be some sort of non
curse in the marital sphere.

But it hadn't been in Edward's hand. In fact, sh
had no idea whose hand it was in. It seemed lik
something the popular author Eleutherios woul
write, but that was a beyond strange thought
Maybe one of the men in the hell? Who knew tha
a poet existed somewhere in hell's depths.

But someone would have had to speak t
Edward, and that limited the playing field im
mensely.

It couldn't be Andreas. He would have had t
have spoken to Edward *and* asked personal ques
tions. Besides, Andreas had been busy with some
thing else. Her heart thumped.

He had called her to his office and presente
her with a document clearing James Pace of an
wrongdoing in the eyes of the Crown. A com
plete pardon for matters discovered and eve
better, those not yet uncovered. She had quickl

locked the door—*and slowly and demonstratively* showed her thanks to the person she knew was responsible.

But another piece of poetry dedicated strictly to the glory of her determination came a few hours later. Then another glorifying her large eyes and luscious lips. Disturbing.

She had started darting paranoid glances at everyone she passed in the halls after that one, folding her lips between her teeth. When another had shown up praising the ecstasy of her smile, she decided that she was going to tell Andreas she had acquired a strange stalker.

But he simply raised both brows when she'd shown him the note before handing her a sheaf of papers that signified the continuation of Pace Industries, healthy and whole. With a contract from His Royal Highness, Frederick. She had blinked at that. When pressed, Andreas had demurred.

Demurred.

Things were getting odder.

Word was sent that the new house in Bath had been readied and their servants summoned.

A note from Henry said that he had been cleared of any wrongdoing. That the sixth viscount Garrett's death had been labeled accidental—the funeral to be held that weekend.

And another bit of poetry had been presented by her bemused mother, who had found it shoved under the door, words blessing the value of her friendship.

As unbelievable as it was, after assembling all of

the notes to determine the identity of the mystery writer, she really only had one suspect, but . . . she didn't know what to do about it.

Phoebe was a bit dazed by the time she lifted her fist to knock on Andreas's door.

He answered right away. He always knew where she was when she was in the building. She had stopped questioning it.

She waited for him to close and lock the door before pressing him to it. "Have you been sending me notes?" She pinned him so he couldn't look away.

"Of course. I send you notes all the time."

"You send me *summonses*. There's a difference."

"Summonses are still notes. Written on bits of paper with ink."

She looked at him incredulously. "Are you . . . playing word games with me?"

"No."

"You are." She tapped on his chest. "Which means you have been sending me those secret admiration notes. Why?"

"Perhaps I admire you. Secretly."

"While I am flattered—beyond flattered, now that I know it is you and not some stranger—you already have me, you know."

"Do I?"

"Yes." She nodded emphatically.

One set of muscles loosened beneath her hand, another tightened. "I can still send you notes of admiration. I've been told ladies like those."

Her lips twitched up. "It is nice to be appreciated, it is true."

"Exactly. I don't want you to feel I do not appreciate you."

While she was having fun, something said he was being entirely too serious.

"Andreas, I know you well enough now that simply having you pay me attention when I'm speaking to you shows you care."

He frowned. "But . . . that is not enough."

She stepped back and observed him. "What is bothering you? I have never seen you so uncertain."

"I want you to be happy."

But whereas when he said it of Roman, it was a steely concern, carved in stone, there was a wistful, sad nature to how he said it to her.

"You think I cannot be happy with you."

He didn't meet her eyes. "I am a terrible person."

She sighed. It was time to take her courage in hand and wipe the slate bare. They needed to erase the secrets between them before they could be on truly even ground.

"What happened to my brother, Andreas?"

He stiffened. "What?"

"I know you know," she said softly. "And I have waited these many weeks, thinking you would tell me, hoping that it wasn't because it was such a horrible story that I couldn't bear to hear it."

No, no, don't say a word. Lie. Prevaricate. Misinform.

But he looked in her eyes and couldn't do it. "Your brother was about to be shot by Garrett's man. But someone else shot him instead. Your brother fell into the river."

He could feel her despair.

Say nothing more. Don't give her false hope.

"He was dragged out of the river a few minutes later."

He could feel the upbeat of her heart against his chest. *Dammit.* But he couldn't keep the words back after seeing her despair. He would drag Christian Pace from hell and glue him back to his mortal coil if he had to.

Her lips disappeared into her mouth, then reappeared. "He is alive?" Her voice was steady.

"I don't know." He said it even more stiffly. He didn't. "He was put on a ship to Australia." He was careful to keep himself out of the words.

Her head shot up. "You put my brother on a ship to Australia?"

It felt like his entire body was made of lead. "What?"

"I thought I must be crazy to think such thoughts—that he might have been transported. But I had the dockets checked anyway, and there are a lot of anonymous passengers. It gave me hope. What ship? What was the name?"

He carefully wet his lips. *You put my brother on a ship to Australia?* She knew that he was involved.

"I already have people searching for him." His voice sounded strange, even to his ears. "I dispatched someone weeks ago. I . . ." He swallowed. Do it. Just *do it.* "I don't know that he made it, Phoebe. I . . ." He cleared his throat. *Do it.* "*I* shot him."

For once, her open eyes were shuttered as they connected with his. It was a little like a vise cutting the rays of warmth from the sun.

She looked away after a moment. "Yes, I believe you. You look at me with such guilt sometimes." She examined him. "You didn't want his death, though."

"I shot him."

"But you don't miss. There would have been no passage aboard any ship if your intention had been death. Another man was going to shoot him—Lord Garrett was truly desperate then, I remember that time with the clarity of a crystal memory, he had outright threatened Christian—so you shot Christian before the other man could." She nodded as if she had finally pieced it all together and was now wiping her hands of the puzzle.

He felt the urge to shake something. "I may not have aimed to kill him, but I *wanted* him out of London. I was willing to do what I thought necessary to our—the Merricks'—best interests at the time." Though that was not entirely true, even then her smile had been embedded in his mind. "He was too dangerous. And I put him on that ship. He might have died of infection, disease."

If only he had tucked him away in the country . . . but he hadn't known then what would happen. Hadn't thought of the consequences. Why would he ever think he would be standing here with her like this—wanting so desperately to hold on?

"He didn't," she said confidently. "I know he is still alive. I feel it. I have always felt so. I will see him again. Putting him on a ship was likely the right choice. Otherwise, he would have popped back up and been more annoying to the people who wanted him dead. I know my brother."

He gripped her arms, trying to make her understand. "I shot him."

"I know," she snapped. Then took a deep breath. "But you didn't kill him. There is a difference." She tilted her head at him. "And now, you would do anything to save him. I know this too."

He stared at her for a long moment, and she held his gaze, as she always did. "Yes. I would."

He moved away from her, back to his desk. "You should go to Bath tomorrow."

"You want me to leave with my parents for Bath tomorrow." There was an odd note to her voice. "Does that mean that you don't trust me?"

He stopped and looked up at her. "Trust you?"

"To love you. To make this work."

The emotions bit into him. He wanted her love in a way that he hadn't wanted much else in his life. More than revenge. More than anything in his memory. For a man used to taking what he wanted, it was a sharp double-edged sword to find the one thing he wanted most was the one thing he wanted to protect most keenly.

He had been scrambling this past week to try and make amends for every slight or hurt he had ever done to her. With the thought still hooked and buried quite firmly that she would never forgive him should she discover everything about him— and all he had kept hidden.

It had nothing to do with his trust of her. The devil knew that she was one of the few people he trusted. It was that he couldn't trust himself to accept what she was offering. Didn't feel it fair.

"It was never fair for me to think you would

stay with me after discovering the truth about your brother. I betrayed your trust by not speaking of it earlier."

"It is a complicated matter." She drew her hand along her desk. Would he be able to get rid of it after she left? He wasn't sure. "I don't think it is fair to make it black-and-white as you are trying to do."

"I make everything black-and-white," he said, a bit stiffly.

She smiled gently. "I know. It makes you uncomfortable otherwise. But emotions are messy."

She gifted him with *that* soft smile. And it did that strange thing to his insides. He would probably lead a revolt against the king if she asked him to do it while wearing that smile.

"You work in a world where you have to rely on black-and-white information. But," she said, in a somewhat oddly gentle tone of voice, "I like you in all shades."

"You don't know that," he said stiffly. "You've been stuck here, with me, your project, for the last few weeks."

With perspective, she would change her mind. Getting away from him would give her that perspective. He needed to give her that.

It would be his last gift to her.

She would find someone worthy of her. He curled his fingernails into his palms. And he wouldn't interfere. He would need to swear it to himself.

"You are wrong," she said calmly. "I have chosen to stick myself to you. Do you really think I would have stayed had I not wanted to?"

He wanted so desperately to believe it that he couldn't trust his own truth on the matter. "I think you need to experience life without me."

She watched him for long moments, then nodded. "Very well."

His stomach dropped and he grew cold. That was it? She was leaving him? He nodded tightly back. Of course she was. He was being foolish again.

"I will let *you* have your solitude for a month. I hope you miss me quite keenly, for I know I will miss you."

Warmth slowly seeped back into his limbs. Dare he grasp hope?

"In fact, if you feel the need to whimper at my loss a bit before I leave, it would not go amiss." She watched him closely. He could only stare back, as usual. The drop in his stomach turned to something close to . . . butterflies.

She nodded, satisfied, as if he'd produced an actual keening noise. "And you had better come for me in a month's time, or I will be forced to return and drag you home with me."

Home?

"Yes, you stupid man. *Home*. With *me*."

He didn't know if he'd uttered it aloud or if she was just able to read him that well now. Either option was horrifying. And it made him feel . . . warm.

"You asked me to marry you. I accepted. You can't take it back." She walked forward and took his chin in her hand, her eyes holding his. "Decide what you want to do about your business interests, then do whatever needs to be done. I will be waiting, regardless—even if you decide to continue ruling the world. The only way you can possibly disappoint me is if you don't show up to claim me."

She gripped his chin harder. "I am yours. You are mine. And I love you. Don't forget that."

She pressed a quick kiss to his mouth and walked from the room. If someone had entered with a sword, a gun, a bayonet, a *penknife,* he would have simply stood there while they slaughtered him.

Chapter 25

It was exactly a month later, and the clock was ticking toward midnight, with no dark and deadly visitors to be had. Phoebe was unsurprised to find what felt like a pit of snakes twining in her belly. She smoothed a hand over her midsection. She would book passage on a stage and drag him back tomorrow. She wasn't about to give up.

They had settled into Bath well. Christian had returned two weeks after they'd arrived, to many tears and chastisement. He had escaped from the ship in Africa, when it had docked for supplies, and been working on money for passage back, when Andreas's men had finally found him. He had been surprised—and leery—to say the least. He said he had been given a note from Andreas Merrick himself. But to this day would not reveal what it had said. She only knew that he had boarded the ship back for England with considerably less reserve.

And the treatments for Father were going . . . well. She had a feeling it would be a lifelong struggle, but that was fine. That was what family did, they struggled together and found happiness even during the most trying times.

She hadn't sent any notes to Andreas those first two weeks. She had actually given their relationship considerable thought during that time. She had written to him at the start of the third week, then each day since. He was a smart man. If he wanted to understand and make things work on his end, she knew he would.

She wasn't the only one with determination.

Roman and Charlotte, and their large entourage, had stopped to visit them twice in the past four weeks. Roman always had a gleam in his eyes. He said very little about Andreas. Only that he was "cleaning." Though a murmured comment about "retirement" had made her a little nervous. He wouldn't retire, then disappear, would he?

No. She was determined to believe he would come for her. And if he wouldn't, well, she would track him down and make him regret leaving. It was crossed thoughts like that—wanting him to choose to come, so they would finally be free together—and wanting to drag him back to her by his hair, if he didn't—that she struggled with the most.

She looked at the clock, ticking those last beats. She had a feeling that the latter, grabbed hair and all, would win. And she'd make him pay for it.

A knock sounded on the door. Her heart leapt. She opened the portal as the clock began to chime. It wasn't so much relief as simple happiness that struck her as she smiled at him standing in the doorway.

"You are punctual, Mr. Merrick."

"You seem a punctual sort of person, Miss Pace." He raised a brow. "Or at the very least, one to expect punctuality."

"I prefer *early* these days."

"I will remember that."

She was almost hopping from one foot to the other in anticipation. Only the long-standing desire to settle things once and for all keeping her from pouncing.

"I hear that you are hiring servants," he said, smiling. *Smiling.*

"Yes." Her smile grew as she looked at him. "Only the most loyal and stubborn."

"I'm here to apply for a position then."

"Oh?" She couldn't help the lift, or the break, in her voice.

"I will likely be the worst, most foul-tempered employee—or husband—you will ever hire, though."

She smiled and stroked his cheek. "I wouldn't have it any other way."

He leaned into the touch, his fingers sliding along the edge of her lips. "I've missed your smile. It is the most beautiful thing I've ever seen."

And he kissed her. Not a farewell kiss, or an evening kiss, or a friendly kiss at all. It was a forever kiss, and it was everything she'd ever wanted.

"And I love you too, Phoebe."

Twenty years later, Phoebe Merrick still anticipated weekly notes, placed in different spots where she had to hunt to find them. No one had ever said the man was not difficult. But now he always smiled readily and laughed when she chased him down.

The twins were a constant joy. Gregarious and adventurous. Independent Frederica Jane and her cousin Viola were the toast of the new season. James Andrew had soared through Cambridge. A financial wizard, he worked beside his uncle Christian, expanding Pace & Co. of London, Dover, Sussex, York . . . etc.

And every debt had been paid.

Kissing was still Phoebe's favorite way to do it.

And though he would never admit it under threat of outside torture, it was Andreas's favorite too.